BLOODKNOTS

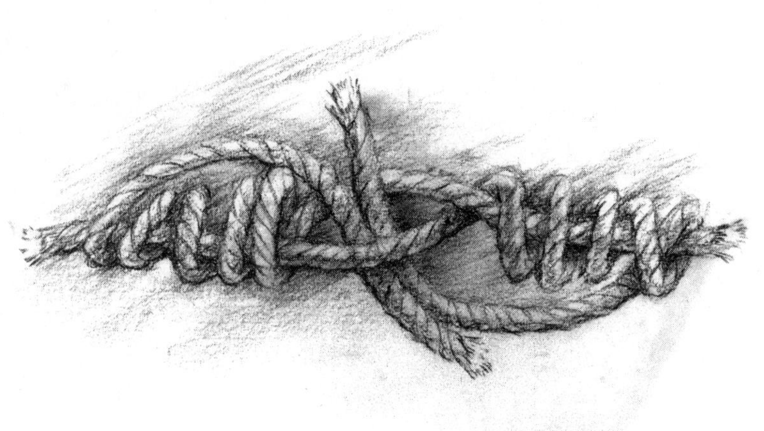

BLOODKNOTS

AMI SANDS BRODOFF

ARSENAL PULP PRESS
Vancouver

BLOODKNOTS

ARSENAL PULP PRESS
103 - 1014 Homer Street
Vancouver, B.C.
Canada V6B 2W9
arsenalpulp.com

The publisher gratefully acknowledges the support of the Canada Council for the Arts and the British Columbia Arts Council for its publishing program, and the Government of Canada through the Book Publishing Industry Development Program for its publishing activities.

Text design by Shyla Seller
Cover design by Solo
Cover illustrations by Jaye Lyonns
Editorial assistance by Linda Field and Nicole Marteinsson

Printed and bound in Canada

This is a work of fiction. Any resemblance of characters to persons either living or deceased is purely coincidental.

Library and Archives Canada Cataloguing in Publication

Brodoff, Ami Sands
Bloodknots / Ami Sands Brodoff.

ISBN 1-55152-182-2

I. Title.

PS8603.R63B49 2005 813'.6 C2005-900313-8

for Michael,
who believes,

and for

Tobias and Rosamond,
mi corazón

It was vague being born and a slow business being truly born. . . .

– Pablo Neruda, *The First Journey*

Fue impreciso nacer y fue tardío nacer de veras. . . .

– Pablo Neruda, *Primer viaje*

ACKNOWLEDGEMENTS

I am grateful to The Corporation of Yaddo, The Virginia Center for the Creative Arts (VCCA), The Ragdale Foundation, and to The Julia and David White Artists' Foundation, for the gift of time and space in which to work.

My special thanks to Brian Lam, Robert Ballantyne, and the amazing Arsenal crew. I cherish your goodness and guts. Thanks for stepping outside the path, thanks for not being afraid of the dark. You help us remember what independent publishing is all about.

As always, my deepest thanks to Michael Atkin, who enters my imaginative world, even those dark and difficult places, and helps me find my way back again. And to Tobias and Rosamond, our living light: thank you for being patient while I listen to the voices of my characters, as well as to your own.

The author wishes to thank the following publications in which these stories first appeared:

The New Jersey Review of Literature: "Extremadura"
Denver Quarterly: "The Jewish Giant"
Mississippi Valley Review: "Babylust"
Triquarterly: "Love Out of Bounds" and "Bloodknots"
Hawaii Review: "Green Avalanche"
Beloit Fiction Journal: "The Haven" (originally titled "Shelter")
River City: "Shrine" (Winner, The River City Fellowship in Fiction Writing Awards)
Quarterly West: "Tunnel Hill"
Confrontation: "Soul Name"
The Best of Writers At Work: "Soul Name"
Other Voices: "Wishbone"

CONTENTS

EXTREMADURA

Spain was the rainbow in our lives, arcing into the future. We dreamed, treading water in jobs that left only our minds free. My mom, Lennie, sold red leatherette encyclopedias over the phone, word processed at the Elevator Company, hostessed; I checked-out at *Shopsmart,* scooped *Carvel,* storing our nest egg in the decoupage hatbox on the kitchen window ledge, a smooth shellacked box of hearts and flowers, bodiless angels and stray wings, all pink and gold and green. We always put something in that box, even when we couldn't pay our bills.

After my father left, we neglected our small, dark house in the valley of the Naugatuck, neglected it until it became inhabited. Dust webbing corners, ghostwriting in smudgy panes of glass. A ragged eye of light piercing through the broken bedroom keyhole.

Lennie kept busy, furiously sliding pictures of her favourite places between laminated sheets – Catalonia's human pyramids, the Canelobre Caves – stuffing scrapbooks till their pages buckled, spines split. She then papered the walls with her cut-outs, plastered maps of Spain across the ceiling, varnishing them into a golden tomb.

Our rowhouse behind the lumber company got so cluttered, we moved things out onto the lawn: my father's favourite chair, its brown seat nubby and pilled, the husk of his rowboat, the one we went out on nearly every day, spring, summer, and fall. Dawn and dusk, we were out on the river. Dad fished, caught Atlantic salmon with a fly. Anything smaller than nine inches he threw back. When he got a good one, he pan-roasted it on top of the stove in sweet butter. We ate the salmon with our fingers, piping hot from the pan, dipping it into the sauce he made with mustard and dill. I remember his dark downslanting eyes and thick black hair, edged almost like a blade.

Twilight was his time. He'd let the boat drift; with both arms around me, crossed tight, he pulled me in against his chest, resting his chin on the top of my head. I liked its warm weight, the sharpness of bone. For years after he left, I couldn't look out toward the river; its sparkling seemed sad and shameful and cruel – painfully alive – now that Dad was gone, maybe dead. He left eleven years ago when I was five, took off for Spain and never came back.

My father had travelled before; he managed a Spanish-owned construction company that renovated ancient buildings and castles into *paradores.* Whether he thought of his work as rescue or destruction, I'll never know. Dad took his first business trip when I was two. Before he left, he gave me a tape recorder, which I still have. It's shaped like a transistor radio with a bright red handle molded to fit a toddler's hand. One side is blue, the other gold. The blue side is a music box, the gold side a recorder. Each time Dad left, he taped a message for me. Something like – *Daddy loves his Gemgirl* – strange, how he spoke in the third person, as though neither one of us were here. Or there. *Daddy will be back soon. Gem and Dad will row out on the river. Everything'll be okay.* I still have the one worn tape which contains every message he ever left me. They overlap, leaving a run of fragments. Over the years, Dad's voice thickened on tape – as if his absence had sped up time instead of halting it – his voice laced with static, broken and staggered as an old man's.

My father's voice was the key to him. After he'd been gone a year, I lost its true sound and couldn't get it back. I listened to the old tape, but it had as much connection to my father as a scratchy record sung by a stranger.

We have Spanish blood, Lennie told me night after night, after Dad disappeared. On both sides, she claimed. *Federico came from a family of fishermen. Along the coast of Coruna. You were conceived right there, a deserted stretch of beach – Ria de Camarinas – the last night of our honeymoon.*

Lennie's own father left before she could walk or say the simplest words. In a whirlwind rage, Grandma Mo tore his face from all the cherished family photos – I've seen those pictures – strong, sheltering arms cradling my mother who smiles up at a torn space. A blank where there should have been a father's face. Grandma Mo's hand enfolded in a veiny, disembodied one. Blanks and spaces which left Lennie's famished imagination room to roam. *My father was a runner for the bulls, at San Fermin.* She described his slim agile form, decked out in red and white, lustily singing to a statue of the saint, gesticulating with a rolled up newspaper he used to direct wayward bulls. . . . In truth, my grandfather was a welder from Puerto Rico. When he left Grandma and Lennie, he returned to the island he loved more than either one of them. Like my Dad, there was this pull back home.

Yet my Dad was attached to this place too: the high hills, a deep valley, the broad river and falls. Its ever-changing names made him feel right at home, made home seem like a new place – Nawcatock to Amaugsuck to Chusetown; Rimmon Falls, then Humphreysville; and finally Seymour, reinventing itself, yet at its core, remaining the same.

Our last winter here, I'd come home from school and find Lennie at the kitchen window, staring out, her coffee gone cold, hands cradling the hatbox where we kept our savings. Her dark blue eyes had an overbright glow that made her gaze seem far away, beyond what could be seen.

"What are you looking at, Lennie?"

Without turning to me, "I see the River Duero."

Over the years, waiting, Lennie became fixed on small details, like what she'd wear on the plane. She'd get that burning look in her eyes and pick out an outfit, sliding it into cleaner's plastic, stuffing the matching hat with tissue, laying her gloves into a slim white box, jewelry into suede bags. There was an ensemble for each season; we didn't know for sure when we'd take off.

Lennie and I never spoke of why we were going, or exactly where. I needed to see the place that drew my father in and never let go. It's true I suspected that Lennie knew more than she let on.

Just before my sixteenth birthday, the hatbox was filled to overflowing – suddenly, the journey was here – startling as the sunflowers that sprout up on our scrabbly lawn each spring, stretching five feet tall, stooped by the weight of their fiery, orange-gold heads.

It was officially spring, but still below zero, with high soiled snowbanks flanking Seymour's streets, mountains that never melted, just crusted over, bracing for the weight of the next new layer. Crisp brown leaves caught fast in sheets of ice like insects under glass.

I packed slowly, as if for a funeral; my mother put our plane tickets into her purse. It was April, a week before Easter vacation. I'd miss school. We'd waited a life, why wait any longer? It started to snow again as we left for the airport.

On the plane, I was calm, for Lennie's sake. I sat by the window and looked out at the familiar landscape, a checkerboard of green, gold, rust, and violet, the curving river like a lifeline along a palm. We lived near the airport and I'd heard the roar of the planes as my father took off and landed, again and again, a roar like a runaway fire – I was inside of it now – and when the sound dimmed, I saw the silver plane with its vapour trail rise in the sky, and my heart galloped, I couldn't get a full breath: there was my father, suspended forty thousand feet above the earth, held aloft by nothing I could see or understand. Now *I* was there.

Evenings after supper, my Dad and I used to build model planes on a long work table in the playroom. Dad described the features of each new one – the delicate sweep of a wing, the speed of a propeller, the beauty of a tiny window made of green glass – as if he were evoking the features of a lover's face. I remember specific models: Dad's vintage Barling Bomber, with its three wings and six engines. His Fokker triplane. The Hawker 800 rescue aircraft with wing skins and ribs milled from aluminum billets, a scarlet candy stripe down its middle. They were lovely, sleek on the work table, alive in the air. Dad and I would go out to the field behind the middle school and he'd fly his Hawker, making it loop the loop, tracing arabesques, an air ballet above our heads. Strange how he lost interest in a plane after he'd flown it once. Then it was on to the next one, which lay in a box, in pieces and parts.

When he'd been gone a full week without word, Lennie smashed the planes, crushing the first one under her feet, breaking the second against the side of the work table, snapping a third above her head. I fought her, then ran from the room with a half-built helicopter . . . it's a horrible sound, the crack of plastic, far worse than glass, for there's no music in it. When the last one was in pieces, Lennie's eyes filled; I turned cold.

Looking at my mother's white face, I saw a stage – like the one where I'd watched *Nutcracker* – her dark, red hair was the velvet curtain. I watched one eye tear and blink, till the auburn curtain swept closed.

My Dad would be back for me.

At last, Lennie sat in the aisle seat, silent, staring straight ahead, her hands folded in her lap; she leaned slightly forward, expectant. Other passengers turned and examined her; I stared them down. My mother had dyed her hair jet black and it looked wet, pulled straight back off her face and fastened into a tight coil at the back of her head. She wore a starchy black dress, fitted at the bodice, swirling into a full skirt, unexpectedly spattered with red polka dots. It had bell sleeves, a low cut neck adorned with a ruffle, stiff and fluffy as meringue. She had on long gloves and a wide-brimmed hat, black straw with a red silk carnation pinned to the crown, shoes and bag to match. My mother looked like something that had popped out of a cuckoo clock.

She'd picked out a costume for me too, but I'd dressed as always, for comfort. High above the clouds, I reclined my seat, put on headphones and listened to a Mahler symphony; we couldn't touch down.

We landed at the Santiago airport in a cool, pelting rain. Lennie hustled me off to *Atesa* where we rented a sand-coloured *Seat*, though my mother was rusty with a clutch. We sped Northwest along the coast on a narrow two-lane road, windows wide, the Firestone map spread across our laps. *La Costa de la Muerte* was carved with inlets and lined with steep cliffs, forests faint in the distance, the whole landscape green and black and grey. Lennie drove fast, whipping around sharp curves. Far below, I saw a wild horse galloping on the beach and told her to stop.

"We haven't time," she snapped, but when the car bucked, nearly careening off the road, she pulled over. We climbed out on the rocks and looked down into the waves crashing against the cliffs. Below us, an old fisherman attached to the cliff by a rope pried goose barnacles from the rocks.

"*Percebes*," Lennie said, "just like lobster."

The goose barnacles had pearly white shells and black leathery necks, shaped like the fingers of an ancient, shriveled hand.

"This is where Grandpa died," my mother whispered, staring into the waves, her arms outstretched, as if offering a blessing. "A wave smashed him against the rocks, washed him out to sea." She dragged her palm across the face of the cliff. "The same way for Federico."

"No." I pried her fingers from the rock; her hand was cold, small, and rough in mine. My mother pushed my hair back from my forehead and waved at one of the fishermen below, *"Hola! Perdone!"*

"Don't!"

The fisherman looked up at us, bracing himself against the rocks. "*Buenes tardes*," Lennie called out. "*Valle? Valle!*"

She was looking for relatives. My father had a younger brother – also a Valle – who still lived here, supposedly, and worked as a fisherman, but he hadn't answered any of Lennie's letters. The fisherman offered us directions to the valley.

Lennie shook her head impatiently. "*Gracias,*" she said, as we climbed back into the car. My mother consulted her map, then an old, crumpled paper. "Itineraries," she said mysteriously, but it appeared to be a letter, written on blue-lined paper, stapled to its envelope. I tried to get a look at it, but she put it back into her purse, and headed southeast.

We passed Galician farms with boxy grain stores, the *horreos,* which looked like prehistoric beasts with stilts for legs, gouged holes for eyes; they lounged on mounds of hay, soft and downy from a distance.

I glanced at the map. "I want to go to Zamora," I said. My father had worked on several *paradores* there – I'd seen pictures.

"Of course," Lennie answered matter-of-factly. "You have relatives there."

"Who?"

"We'll see."

I knew it was hopeless to try to get any further with Lennie, so I tried to take in the scenery, which was lush and mountainous . . . but my mother was going nearly eighty, the car lurching and bucking with her clumsy gear shifts. "We'll never get there, or *anywhere,*" I said.

Lennie floored it.

I held my breath. "Fool." A moment later, two policemen in olive green uniforms and tricorn hats waved us down, as if I'd summoned them. The Guardia Civil were calm and firm and never spoke a word of English. Lennie smiled sweetly; once they were out of sight, she drove on in her usual way.

Late that afternoon, we stopped at a small restaurant. Its stone wall was painted with the promise of feasts within: a whole lobster, a quail, peaches, pastries. I ordered for us, but Lennie had no interest in food. She asked the bartender about a particular street, *Calle Rioseco*, a specific family, the Escamillas; he drew us a map on a cocktail coaster.

We reached Zamora that evening. The old city glimmered ochre, the colour of the village stone, cairns, and fields. I closed my eyes and saw my father at the *Parador Condes de Alba Y Aliste,* building the double-arched patio, beam by beam, polishing the crests of the counts. Lennie beeped the horn, breaking the spell, as we entered a dirt road with simple stone houses. She pulled the car over and got out. We were in front of a house made of overlapping slabs like fish scales with a slat door and red tiled roof; she rapped hard on the door.

A tall, large-framed woman came to answer. She studied us for a moment, perplexed, then her gold-brown eyes glowed like lamps, as Lennie said, "I've come after all."

The woman's eyes swept over Lennie, settling on me. She held me in her gaze for a long moment, then said my name: not Gwendolyn, but Gem. My heart beat faster as she put out her hand. "I'm Claribel," she said.

From the dark recesses of the house, a high clear voice called out in Spanish. A young girl appeared in a knee-length skirt and simple white blouse. She was tall like her mother, but fine-boned and willowy, a few years younger than me. The girl stood close to her mother, one hand on her hip, twisting her slender torso from side to side. She was pale and dark-featured, her hair piled carelessly on top of her head. Black downslanting eyes and glossy brows with a high, almost haughty arch dominated her delicate face. She gave me a sidelong glance and a golden wire of current ran through me. I couldn't look at her. I went cold as stone.

Claribel wrapped her arm around her daughter and gently pushed her forward. "This is Pancheta," she said, motioning us in.

We passed through a narrow foyer into the kitchen, where Claribel stirred a stew bubbling in an earthenware pot before turning down the flame and removing her apron. She led us into the parlour. The room had a wood-carved ceiling, two stiff brocade couches, and a glass case filled with mythological figures. Lennie twisted around to see behind a bookcase and Claribel let out a deep ringing laugh; seeing Lennie's anxious expression, she covered her mouth. "You will not find him here," she said softly. "Federico left . . . how many years . . . not long after I wrote you."

Lennie stood motionless as I slipped the letter from her purse. It was dated September thirteenth, eleven years ago, three months after my father left. *I am writing to reassure you that Rico is safe.*

At last happy. Please do not come here: he has followed his heart. – Sincerely, Claribel Escamilla.

The note stung, like a slap. Short and plain, it breathed a confidence Lennie and I had never possessed. Claribel wrote as if my father were a child she and Lennie were fighting over. I hated her calm, the poise between the lines. I didn't understand how this stranger could have been secure enough to include her name and address. I looked at Lennie and her eyes collapsed in a strange mix of hopeless relief. I guess she'd stopped time with that letter, expecting to catch my father unaware.

Nights at home, I used to hide in the stairwell, watching him. He sat at the dining room table, sipping coffee, writing furiously. After a while, Lennie yawned and stretched, said, *I'm going to bed.* She ruffled his hair, threading her fingers through backward, till he pulled away. *You coming up, Rico?* Her voice was yearning and childlike, thinned to a question mark. My father's pen ground across the page. He pressed down so hard, I imagined I could read it with my fingers, like Braille, if only I could get up close enough. Lennie went to him and he kissed her forehead with cool reverence, like a priest touching dry lips to the rosary.

"*Donde está el bastardo?*" Lennie demanded of Claribel, a hiss propelled on the speed of forced breath. And then, in bungled Spanish, "*Donde está la tina?*" "Where is the bathtub" instead of "*el bano*," bathroom.

Pancheta laughed, high and clear, while Claribel put her arm around my mother and led her. Lennie called out for me, then locked the bathroom door behind us, turning the tap on hard. "There's no accounting for your father's tastes," she whispered, running water over her hands, splashing it onto her face.

"He liked us . . . for a while."

"A big, clumsy woman."

I shook my head. "Handsome."

"Whose side are you on?"

I turned off the tap. "Just tightrope walking." I left the bathroom so Lennie could sulk in peace. A moment later she burst out and came to join the three of us in the parlour. "I need a drink," she commanded, "air."

"A stroll, then," Claribel suggested, retreating to the kitchen to turn off the stove. "To bring you up to date."

The four of us made the rounds of the tapas bars along *Calle Los Herreros,* lingering for a while at *Bodega el Chorizo.* The tapas were displayed on the counter under a long, glass case: olives stuffed with slivers of pimento, *serrano* ham and black sausage, turnovers wrapped in cheese, snails, potato and vegetable salad. "*A buen hambre no hay pan duro,*" said Claribel, hunger is the best sauce. Lennie drank glass after glass of red wine without touching the food. The rest of us ate from a common plate, with our fingers.

"There are too many blanks," Lennie said, her eyes fixed on Claribel's face, imploring. "So much I need to know."

"Some things – *cómo* – we can never know," Claribel said, her square face resolute and weathered. She swept her rich brown hair back from her forehead; it was greying at the temples, loosely waved over her shoulders. "*Y algunas cosas* . . . we refuse to see in front of our eyes." She bit into a sausage, oil glistening on her full lips.

"Oh stop, please," Lennie burst out, "with your sayings and riddles. They mean nothing to me."

Claribel licked her fingers, then delicately wiped her mouth with a cocktail napkin. She folded her arms across her chest and swiveled her stool till she faced my mother. I wanted to dislike her, but couldn't; she was too much herself. Years after my father had abandoned her, she still had the fibre of her note – nothing to do with him. Claribel nodded her head once, very slowly, at Lennie.

"How did you meet Federico?" Lennie asked, a vein pulsing in her forehead.

"*Violeta Cristal,*" Claribel answered quickly. "I was manager then. A small elegant hotel, Rico's favourite. He was working on the *paradore* in the Old Quarter. Tomorrow, we must go. A palace with a *Torre del Caracol*, what is left –"

"You were *saying*," Lennie pressed.

"We talked, sometimes every day. He spoke of . . . Gem." She turned to face me.

"What did he –"

"And so you lured him away from us," Lennie cut in, "only to lose him so carelessly."

"I can't take all that credit," Claribel said, folding in her mouth to stifle the smile playing at the corner of her lips.

"I wanted *un bebé*." Claribel pulled Pancheta into her chest and kissed her forehead hard. "A girl." She smiled a long, slow smile. "I already had . . . Federico."

Lennie sighed, her eyes faraway. "I have to tell you," she said, "our beginning." My mother paused for effect, waiting to ensure that she had our full attention. "Federico called the house," she murmured in a low voice, speaking very rapidly now. "Looking for Pilar Rioja, his aunt. Wrong number, but he called back again and again, till we were laughing on the phone, two strangers. We were *734-5658,* the Riojas, *734-5685.* He was not the only one who called, looking."

I imagined my mother first hearing my father's voice before she ever saw him. And then I thought of my tape recorder, the messages, my Dad's lost voice.

"I agreed to meet him at the Planetarium," Lennie continued. "We sat in the dark blue dome, stars glittering overhead. He knew all their names, described the position of the sun, moon, the planets." She waved her hand. "Made it up as he went along. I was seventeen." She closed her eyes. "When I held Federico for the first time, he felt so light . . . as if his bones were hollow."

Claribel pulled her stool toward Lennie. "You know how he always talked to strangers, he had –"

"An open face," Lennie added.

"Still does, I suppose." My voice was cool, not my own.

"People trusted him," Lennie went on, "spilled their guts."

"And he could not put them back in!" Claribel laughed along with Lennie.

Pancheta tilted her face and looked at me through my father's eyes. I couldn't get used to it, never would.

"Don't you miss him?" I asked her.

She shrugged. "Mama is with Juan Toro a long time. We see Rico, now and then again."

"What does he look like? Father."

"He is –" She drew a big round globe with her delicate hands, describing Juan Toro as tall and "*gordo*, like the whole world," the one who stayed, not her biological father.

Claribel said, "We will meet Juan later. At *La Cueva,* his club. To all dance!"

We got home very late and Claribel insisted we stay the night. When Lennie was asleep, Claribel brought me a cup of cocoa in the parlour. "I want you to know," she said, "how much Rico cared for you. He called you – *camarada* . . ." She looked up at the ceiling, searching, then a light came on behind her eyes. "My buddy!"

The word sounded so empty in my ears, after so many years of yearning. And yet when I thought about it, it seemed oddly right.

"I must tell you," Claribel went on, sitting beside me on the couch. "Rico wrote you. Right away, letter after letter. He tried *por un año.*"

"Where are they? *My* letters?"

Claribel put her hand gently on my shoulder and said goodnight.

I paced the house, too angry even to sit. Lennie had kept my letters from me all those years I'd given myself up to her wasting dreams . . . till they nearly became my own. Yet, my father could have called, could have come. He left us both, left Lennie again and again.

The next morning, we slept in late. Over breakfast, Claribel urged us to see Federico. "He has a restaurant, now," she told us, "in Caceres."

I was afraid, Lennie nearly feverish. We had to go; it was the only way.

The four of us left in the afternoon. Claribel drove our rented car South through Extremadura, in the heat of the day. The sky opened out into a high, white silence, pressing in at our ears. The land was gaunt, the earth dry and sun-hammered, with mountains, open meadows, and plains scraped bare or pocked with outcroppings of rock. Here and there, a solitary oak threw pools of shade onto the grassland that had already gone tawny.

In Caceres, there were storks on church steeples, in belfries, atop the spires of cathedrals, perched on disused factory chimneys. They chattered on with an odd rattling sound and careened about the sky, long necks extended. As we drove through the old city, floodlights illuminated the monuments and the disturbed birds peered down from their emblazoned nests with a look of troubled surprise.

"We are coming near," Claribel said. "Rico runs this restaurant with his companion, Manuel Sagrada. *En gustos no hay disputa.*" Every man to his taste. Lennie and I looked at each other, a formless sense given shape.

My father's restaurant, Estrella Ardiente, was on a narrow, curving street. We parked beside the small plaza, guarded by a jade gargoyle spurting water from its mouth. The restaurant was whitewashed with a balcony and porticoed ground floor. The doorstep was filled with clay pots of geraniums, marigolds, and salvia, in scarlet, gold, orange, and mahogany. We climbed out of the car and walked single file through the arched doorway. The interior was illuminated by candles in garnet glasses and cast a warm wine-coloured glow. We stood side by side. I felt sweat gathering in my palms, at the back of my neck.

The trip before the final one to Spain – when my father left us for good – he arrived home a day late. Always before, he'd been on time. His first broken promise crushed my heart. When he finally walked through the door, I felt dead, numb with waiting. I wouldn't come out of my room and barricaded the door with books and boxes. He forced the door open and I felt his anger in the tautness of his arms as he lifted me, like a baby. I was five, already a little girl, and kicked and pounded at him with my fists. I remember the painful grimace he had, as if I could really hurt him. Then in one fluid motion, he hurled me over his shoulder into the fireman's carry, though I kept on kicking and punching and screaming, *Let me go!*

Without glancing at Lennie, I took her arm as Claribel reached for mine, and Pancheta grasped her mother's hand. Standing four abreast, a shield, we made our way up to the bar.

THE JEWISH GIANT

I was born with a pituitary tumor. The doctors discovered it when I was ten years old, but couldn't operate until after puberty. At twelve, when I was sent away to the Stapleton School, I was six-foot-four; by mid-adolescence, nearly seven feet. Fugitive growth, nothing in this world built to my scale. I broke something precious of my father's nearly every week: shattering his glass-blown dolphin, smashing the crystal of his pocketwatch with enormous thumbs when I snapped closed its gold case. I would have kept on growing until the process itself killed me. Thanks to my operation at sixteen, I survived. A frail giant.

Perhaps that's how Simon Downing saw me. His persecution shamed me, made me believe people were going to make fun of me, had a right to, but also taught me that my life was different than most people's. Essentially my own. My height was an opening, to see what others would reveal to me.

As a boy, I believed in the dark, Jewish God, *El N'kamott*, God of vengeance. He taught me that if you pity the guilty, you will harm the innocent. Truth, fact, faith, belief, were all one, and this, my comfort. *El N'kamott* was a living God, not an old, white-bearded face floating in a cloud: He had a bald head, rough-hewn features like weathered stone, steel eyes. My God was small and lithe with the impatience of the very lean. At night, He appeared to me and spoke, raising the hair on my forearms, a voice with the force of an undertow. *Noah Avrim Levinson, your day will come.* Of course, I had no idea what He meant. His vagueness, too, was my comfort.

I arrived at the Stapleton School an orphan. My mother died when I was two. I have no memory of her, just a few bare facts: her name was Alma, she sewed exquisite costumes for wealthy people and their dolls, she was tall, with black hair, dark eyes, and slender hands. My father raised me in a small town outside Philadelphia until I was twelve. He was a survivor of Auschwitz and developed a bad heart there. When he was physically ill, he was lucid. When he was well, his mind went. Father's temperament was changeable as weather, but with me, he was always gentle and kind, mixed with unexpected flashes of humour. Late in life, he became religious, but this only added to his suffering. He was a man who saw the light passing through his blown-glass dolphin, the shimmering rainbow it cast on the wall, the black shadow, too.

Father was trained as a physician in Prague, but never practiced. After the war, he worked briefly as a medical illustrator, but could not draw from life. While in the sanatorium, he did his own illustrations – marvelous bodies, figures, and animals with wings and scales like coloured glass – these were published in a book after his death. My Uncle Axel, by then a British citizen, became my guardian.

Uncle Axel sent me away at once to the Stapleton School, outside Oxford. I clutched the steel box – my father's old Army medical kit – containing the finger puppets I'd come to call the Bloodkin. My father had made them for me when I was small, with clay heads and hand-painted faces, clothing them in old doll's costumes my mother had sewn. They were my favourite toys, the only ones that grew with me.

There were five Bloodkin. I liked the way they fit snugly over my fingers and became part of me while retaining their own personalities, five that could easily become fifty. That first school day, I clutched their steel box tightly under one arm, carried it like something living, afraid – as if entering prison – of being stripped of all personal belongings.

We entered a parlour smelling of freshly polished floors, leather, and damp flannel. The headmaster poured my uncle a glass of sherry, which he set on the mantelpiece, untasted. Uncle Axel stood behind me and reached up to grip my shoulders, kneading the slouching muscles until I stood straight. Then he vanished.

Boys stood in clusters, trading prize marbles, showing off card tricks, playing board games, but I took them in as I would a scene out a car window. At the far end of the room, by the trophy case, was another boy. He held me: his staunch look, his outrageous carrot-coloured hair, the fact that he held an army medical kit, a near twin of mine.

He swung it from hand to hand, each time nearly letting the steel box crash to the floor, its contents clattering above the muted voices of the homesick boys.

This boy strode over. Built short and thick as a fireplug, he had a great walk, springing on the balls of his feet like a prizefighter. Being ungainly, I envied his physical assurance. Back then, I was ghostly pale, with long brittle bones and barely skin to cover them.

Reaching for my box, the boy said, "Hey, Frank, give over."

"My name's not Frank." I clutched my box more tightly.

"Sure it's Frank."

His naming unnerved me. I was like Frankenstein, a monstrous body, inert, awaiting the spark of life. The boy ran a hand through his red porcupine hair, his eyes narrow, bottle green.

He put out his hand. "Downing," he said, then shook his box hard. The housemaster shot him a look, pure poison, and Down just smiled. He had a warm, open grin, regular white teeth. Mine were grey-tinged from antibiotics and made me feel rotten to the core; I kept my lips sealed.

"What you got, Frank?" He tipped his head at my box, then pounded his fist down on it, so the kit fell to the floor, the Bloodkin scattering about my feet. "Frank's dolls," he whispered loudly, as if on stage. I knelt and picked up my puppets.

"Know what I've got?" he asked, tapping his box.

"Who cares?" My curiosity grew.

"*You* do." He rattled his box harder. "Bones," he said. "Bird bones. Birds I've snagged with my bare hands." He balanced the steel box expertly between the crook of his elbows, laying his palms open. "I have a way." He demonstrated the sharp twist, like opening a too-tight cap. "That quick. I have a taste for swallows." He shrugged, modest.

Whether what Down said was true or a tale barely mattered: it had the force of his will behind it.

We were shown to our dorm by the housemaster. It was in a huge, decaying mansion with a Latin phrase engraved above the doorway; I hadn't a clue what it meant. (The headmaster had already informed me that I would be relegated to a Latin class with eight-year-old boys.) I was at the back of the group, Down a few steps ahead, when he barred my way.

"Crawl in."

I stretched up to my full height. Stepping into the entry, I fell to hands and knees to the sound of his low, monochromatic laugh. Turning around, I saw the tripwire he had rigged while I was downstairs: a gossamer-thin thread.

Down had the bed next to mine, our names on stickers taped to the end of each iron rail. I tried one position, then another, my feet dangling well over the edge, the cold metal press of the bedrail against my calves. Down watched me toss and turn; I remember his words, *Night, ugly girl*, whispered just before he fell asleep.

At our first tea, the boys chanted grace, words mouthed of meaning. I sat silent, missing my father, homesick for a home I no longer had, as servers set out bowls of aphid-seasoned salad and plates of mystery meat and Down hectored me to *say Grace, Grace Frank, or die.*

I stared at the food in total disbelief. "What's that?" I asked anyone who'd listen.

"Toad-in-the-hole," someone said; it was a decent fellow called Mallory.

On closer inspection, this toad looked like rancid sausage embedded in a baked yellow-brown batter. "And that?" I pointed to a small side dish containing a speckled mess.

"Spotted dick," Down said.

This was suet pudding covered in a gelatinous white sauce with raisins dotted all over it. Some boys poured a warm yellow custard on top; Down and Mallory poured the custard over everything.

I escaped to the bathroom. By the time I got back, there was a cover over my plate. When I lifted it, I found a blood-brown piece of flesh, steaming in its own juice.

"Le coeur de chat," Down said. "Chef's special."

My stomach heaved as the other boys roared with laughter and Down sang out: "Cat's heart, makes Frank fart. Eat all of it. Then shit, shit, shit."

I shoved the bowl at Down, its contents splattering into his lap. Lunging across the long wood table, he forced my head down; my face pressed into the tableboards, my nose flattened against the grain: his puppet. A moment later, there were the voices of the masters. One took Down away for six of the best I was sent back to my dorm.

I sat on my cot, wondering how Down intuited my fears. Cats, for one, how they slink up too close, barely noticed, then rub up and down one's bare leg; sensing discomfort, they take pleasure in witnessing one chafe, then pounce with sharp teeth and claws, all of their movements unexpected. Yet cats are beautiful creatures with their sudden grace, marble eyes, and electric fur. Sublime. Cool in a pinch.

The next day, and in the days that followed, Down stalked me from chapel to meals to mail call, from games to bun break, even out on runs and field trips. Neither insider nor outsider, Down was caught between: a Catholic in a sea of Anglicans; part Scottish, part Welsh, in a school of blue-blooded English. Fatherless, with a mysterious mother rumoured to be insane one day, lewd the next, both on a rainy, bored Saturday. The other boys called him bastard, said his mother had the clap *and* syphilis, that he was destined to go mad, that he'd gotten a dose in the womb.

When Down passed boys he wanted to impress, his taunting of me escalated, boys who let him in, then shut him out: Wilson, the brawny Captain of the Eight, Marksby, the best debater. Down drew their attention with his burlesque. He was a genius at ambush, setting traps for me, and I was often laid up in the San.

Down visited me there at odd hours, and when the nurse was out of sight, he would look at me, just look, his gaze free of judgment. Some days he actually brought me treats: a chocolate bar, a hand warmer, a killer conker, radiator-dried all winter, its middle hollowed and filled with hardened glue. After, Down always asked to see the Bloodkin. Once, I took them out and set each man down on the small, hard cot. Down took out his kit, too, upending it on the bed so the spindly white bones fell about the Bloodkin. There *were* bones in there and Down set about forming a group into a bridge, another made a gate, a third clustered into a wood fire. Once we tired of the game, Down reached out and stroked my face, as if reading my features.

His hands had a smell, cool and dry as pine, except when he couldn't get to sleep and took out the bottle of his Mum's perfume that he kept concealed inside his tuck box, and dabbed a touch on his wrist, so she'd be near to him all night long.

In the morning, we pretended things were just as they'd been. Only Down was crueler. I wondered if I'd imagined that moment of gentleness, the tenderness in his hands; it had the quality of a deeply pleasurable dream, vanishing, then reappearing like silverfish. My real dreams were of weightlessness, of flying, of grace.

I startled awake from a flying dream the night Nigel Weber arrived at school: in the middle of the term, the middle of the night. Soaring above the clouds, I careened to earth. To calm myself, I took out the Bloodkin and played with them under the covers lit by my flashlight. Just then, I heard the sudden whisper of the housemaster as he led a new boy into the dorm by the hand.

He was a small, shrunken thing, with wide, dark eyes that glistened in the amber light that fell in from the hall. The housemaster settled him in the cot nearest the door, next to mine.

I glanced at Down; he lay in a deep sleep on my other side, his mouth loose, arms flung upward.

After the housemaster left, the boy turned to me and said, "Let's see," his voice thin and clear, wavering at its edges. He reached over and lifted the covers, then slid over and sat cross-legged at the foot of my bed. From the pocket of his baggy pajamas, he took out a penlight and clicked it on. His face was heart-shaped with large, pointy ears, like an elf. He said his name was Weber.

I unearthed the Bloodkin one by one. While Web studied each man, I studied him: nearly bald, with pale tufts of hair, patches of scalp showing through. He had very white skin, visible branchings of veins, and the boniest ankles I'd ever seen. His ears had down on them like rabbit's fur, which made him look like a soft, fuzzy-felt animal.

"There are two kingdoms," he said, naming them the way Down had named me. "Mountlantis, a mountain range under the sea. Big and high as the Rockies in America. Gloudseah," he went on. "That's an island floating in the sky." Two of the Bloodkin were from Mountlantis, he explained, one from Gloudseah. Only the last pair moved between both worlds: Web named them Nye and No.

We heard the housemaster walking the halls and I put the Bloodkin back in their box, snapping the lid shut. Web went to sleep. I listened for a long while to the gentle gusts of his breath, then glanced at Down on my other side, feeling a twinge of disloyalty.

Some time later, I heard an outcry, a high staccato wail. Web rolled to the floor between our beds. His eyelids fluttered, he murmured unintelligible sounds; his body thrashed, convulsing; his head banged down on the floor, while his limbs contracted and released. I jumped from my cot, put my pillow under his head, and loosened his top, which was constricting his neck. Then I rolled Web onto his side, as everything inside him spewed forth.

After, I held him, as my father had once held me. Web's skin smelled both sour and sweet, new.

The other boys woke up and were staring at us; no one said a word. Mr Worrel, the housemaster who slept like a stone on the top floor of the old house, was nowhere about. Down threatened to get him, then he said, "Doesn't belong here," his voice clotted thick. "He won't make it."

To get away from Down, I led Web into the bathroom and washed him clean. There was blood on his lips and cheek, already drying to a brownish paste. I'd never taken care of anyone before, not even my father, but I wanted to look after Web.

When we returned, the other boys were gathered around Web's bed, whispering. Both Mr Worrel, looking bleary-eyed and dizzy, and a matron called Fiona, were there too. Fiona shepherded Web to the San.

He was back with us the very next day, for little could be done for him. The seizures would come in their lawless paroxysms, despite medication. However, a strange thing happened between us. After that first seizure I experienced an aura – sensed Web's fit coming the way one smells a rain. It didn't matter whether I was asleep or awake, the warning came. A fuzzy black shape bled into my line of vision and grew until it enclosed my whole visual field, then the shape shattered into halves, scintillating along the zig-zagged edge. I knew then to go to Web. By the time he needed me, I could see clear.

Watching the inner volcano erupt inside him, a strange power took shape within me. I was released by the seizures; I began in an odd and perverse way to need them. Web's fits usually lasted only a few minutes, and afterward, he fell into a deep sleep. Once the dorm had settled, I climbed into his bed and held him, stroking his soft, tufted hair, shaping it around his ear.

Soon Web and I found a secret place: a fir at the edge of school grounds, partway into the woods. Our tree had brambling, low-lying branches, and beneath them a bed of needles weathered into soft mulch, a cool, dark den to hide out in and play.

Web owned a Swiss Army knife, which he carried on a cord attached to his jacket. He carved winged creatures for Gloudseah and molded birdfish for Mountlantis. Eyes to the ground, we spotted the spiked balls of horse-chestnuts, a quartz crystal, old beer bottles filled with rainwater, things we incorporated into the world of the Bloodkin. The hockey rink was a glacier, Web's cloggy shoes were rescue boats, ordinary tennis balls became missiles. The yellow walls of Latin class melted into liquid sun that kept Mountlantians warm, the clots of fog that hung above the rugby fields composed the veil that protected Gloudseah from earth. Together, we made up a quest for the Bloodkin with riddling clues and internecine rules: The kinsman who completed our perilous journey gained the power to see inside opaque surfaces – mud, minds, rock, clouds. . . .

Before long, Down discovered our cave and carved obscenities in the dirt with a sharpened stick. He laid the mulchy bed with nails and fouled the earth with excrement. As we cleaned up after his ravages, I dreamed of getting him back: grinding his bird bones into powder with mortar and pestle, smashing that secret bottle of his mother's scent.

The first night of half-term break, there were just a few boys left in the dorm. Sometime near dawn, Web had a terrible seizure, his longest and most violent ever. I rushed to him, placed a pillow under his head, shoving objects out of his way. From the corner of my eye, I saw Down scramble onto my cot and reach under the covers. He snatched the smallest kinsman – Nye – who barely fit over my pinkie. Then Down grabbed my arms, wringing them around my back, twisting as hard as he could. I watched Web, but could do nothing for him. He was lost, haunted.

Down whispered, "Noah, let him go." It was the first time he'd ever called me by my real name. He held my arms fast.

Swerving around me, Down straddled Web, thrusting the smallest finger puppet down Web's throat. I fought Down, as Web struggled. Freed, I found the space below Web's ribs and gave sharp, upward thrusts with the heels of my hands. There was a horrible choke and rasp as Web gulped then swallowed. I saw the shape of the puppet bulge against his pale throat and go down. Nye was Web's favourite kinsman, one of the pair who navigated between both worlds.

When I caught my breath, the few remaining boys were gathered around us. Mr Worrel separated Down and me. I looked at Down across the room. In his eyes was a contraction of light, then dark, and I saw my father's flinch when it was just me, reaching for a glass, or his arm, a look I hated and pitied more than the one that followed, an impenetrable glaze, when my father went to a place where I couldn't find him. Down bowed his head.

The next morning I left for Uncle Axel's, while Down and Web remained at school for half-term break. Web's father, a diplomat, was in Singapore, while Down's mother was ill and staying with her sister, where Down was not welcome.

I had been at my uncle's for three days when the aura seeped into my dreams, its shape darkening the sky, clouds, and reeling stars I'd seen so vividly, until I clambered to the edge of sleep and rushed to Web, only to find myself alone, in a strange and unwelcome place.

I got back to school the tail-end of break, a cold blustery day with snow slanting down. I remember the dry heat in the dorm, the stale smell of the radiator, its gravelly bursts, all of the metal cots neatly made, but for two: Down's, which was piled with dirty clothes, and Web's, its mattress stripped and discoloured by a stain. His tuck box was empty, its padlock cut apart; the metal door of his locker was flung open, his belongings were gone.

I ran through the snow to our cave, carrying the steel box containing the Bloodkin. Snow covered the buildings, the playing fields, the woods and sky, everything blanched and smoothed of its own form and colour. I kneeled on the floor of the cave, looking for any sign of Web: his knife, coat, then felt Down's arm on my shoulder.

"Hey," he said. Web's knife hung around his neck, motionless, the knife that had whittled creatures for the Bloodkin, shaped toy trees and kayaks, sharpened spears from still-green branches.

"Where's Web?" I asked.

"Gone."

I shook his hunched shoulders. "Gone *where*?"

Down looked away, and I realized he was crying, first into his hands, then openly. I turned him toward me, but Down wouldn't look at me. Instead, he reached into his shirt pocket and handed me a note. Immediately, I recognized Web's writing paper, the thick cream-coloured stationary with his name engraved at the top. I unfolded the note and saw's Web's handwriting, the shaky black letters forming one word: *Enough*, and his signature.

"I did it," Down said. "This time, really. Noah, you're the only one I can tell." In his eyes was that awful flinch and I wondered how one person becomes another. "You know the pills I've got?" He went on. "The death-sleepers?"

I nodded. Down had stolen Seconal from his mother's purse and kept the bottle concealed inside his tuck box. I knew he took a half-tablet now and then to get him through the night.

"Web had a bad one, this last," Down said in a soft, flat voice. "Messed himself. Web knew where to find the sleepers," he went on. "I made them handy. Told Web they were ready, waiting for him."

I held onto the steel box containing the Bloodkin, imagining Web going through his last seizure, wetting his bed, the warm urine flowing down his legs and dampening the sheets. Web drags the sodden sheets to the bathroom, tries to wash them out in the sink. Water everywhere now, the sheets drenched, waking Down with the sound of it running. Down is beside Web, taunting, threatening to tell, *they'll give you the plastic one. Everytime you move, it'll crackle. Everyone'll know, the whole house, the whole school. . . .*

"I told him you were off," Down said. "Gone for good."

I felt it coming up again, Down's eerie one-note laugh and lunged at him before the sound escaped, backing him up against the tree, one hand spanning the width of his head, the other around his throat, imagining the thin birds' necks twisted, as my hands squeezed, their spindly crack; small branches breaking, trees crashing to wet ground, insects seething inside stumps; ants and spiders on their bellies, some with poison lances, others skittering helpless, the devouring and devoured, utter stillness at their center; blackness filling my old room, my father's footsteps coming into the yard, up the steps, closing the gate, the contraction of light in his eyes, fiery and forlorn – looking right at me – and something turned within me, loosening.

Down dropped his head against my chest, heavy as a stone, and I remembered being on holiday with my father in Maine, just before his death. We stood together on the cliffs of Pemaquid Point hurling rocks into the curling waves. "Come," my father said to me, "let's throw away what we don't need." He crouched, picking up a small stone. "I throw away confusion!" he called out, the stone spinning and landing soundlessly. "Go on, Noah. Something you want to get rid of," he coaxed.

I pried a fist-sized rock from the sandy crag and felt the sharp weight of it in my palm.

"I say goodbye to –"

"Shame." My father spoke for me.

"Gravity!" I tossed the rock underhand and it made a barely perceptible plop as it landed, a silvery splash. We went on like that until we'd hurled two handfuls of rocks into the dark, swirling water below, and then my father made his way down for a swim.

The sky was high and light, the wind billowing, as if washing it. I played on the cliffs by myself and when I looked down, I saw my father riding a wave, his body curling in on itself, tossed and hurled, pulled out to sea, then sucked back on shore, and before the unbearable loss closed in, I wondered how the water must have felt to him as his heart gave out, barely there, like the fluids of his own body, as he floated and bobbed, an organ in the bloodsea.

I sat down on the cold, hard ground of our cave, under the low-lying pine branches. Scratching with my nails, I tried to dig a hollow for the Bloodkin, for I was through with them. But the ground was rock solid, I barely made a dent.

Down slipped Web's knife over his head, opened the blade and dug into the frozen earth, making a small hollow; gently, he laid out the four puppets that remained. We filled our arms with new snow, sweeping it over the Bloodkin in thin powdery layers, tamping it down until all were covered. Filling my hands again, I tasted the new powder, letting the white dust melt against my tongue.

Walking back to the dorm, the sky turned from blue to black, lowering in around us, and I swung my medical kit from loose fingers, empty as air.

BABYLUST

I didn't know my grandbabe existed till I held her in my arms. My daughter called her Belle, after my mother, and I wondered if every time we said her name, we'd both feel pain.

I rock Belle and old phrases sound in my mind, truth in their echo. *Enjoy her. They grow up so fast. The days go slow, the months pass.*

I'd like to believe I had Greyson when I was young, just a girl, but this isn't so. I wish I could conjure being unsettled – Lord, I was as settled as I was ever going to get. An accident? Franklin and I would sneak into Mount Sinai on visitor's hours and look through the glass at a blooming field of babies, so new and old and wise, eyes still slitted against the world, we wanted one so.

I look into Belle's black eyes, lashes grazing her cheeks and think, every mother is a daughter. "You'll learn her," I tell Greyson. "You'll learn her cries." I want to pamper Greyson the way Mama pampered me. She died three months ago, a few days after Belle's birth. Greyson left the hospital for the funeral home and put Belle into my arms, the baby still spotty and scurf-scalped, skin peely as bark. We hadn't spoken for twelve years, Grey and I, not that I wanted silence – I ate humble pie till I was sick on it – but Grey had an anger toward me that spurted up from underground, a boiling hot spring. Once her heart gets set against you, she don't turn back . . . till she had Belle. The circle goes around and comes around. Thank God for that.

Franklin and I, we argued over names. I still remember us leafing through baby books while I nursed my new girl in the recovery room. I wanted to give my daughter a strong name, something different. Franklin liked Grace, but it was too Puritan for me, too religious. I'd had it with a life as Charity. We settled on Greyson – my mother-in-law's maiden name – Franklin called her Grace, I fixed on Grey, a strong, cool hue, like the scaling notes on Franklin's sax.

He composed and played, I sang. We had our own band. My voice isn't pretty, but I can bend a melody. When I was separated from Grey, I couldn't count on my voice no more, it played tricks on me. Some nights it broke, I just didn't have the heart for a song. Other times, the ache I had would get inside the notes and I'd soar. There was no knowing what would come out.

I brush Belle's hair which is going every which way and up. Her nails are long and sharp with grime next the skin – got to speak to Grey about that – she's afraid to clip them; you know, you can chew them off.

It's windy outside, windows rattling, less day than night. This cold just goes on and on.

Grey was a winter baby, February. I remember walking her in the carriage down Amsterdam, thinking, I've got a bomb swaddled in blankets. Everyone loves a baby and everyone's an expert. Old biddy peering inside the stroller, "You need a snowsuit on that child," or, "She a good baby?" Good baby, bad baby, me feeling that old gizzard be dead meat if she so much as make my baby blink.

See, Grey had colic. Knees jack-knifed to chest. Purply, wet, scrunched, screaming face. Uglymad. You don't understand 'less you been through it. My daughter screamed straight through the first twelve weeks of life, then shut off, like a light switch. If only I'd been there, but she already jumped on Franklin's last nerve. We had no idea what the venture entailed, the hard labour of it, before, during, after. We were naïve.

Her squalling. Franklin took to wearing earplugs, sleeping in mornings at Dean's, our drummer's apartment. I felt so helpless, couldn't do nothing for her. Tried rocking, walking, singing, swinging; bicycled her legs, put her on her tummy, flung her over my shoulder; rode her in the subway, on the bus, soared her through the air; tried every formula ever invented, chamomile tea cold, brown sugar and water hot, rice cereal in the bottle, gas drops, Gripe Water, bay leaves. Tried *everything*. She cried, I cried. We cried, what else could we do?

One night, I was determined to see the news through. Since motherhood, the world was passing me by. Announcer got up to Siamese twins separated and the littler one dying to save her sister and I'm fainting through clouds. Then I hear Grey's cry carving up my dreams, wake up sweaty and panicked, rush to the bassinet where my daughter is still *screaming*, the girl never stopped!

I yank her up, a windmill of arms and legs, and for a big bright-eyed second, my daughter just looks at me, silent, then gears up again and I'm by the window, shaking her. Hard. Shaking her something furious.

When I came to, I brought Grey straight to my mother's, still screaming in full voice. (You hadn't heard nothing till you heard my Grey in full voice.) Mama took her from me and started in with a stomping dance to an Ethiopian cradle song, jazzing up the rhythm, singing above Grey's screaming notes, the baby swung way over her shoulder, the child's tummy smack against the bone. And Mama rocked and rocked and bounced and rocked till Grey's eyes opened and her miserable purply wet screaming face calmed and quieted, and she looked around as if she'd just been born that minute, surveying the world from atop her perch.

I tried to imitate that song and dance routine – it was Belle's dance.

Grey stayed with my mother that night, and the next. Franklin found us a bigger place across the bridge in Williamsburg and Grey stayed with her grandma while we settled in. That took a while.

I visited Grey every day, then every other. It was like going on Safari getting uptown. Harder other ways. I missed Grey so bad . . . or she was a stranger to me. My visits spaced out. Ever not let yourself cry 'cause you know you never going to stop?

Spring came. Franklin was talking about opportunities in Miami, playing the hotels. That's when I knew I had to choose.

Thousands of miles away, I heard Grey's cry, a siren, an alarm going off in my body. Her cry shaped my quiet, made the mewing of a cat new, changed the whine of a stupid door.

My mother wrote me when Grey hit three months: no more crying 'less she was hungry or tired or wanting to be picked up. Needs you could satisfy. On crackling phone lines, I heard Grey's *ah goo*, a long beautiful sound, through static. I missed her first smile. She smiled for Belle.

My Belle opens her toothless mouth in a big fat "O" and her whole face is a silent squeal of joy. I change her and tickle her belly to get a chuckle out of her. Before her bath, we dance to Najee. Belle's bare dimpled back against my palms, juicy froglegs, triple chin. My grandbabe's a bruiser. Now it's combed, a helmet of hair like James Brown. I see Grey in her.

Grey's a nice looking girl, but she don't take care of herself now. I never featured the popular view – pregnancy, I believe – is an *assault* on a woman's body. I'd have cautioned my daughter (had we been speaking) anything over twenty-five pounds is yours to keep. I tell her, you don't get that off now, it going to stick like cement. She tells me, mind mine.

I see the situation like it were in front of me. After what they call the rondo of calming feeding changing bathing calming feeding Belle, Grey and Alexander, well, they just too pooped to pop. I hear them squabbling over the right way to do for Belle. Yesterday, Grey was so frazzled, she put the baby down on the dirty cold lino, so she could mix formula in peace. Alexander slapped her face.

I'd like to give those kids a break. She and Alex need time, time to themselves, to remember what made Belle. She stares up at me and I see my own worn face, the most beautiful thing in her world.

Now I hear Greyson on the stairs. Not her usual light step, my girl is running, rumbling, leaving me thunderstruck. I hug Belle, crushing her against my cheek to smell her milk-fresh skin, even the fusty smell of her diaper which I only just changed, and when she yelps it pierces through the skittering panic in my heart, her cry sets us both rocking, for any second now Grey will stride through that door like she owns the place, and claim Belle, my baby girl, leaving me alone without my flesh. Sloughed skin. Bloodache.

LOVE OUT OF BOUNDS

I

I don't live here anymore, but my old key still jingles on the chain mixed in with all the new ones. The deadbolt slides back without making a sound and I'm inside, feeling like a burglar.

Doren is standing at the top of the stairs, a beam of light touching his hair and beard. He's holding a doll I recognize immediately. That delicate ivory lady is Mom's favourite from her collection of doctor dolls. I wonder how Doren slipped her from the glass display case since our mother is the only one with the key.

"Hey D," I call up to him, trying to sound bright and normal. My brother runs down the spiral stairs, his upper body erect and still, just like Dad's when he jogs in place before bed. "Dory, it's good to see you."

"Hey, Sarah." He looks at me expressionlessly.

"I heard you were home and I wanted to come see. . . ."

"See what?"

I look at my older brother. He is all sucked out, whippet-thin. Last time I saw him he was almost stocky like Dad. Now he's sinew and bone. His eyes are as beautiful as ever: hazel with a dash of yellow in the center, changing colour depending on what he wears. Today, they are a startling green that makes me think of traffic lights. His new beard is streaked russet, crusted in places with a dry yellow resembling egg yolk.

"I wanted to see you," I answer, moving to hug him. Doren's body stiffens as though he's about to be struck, but I embrace him anyway. He mimics my hug, thin arms like a robot's.

"What have you been up to?" I ask.

"Thinking. Just thinking." His eyes stare into blank space, unfocused and glassy.

"That's good. You're better, Dory, you're home."

"That proves my mind doesn't sound. They disguised those controls but they still snap."

We are both quiet for several moments. "What are you thinking, Dory?"

"I have too many thoughts. All sorts of thoughts come to me. Take that ashtray." He lifts the heavy crystal ashtray from the marble elephant whose back is a coffee table. "They put my ashes in there, but there are hundreds of other things I'm connected to simultaneously."

"Like what?"

"I can't get specific." He looks irritated. "North, South, East, West. Thoughts stream in four different directions." He shrugs. "These thoughts don't mean anything to me, but I get distracted. They forget what I'm saying."

"Who? Mom and Dad?"

Doren's lips work, a gesture between chewing and speaking, though he does neither.

"They coming home tonight?" I ask.

"Still shrinking in Vegas."

"Oh, yeah. Mom delivers her paper tomorrow. Boredom and Anxiety: The Ineluctable Link." I look to my brother for a smile or a snicker, but I've already lost him. He gazes out the bay window toward the spacious, manicured lawn that sprawls away from the house. It is blazingly green, as if lacquered. Late afternoon sun streams in, casting a funnel of light on the hardwood floor. My brother stands in the orange light rubbing his hands together, as if to warm them over a fire.

"Over here," I say, not making much sense, thinking how lonely and unreal it is to miss someone who's right there. Doren comes over to me, tenderly rubs his face against mine, then pats my cheeks with both his hands, chanting:

Ah sista goah, I love you and the pack
I give you juice and candy to make the bad go back

I join in and we chant and chant and chant. When we were kids, our private language muffled the sounds of Mom and Dad downstairs, their voices sharpened like instruments. Doren caresses the scarlet sleeve of my sweater. "I have one for you, Dory, in green. Extra tall. Shall I get it from my suitcase?"

"No. Stay. Right. Here." His eyes get vacant, then dart and flash. "Can you see me?"

There's a burning behind my eyes. For a moment, the tears feel like someone else's. "Yes, Dory, I can, even from far away."

My brother smiles. "'Home is the place where, when you have to go there, they have to take you in,'" he says.

"Was it horrible at the hospital? How did you get out of there?"

"No bolt was necessary. When I'm without, she's gone kidnapping. I reimburse that equilibrium. But you," he finishes, "I love out of bounds."

For me, it's his most lucid sentence all afternoon.

That night, I dream of Doren's car. I see the headlight eyes, hood ornament nose, and wide grille mouth approach me on the road. I get in, zoom down the highway, Springsteen's "Spirit of the Night" on the radio. Suddenly, the car stops, its motor still running, ragged and guttural. I get out, open the hood, tinker with the car's innards. Soon I'm tangled in a sinewy web of wires: one tube is fastened to a vein at my wrist; another feeds me through the nose; a thick, bandage-coloured cylinder pumps air in and out of a perfect hole in my throat. A shadowy figure unhitches me from the car. My body writhes and twitches in rhythmic spasms. Ghost-Man stands by, transfixed, like he's watching television.

I wake up, shivering and sweating, the sheets cold, damp towels over my body. Downstairs, I make a cup of hot, sweet tea and drink it in a bubble bath, imagining pure black space, a deep and dreamless sleep.

II

Morning brings one of those dazzling days of early spring and I take my coffee out to our circular driveway. Sun glints off Doren's derelict red Chevy, its body bruised and cratered from a series of crack-ups. Take-out coffee cups, squashed beer cans, piles of clothing for every season, an upended box of kitty litter, and butts and ashes from dozens of cigarettes coat the upholstery and carpet. The car looks like an SRO someone hid out in for a while, then abandoned. On the dash sits my first princess phone, severed at the cord.

I toss armloads of junk into big plastic bags, working up a sweat. Just as the nightmare's hangover begins to evapourate, Doren comes out front, smoking, the cigarette burning dangerously close to his fingers. I spot Mom's doll – an elegant lady in miniature – peering from his pocket.

"What a mess! Want to help?"

"Not really." Doren drags deeply, sucking in smoke like breath. "Chaos escapes the boundaries of my mind and finds expression in this car."

He snuffs the cigarette out against his wrist, not seeming to feel much.

"Don't!" I stop working, take a sip of coffee. "I know it's been a while, I'm sorry." The truth is I haven't been home in over a year, haven't seen Doren since he was admitted to Stillwater Hospital. That was about the time I graduated from Parsons, about two years after Doren's third and final drop out of Oberlin, an anniversary he liked to celebrate.

When I heard he was in the hospital, I went through my daily routine on automatic. The F train from Brooklyn to my sealed-windowed office at *Heat and Fridge News.* Paste-ups all day for the "Story of the Soft Switchover," a micro-processor-driven, set-up, set-back, heating-cooling system for the whole household. Back home on the F to my studio. Evenings and weekends, I holed up in that studio sorting through stuff in Doren's old Superman lunchbox. Growing up, he'd given me all kinds of things: a slab of mica from a cave-in accident; arrowheads, marbles, and bits of quartz; a leopard-print seashell and coloured-glass unicorn. When he was in the hospital, I pored over the stuff in that lunchbox like a young girl pores over mementoes in a hope chest. I didn't visit him, didn't speak to him.

Staring at patterns of sparkle in the mica, listening to the whoosh of the sea inside the shell, I lost myself in a videotape loop of saviour fantasies. If a chunk of masonry came loose from the Flatiron Building, I would whisk Doren out of its way; hoist him onto one shoulder and pull him out of a burning brownstone; lift him from the brackish waves into my rescue dinghy after his kayak capsized, paddle and boat having floated away!

Embarrassed, I crush several styrofoam cups, then toss them, avoiding Doren's eyes. "I don't have a good excuse. Will you forgive me?"

"Let bygones be gone by." He rolls up his sleeves and finishes the job with the careless whirlwind motion he reserves for all household chores. After we cart the last garbage bag out to the dump, Doren looks at his wrist, though he has no watch.

"C'mon," he say. "Time to blow this insalubrious locale."

"I'll drive." He tosses me the keys.

We head southwest on the Deegan, cross the George Washington Bridge, and continue on the Jersey turnpike through the flatlands.

"Uglification, next twenty miles," Doren says, and he is right. We are deep into a geometric wilderness of plant-works and manufactory. Oil refineries spew forth continuous eddies of smoke and blue-orange orbs of flame seem to light the grimy sky from within. It's an iridescent play of colour you just don't see in nature. Just as we're beginning to appreciate the surreal beauty, the landscape turns lush, quick as a scene-change in the movies.

My brother points to a gargantuan billboard that nearly takes up our whole visual field. A colourful globe whirls bull's-eye center.

COLOSSAL COSMOS
LAND OF FANTASY AND WONDER
2 miles

Doren makes the thumbs-up sign and I follow arrows around several sharp curves.

500 ELECTRIFYING RIDES
FAMILY FUN AT ITS BEST!
COLOSSAL COSMOS – 1 mile

We hadn't planned this as our destination, but these corny signs have me hooked. When we finally pass through the gilded, curlicued gate, I want trumpets to sound, feeling like Dorothy entering Oz. We can already hear the low, thunderous rumbling from the killer coasters, long, drawn-out shrieks and cries, and disembodied Muzak lilting out of hidden loudspeakers everywhere.

2000 ANIMALS ROAM FREE
NATURAL LANDSCAPED SETTING
DRIVE-THROUGH SAFARI – ½ mile

Doren starts jumping up and down like a kid, guiding the wheel toward the Safari – *the world's largest*, another sign proclaims, *outside Africa itself.*

With tickets, we pass through an ersatz wilderness in convoy where bison, llamas, elk, and deer whiz-bang by, inhaling dust fumes from dozens of cars. Doren reaches his leg across to the driver's side, pressing on the brake. A long-legged bird has already come right up to him, beating mottled wings. She bends her sinuous neck inside the window, rubbing her head back and forth against Doren's cheek. He opens the car door a crack and rips up a handful of Safari grass; it makes a sucking sound as it comes uprooted. Chewing on a blade of grass, he feeds the bird from his open palm, mumbling made-up words and sounds, a lover's language I've only heard him use with animals.

In "Africa," monkeys fasten themselves to the sealed capsules of cars, claws scratching, jaws gnawing. Behind electrified fences, leopards and tigers move in suspended animation, languid and dazed from the unrelenting sun, the snaking monotony of cars. I stare into the marble-green eyes of a tiger. He stares back. A dull, hooded gaze, lifeless as the torpid tiger at home who doubles as a chair.

When we were kids, Mom redecorated our house as a jungle. A dense, long-haired scarlet-and-green rug stretched from wall to wall like untended grass on fire. Plants on every surface, in every corner, suspended from windows and ceiling. Huge Wandering Jews and snakes, asparagus ferns and gloxinia.

I remember those days we were left alone in the house from first light and dawn chorus till the mosquitoes began to bite. The notes signed with XXXs love mother pinned to the fridge door with animal magnets.

First, we'd let out Elixir and Rosmoor, Monty and Nightsprite, who were screeching and yowling behind the utility room door. Sounds that made me imagine an ambulance coming. Elixir sharpened her claws in the plush giraffe's flank; Rosmoor burrowed in red-green shag; Nightsprite swiped at tropical birds, making Mom's mobiles fly.

We crawled around through rooms and rooms, playing snakes, tongues darting like flames. One day, Doren started a new game. He ripped leaves off Mom's plants, chewing on buds, laughing and laughing without taking a breath. He crammed leaves in my mouth – his laugh just like a yell – by dusk, we'd stripped Mom's jungle bare.

Out back, we stretched out on the close-cropped lawn, wet and steaming in the twilight. Soon everything turned black. Doren held my head between both hands, as my stomach lurched and I retched up green.

III

Doren's hand over my eyes is cool, so large it wraps around both temples. We pick up speed, whirling faster and faster, our car swings out sideways, lifting, revolving, till we're vertical, spinning madly upside down. Between Doren's fingers are slats of light. In the orange darkness, I see us shaking and spinning, flying right off the rail. My brother pulls his hand away and the sunglasses on top of my head clatter to the car's ceiling, the world turns blindingly bright and blurry till Doren retrieves them, hair fluttering against my cheek.

Down on the ground, the crowd is dense and teeming. All the good rides have endless lines and it's just too hot to wait in the stinging glare of the sun, so we stroll off to the Garden of Eatin', choosing a canopied table overlooking the big pretend lake.

Doren eats like a blind man, touching everything on his plate before beginning, as if to memorize its position. He takes Mom's doll where he's wedged it between a couple of corn cobettes and a giant-sized Coke, carefully wrapping it in a napkin and laying it on its back. Swathed in white, the doll stares out of sightless eyes into the unvarying blue sky.

"They're not ordinary dolls," Mom once explained while dusting her collection lovingly as she always did on Saturdays. I was maybe eight. She told me how an elegant lady would use the doll to show her doctor the part of her body that hurt. With fingers manicured pearl-white, Mom lifted the doll's hair, which was carved into a bun. She swung that bun open on its hinge like the lid of a box and pulled out the tiniest silver spoon I'd ever seen. "The lady who owned this doll used the spoon to take her medicines" – my mother pointed to the pillbox inside the doll's head – and with a lingering look, she replaced her favourite in the case and clicked it closed.

"Why did you take it?" I ask my brother.

Doren pockets the doll, then sips his Coke. "There's electricity coursing through my veins." He is matter-of-fact. "If IQ doesn't circuit short, I'll shock people.

I concentrate on figuring IQ, blocking the rest. Ivory Queen. An easy one. Doren upturns the doll like a salt shaker, spilling the tiny coloured pills from inside its head into his palm.

"Wouldn't it be better if you took those?"

He pours them back into the Ivory Queen and smiles. "I already get medicine secretly. She's got a syringe inside her, pumps it right into my bloodstream."

I feel a funny pulsing in my neck. "C'mon, Dory. You don't have to pull that on me."

Doren signs deeply.

"Doesn't the medicine help?"

"Yeah. If you like being buried thousands of miles below the earth and windowless." Doren double-crosses his legs, wrapping himself into a caduceus.

"That's awful. Maybe the dose is too high."

Doren unravels his legs. "I forgot," he says, getting up from the table. In five minutes, he's back with coffee and a handful of gem-coloured swizzle sticks, their tips molded into tiny figures of Adam, Eve, and the Serpent.

"Adam and Eve in the Garden of Eatin'. Can I have those?" It always calms me to collect things for the Superman lunchbox. I reach for the mixers, but Doren pulls them away.

"You can't go on saving so many . . . *things*," he says, snapping them in two. "Now that's better."

"I can't stand you." Can't stand, don't want to know, like in high school at Treemont. I'm waiting by my locker. See Ross coming, Doren just behind. My brother's wearing stuff that doesn't fit or match; he's shaved his head for no apparent reason. He stops, freeze-frame, listening, as if to a voice out of earshot or some pressure beneath all the other kids' voices. I link my arm through Ross's, Doren's breath at the back of my neck, that funny pulsing as if a small animal were trapped there. I want to blast off, out of my own skin. I pull Ross down the long, dark hall, turning back before we round the corner. Doren gives me a weird smile, his mouth stretched tight, all his teeth showing. He makes me think of that painting, "The Scream," the woman suspended in the road, she's shutting her ears to something deafening, though all around her is silence.

Hundreds of kids went to Treemont High. At least ten of them were Solomons. Only a few knew for sure Doren and I were related.

I feel my brother's knee tapping restlessly under the table.

"Ready for the mind-bending, brain-blowing Blockbuster Buccaneer?" he asks, putting an arm around my shoulder.

"You know I'm a wimp about scary rides," but before I can protest further, he's pulling me toward a line so long and labyrinthian, I can't see where it begins or ends.

IV

The ticket-taker rips coupons from our booklets and we're part of the line, enclosed behind velveteen ropes. The queue is as dense and long as any line for a newly-released film, Saturday night, in the

Village. Up ahead, an outsized owl consults a Salvador Dali watch. *One hour till you board the Buccaneer.*

"This is nuts, Dory." I consult my watch, as if we're due somewhere soon. "We've got better things to do. "

Doren shakes his head, gives me a toxic look. "Patience, patience," he says. "The day is a clock without hands."

A middle-aged woman on her own turns around, stares at Doren, then winks. I catch a glimpse of what she's reading; it's Kafka's short stories.

I see people getting off, lining up again. Incredible. I'm trying to fathom the pull of this place, a come-on that breaks through all kinds of boundaries. Everybody's dying to relinquish control, to surrender.

"No matter how many times you zoom up and down this thing, you know you'll get to the bottom in one piece," I say hopefully.

"The velocity's the same, the peril's predictable," he answers.

The woman ahead of us turns around again and smiles winningly at Doren. There's some rapport there.

I fall into a trance observing a cool-looking androgynous couple in peekaboo Spandex. They're holding hands, each in separate worlds. She's eating a candy apple layer by layer, picking off the nuts, then chewing on the caramel. He's got headphones on, and is bopping to the beat. It's so loud, I can hear the tinny rhythm of golden oldies seeping through the phones. *Dontcha want somebody ta love. Dontcha need somebody.* . . . Watching them makes me lonely as hell, but like picking a scab, once I start, I can't stop.

My worst days these past months, I've lived my life from inside a spacesuit. Everyone's voice sounds metallic and strange, distant, without colour, and muddled like bees buzzing. It's the background noises – traffic horns beeping, trees rustling, children whispering and weeping – that are deafening. It takes all my concentration to make out what people are saying. My own name – Sarah Solomon – starts to sound strange too, like I've never heard it before. I repeat it over and over in my head, but the name has been cut off from the language by a knife. I can't picture my face, either. I have to reconstruct it the way you do when you've just met someone and want to visualize their features. I pretend I'm in life-drawing class, with me as the model. First, I draw in one almond-shaped eye, then another; next, the thin straight nose, small mouth, upturned chin and long neck. While I draw, I recite out loud the story of what I'm doing, third-person-journal-style, everything happening right now. Just a few minutes of head drawing and third-person journal is usually enough to do the trick. I coalesce.

What's important, I can always function on the outside, even with all this cacophony going on. At times, I wonder if this is the only thing that makes me different from Doren. I admit, it's a struggle, like trying to sing a favourite song in your head while another one is playing. But I can do that. It's my gift.

I hear a pealing roar reverberating from the coaster; it sounds like an airplane about to land on our heads. Only ten people are ahead of us now and each car takes two.

A big sign in bold block letters warns that this ride is not recommended for pregnant women, people with heart conditions, people with back or neck ailments, people with disabilities, those subject to motion sickness, or anyone under the influence of alcohol or drugs. I begin to panic.

"You go." I touch Doren's shoulder. "I'll watch, take pictures." I rummage in my shoulder bag for the portable camera.

"No way, SOS. You gotta get dirty with life."

I notice all the cars have headlights, though under the bright glare of the sun, they're barely visible. A red car glides up, jolts to a stop. Only one headlight. A cyclops. I want to mention this to the guard but feel stupid. The headlights serve no function.

The watchman puts out his hand to help me into the car. Doren slides in beside me. The safety bar grazes our thighs as it locks into place. Another sharp jolt and we're moving. The car makes a clackety-clacking as it rises up the first steep incline.

At the peak, we idle for a split second; I see the pulse-movement of people way below, one amoeba-like organism, moving, spreading in every direction. Plunging down, my heart rises with a live flutter, leaving me weightless, emptied out, like free-falling in a dream. On the sharp turns left, then right, I swing against the sidebar, then slam into Doren. I feel a cool breeze against my face and a sharp tingling, as if my whole skin has fallen asleep and is regaining consciousness. On the next downslide, I scream, dizzy and exhilarated; I'm getting into this, despite myself. Like motorcycles.

"Look!" I shout to Doren as we reach the crest of the next hill, pointing to the bird's-eye view of the park. "Now, that's something."

He's got his right arm cranked back like a pitcher's, Mom's doll in his fist. "The IQ's kayoed!" he yells, hurling the doll into the blue sheet of sky.

I lean forward against the safety bar, almost standing, following its high graceful arc, then fall, the tiny coloured pills exploding from its head like pool balls scattered by the cue. Suddenly, the safety bar flies open and I'm suspended in midair, screaming, with no voice at all. Everyone is screaming. In an instant, Doren's arm is around my waist, pulling me back into the seat. He holds his arm across me, the safety bar swinging wildly in the wind.

I bury my face in Doren's shirt, hear his blood beating, as I flow into the roar and motion of the car till I can't feel my body anymore.

On a twisting turn, there's a sharp metallic clank. I open my eyes. The safety bar's locked right back in place. Slowing, we glide into the final straightaway, a quick jolt forward, then back, as the force of inertia brings our car to a halt.

"Waddya wanna do, put a monkeywrench in the works!" The guard shouts at Doren as we stumble out of the car.

"There's something wrong with *that* one." I point to our car as the next couple climbs in. "It's the safety bar."

The guard checks the bar twice. "Looks fine to me." He gives Doren a sharp, warning look. "What's the matter with you, chucking things off the top?"

"My mother and father are doctors, both grandfathers are doctors, all my uncles are doctors, three cousins are doctors, and I'm a patient," says Doren.

The man looks uneasy, then chuckles. "That's a good one." He pushes the button on his remote-control box. The car bucks, then lurches into motion.

We weave through the shimmering sea of metal trying to find our car. My legs are wobbly and trembling, the asphalt's turned to Jell-O. I lean into my brother for balance. A few feet ahead of us, I see a shard of ivory, white against the pavement. I remember all those Saturdays I watched my mother dusting her doll collection. It was easy to imagine the doctor's healing hands palpating the doll as meticulously as a miniaturist might work on a prize painting, while the real woman languished in pain. "It's like no one . . . noticed, like nothing happened," I say to my brother.

Doren nods. "'Not waving but drowning.'"

I stoop to pick up the shattered piece of ivory and hold it in my palm. Nothing in its shape or texture suggests the part of the doll it once formed.

GREEN AVALANCHE

Christmas

Light pulses across his face. He shuts his eyes against the bright spasms, a beam dance from *Newspapers, Cigarettes, Wine, Liquor, Lotto* across the street. Hunched motionless on the hospital cot – doctor's white coat mashed between his knees – Justin doesn't see me standing in the doorway of the on-call room, half-in, half-out. His feet look so weird, naked, splayed out in swathes left by the mop. Headlights stream by, wave after white wave, and I see a radial pattern in the wet floor, a child's spiky sun.

This morning, I delivered Alana Calderon's baby boy; Justin checked him over after delivery. Everything as usual – a beautiful healthy boy – so we thought. Exhausted, I collapse on the hospital cot, just as Justin springs up. The cot whines in that baby's language I keep hearing inside every stupid sound. My patient Alana was beginning to learn her new son's language; she named him Miguel Ríos Calderón.

I watch Justin's back, shoulders swerving as he skids across the floor, barely catching himself before a fall. He can examine the raw back of a throat or insert the cold nib of an earscope without making a baby flinch, but this man is clumsy everywhere else. He just doesn't have the time to take care, by choice I suspect. I'm speaking comforting nonsense to Justin's back, a bitter taste in my mouth, eyes and nose streaming from the ammonia. "You should get some –"

"Coffee."

This morning, Alana's room was flooded with light. Cold winter sun. Cleansed away the waxy hospital fluorescence. Poinsettias everywhere. I'd never seen so many together and Alana cursed as the nurse brought in another red-ribboned pot. "Dr Iz, I can't *stand* these. They're so ugly!" she said with laughter in her voice as she burped Miguel on her shoulder, rubbing his soft dimpled back with a circling palm. I looked around and saw the flowers through her eyes. Bloody blooms, little red claws, predatory things, and laughed right along with her, wondering how so many well-wishers who cared about Alana Calderón, didn't know the first thing about her.

We'd become friends. This patient who disliked me, knew I delivered babies, delivered mothers too, asked me during our first meeting, Dr Rosenfield, do you have kids? her voice threaded with challenge. No. I couldn't honestly reply, not yet. My ob-gyn partner, Elizabeth, was the mother of four; I thought I might mention this, but decided not to. Alana had suffered three miscarriages in the space of a year-and-a-half, one baby dying inside her womb in the sixth month. Her last doctor just couldn't pick up the heartbeat one day – and when Alana went to the hospital for an ultrasound she found out the baby was dead. No one knew why. Her doctor couldn't fit her in till the following Monday, so Alana walked around with that sloshing weight inside her belly for six days, then went through induced labour and delivery. Labour to deliver nothing.

Alana wanted a woman this time. Her FP recommended me, but scaling Alana's wall of distrust was nearly impossible. Wanting to be a mother more than anything, Alana must have seen me as wasting a power I was too stupid or selfish to understand. Yet so much can happen in forty weeks to turn things around – for Alana, it was just thirty-two – eight endless months of being a glass house, and me, a fence around her.

Justin turns to me with a sweet slip of a smile I can't catch hold of, though it leaves me warm for a moment after it vanishes, a flash across his face, a round face with the soft cheeks of a child. He sloshes water into the machine, shakes in grounds straight from the can. At the window, we look out over the Avenue, reeling out of this room, outside our heads. Taxis shush through fresh fallen snow. An old woman curved like a question mark pulls a woollen stocking over her head, the legless man rolls into his cardboard box, that same coatless kid lights a cigarette with shaking hands, as if its glow could warm him. *Merry Christmas to all and to all a good night!* Inside, the coffee pot's gurgling, nutty smell lacing into the ammonia.

Justin shoves his paper cup beneath the stream, burning his hand, then shakes off coffee onto the floor. "Cof drops," he says, dumping in four spoonfuls of creamer, three packets of sugar. The creamer bubbles to the top and Justin swishes the mixture with his finger and then licks it.

He's the only person I know who's gone from black to regular, drinking cup after sweet creamy cup, his midnight snack his one real meal: yogurt and peanuts, maybe a muffin layered thick with American cheese and butter and jam. He's so *unhealthy.* Tall and spindly with a saggy paunch; cheeks a little too red, glowing. I wish he'd take care of himself, then remember, he's through, out of here with the New Year – third best hospital in New York – handing over a thriving pediatric practice to his partner, and I know all this abdication is the best thing in the world. For him.

The pot gurgles to a stop as the door opens by itself with a long *meeeow.* I hear nurses arguing, the blare of a page, then shut the door, watch it open – doesn't fit the damn frame – so I lean my back against it to shut it up, keep it shut. Justin slants against the wall, feet crossed, as if he can't support his own weight. Cradling his cup between both hands, he concentrates on each sip, both of us at the edge of this small white room, wanting to bolt, not home, not anywhere fixed and stationary.

I stroke Justin's hair, rough brown curls loose over his ears and the back of his neck, my palm gently grazing the outline of his skull, as he says, "I told Mrs Calderón – I said, you've got a beautiful boy. Healthy. Perfect."

"Stupid word, Jus, why do you say that to my mothers?"

His pale brows arch at *my*, as he rests his cup on the sill.

"What does it mean, Jus? Doesn't mean anything."

His mouth folds over mine enclosing my lips like an ether mask, muzzling me, and then there's the stab of his teeth, silt of my own bloody lip and my hands every which way in his hair, burrowing in the roots, scrunching the curls in my fist, hair that smells like wet earth, the pelt of an animal. He reaches up and squeezes my wrist till I open my palm and see a lock of his hair in my hand. Alana's baby was born with a thick thatch of it, jet-black, slick as licorice and Alana – "I checked her, checked her for Group B in the twenty-sixth week, I –"

"Shush."

There's an ache behind my ribs, and I press the blade of Justin's hip against that space, until the sharp pressure numbs out the ache, at least muffles it. My back against the door, Justin holds my hips as he enters me, but I hear the mothers and the babies and the mothers' mothers, *Dr Iz, Dr Iz-All, Dr Iz-All-Rose, Dr Roses In the Field*, *Dr Just, Dr Just Bloom, Dr Just Bloom a Rose in My Field*, our heaving and sliding and pushing, too much like Alana's, birthing Miguel, and I whisper *I hate us*, and Justin says, *won't let you*, as his hands knot at the small of my back. He yanks me into him and my body ribbons, then snaps, as my shoulders lift away from the door; it opens by itself, that baby's *meow*, a slice of light.

This morning, Alana padded down to the nursery for Miguel. She relished the ritual, fetching her baby for feedings, arriving early so she could watch him through the glass: cockeyed slit-smile, eyes narrow and black as hers, laughing at the world or his own private joke; little swimming motions of his arms and kicks so hard they'd woken Alana from sleep, when there was no boundary between them.

Now he was outside, for real, and she could love him.

I helped Alana get him latched on after birth. We tried the side-lying position: Alana on her side, Miguel on his, facing her. Miguel opened his mouth wide. "Quick! Pull him in close."

I heard Alana gasp when she felt the sucking power of his pursed lips. Put that stupid breathing to use for the first time. Honestly, I don't put much stock in it myself. After nursing, Alana enfolded Miguel in her arms as he slept, and just before she dozed off, she said, "Dr Iz, it's the real thing."

That afternoon, Justin went to see Alana. He told her that Miguel had contracted an infection and he'd moved the baby to the neonatal intensive care unit. Every hour, he gave Alana an update. At five o'clock, Alana returned to her room on the arm of a nurse, her black eyes wild. Justin and I flanked the bed as Alana shook herself free. "Where's my baby?" Another nurse appeared, another poinsettia. "Take that away," I said.

Justin asked Alana to sit down.

"No!" She pulled her robe tight, belting it low. "What's happening?"

"The infection came on hard, hit him like a Mack truck." Justin's voice was quiet, nearly toneless, his eyes fixed on Alana's face, her chin maybe. "The smaller the baby, the earlier he's born –" Justin ran his words together, his raw-boned hands shaping the air, head and body inclining toward Alana. "Miguel was a good weight for thirty-two weeks, almost five-and-a-half pounds. But, he was still – contracted group B strep. A bacteria in –" His voice went metallic, hands stalled. "We treated him. Infection got into the blood before the antibiotic kicked in. Once you've got sepsis, pneumonia –"

"Who let infection in?" Alana shouted, her arms rigid at her sides.

"Infants can get infected before or during delivery and –" Justin's voice broke, the metal melting. "I'm so sorry, Mrs Calderón."

"Get out."

"Alana, *Alana.*" I held her shoulders. "Can I bring you Miguel?"

Later, Alana called me in from the hall. She was still in the papery hospital gown stained with lochia. "Help me," she said, holding Miguel curled in her arms, his eyes open, mouth agape, one thin arm and tiny hand hanging limp down her side. Her husband Luis was with her, dozing on the bed.

"Hold Miguel a minute," Alana said, passing her baby to me as I had passed him to her, after delivery. We made a hammock of arms and hands, wrists and fingers brushing, as Alana slid Miguel's head into the soft space beneath my arm. His head sank into the crook, his scaly feet extending just past my elbow. He was cool, heavy with stillness, his mouth bloomed into an O, as if he knew all this air around him wouldn't give him another breath. Alana shut his eyes, his mouth, like he was sleeping. She took a small scissors from her toilette kit and snipped a lock of his hair, twining the ends with thread and slipping it over her middle finger. Before I knew what was happening, she sawed off a thick swath of her waist-length hair with the scissors, and as I held the baby, she swaddled him in it, tucking the ends inside the tight coil. The abundance of glossy black hair, its keen-edged ends, made death seem impossible. I left Alana alone with a sleeping Luis, and Miguel, holding him tight against her chest, sitting on the edge of the hospital bed, rocking with a furious motion, a circling, round and around.

Sena is etched into the morning frost on my window, an arrow above the name pointing up. The *S* is a G cleft, the tail of the *a* underlining the name with a sweeping flourish. Inside, my little sister's asleep on my couch. She's in denim short-shorts, black tights, scrunched socks. Her commander boots, still tied, are kicked onto the floor. Her note says, *Whippet, boiler's bust.* I cover her and collapse into bed.

Later, I hear Sena cry out in her sleep – a skirl. Growing up, I rocked her night after night, while Mom nursed Dad through MS, or drank herself beyond despair. I rush into the living room and find Sena sleeping soundlessly, just a whisper of breath, in, out. She's thrown off the cover and lies crouched, face down, burrowed into the couch, hands tucked beneath her ankles. A frozen crawl.

New Year's

New Year's Day, I meet Justin for breakfast at the Empire. His hair is caught back low with one of his daughter's ponytail holders. He shares custody of Shoshanna with his ex-wife, Eileen; they divorced five years ago, before Shosh turned one. I've worked with Justin, been close friends for three times that long. The other night was a fluke. We study the familiar menu, look into mirrored walls, up at the chrome ceiling, down into jet formica. Mirrors, mirrors everywhere. We concentrate on *Today's Hedonist Omelette*, drink cup after cup of coffee and fall back on what's comfortable, our separate private lives.

"You know what did it?" Justin says, explaining why he is giving up his thriving practice. He rakes long fingers across his crown, then yanks out the hairband. "I'd invite friends over for Shoshanna. And she'd hide. In the bottom of the laundry chute, inside the washing machine. Once I found her folded into the fireplace."

I picture the little girl I've met with the dark eyes and resolute brows, see her curled knees to chest, comforted by the ashy mouth of the hearth. "She has you back now," I say, a split second before Justin's flinch.

Outside on Tenth, we embrace. Decorously. Our hug is the equivalent of French air kisses, our bodies don't touch, they only appear to.

Darkness closes in so early now. I hate these cold, lightless days that stretch on and on in the middle of January. At four, it feels like midnight. Sena and I are in front of the gold-lit window of *Cup and Chaucer*, a new bookstore/café on Hudson, looking into the scene she's made, "a surprise," she warned me on the phone, "nothing bad."

It's *The Princess and the Pea*, my favourite fairy tale in silent, motionless theatre. The twenty mattresses are iridescent clouds of blue, pink, and pearl, the pea a translucent emerald on the bottom, glimmering.

"You *were* the princess and the pea," Sena says, nodding slowly, "everything just so." My sister has a soft, distinct voice that enunciates every syllable; it sounds both definitive and child-like, a child learning to speak. "Remember when I put that feather in your bed?"

"A tiny perfect feather. Under the quilt and blankets and sheets. Under the mattress cover." I must have been about nine, Sena two. She didn't know I checked under my bed, inside closets, and beneath the mattress cover every night. My bedtime ritual. Less afraid of monsters than of closing my eyes, sure my parents would die if I left them even for a moment, in sleep. "Before you were born, I made Mom read me that story every night. Finally she went on strike."

"No stories? No stories, *ever*?" Sena's grey eyes widen, appalled, as if I'd said Mom stopped feeding me.

"Stories once in a while. Mostly songs."

"I never heard Mom sing," Sena says, her eyes distant, unfocused. "What songs?" She studies her display. Not waiting for my answer, she disappears inside the bookshop, and a moment later enters the window to lift a cloud, which separates into clumps of cotton, and adjusts the pea, which reverts to paste.

Before you were born, they were two different people, I want to explain, watching her work. *As if their lives were bisected into first part and second part.* "Mom made up songs," I answer when Sena returns. "The *Iz-All medley.*"

The sadness in Sena's eyes melts away, becomes a gleam. "Forget it," I warn.

"There's a story-telling marathon Sunday," she says, as we walk around the corner to Barrow. "For kids at *Harbor House.* Want to read?"

"Sure," I say, as we leave the display and head toward Sena's studio on Waverly.

Sena's place is one tiny room on the fifth floor. Unstable piles are everywhere: laundry, scarves, shoes, makeup; the collected works of C.G. Jung and *The Night of the New Moon*, by Laurens Van Der Post; design and dessert books, a *Merck Manual*; sketches, snapshots. I'm trapped inside a closet where the rod has broken, shelves collapsed. Sena takes my black leather satchel and throws it onto a chair stacked with drawings, hose, hats. She scrunches up the sleeves of her sweater. "Now. I could open a Chianti or pour you a Courvoisier."

I feel as if a vapourous cloud cocoons me, removing me from Sena. My head's a helium balloon, threatening to carry me off. I remove winter layers and settle cross-legged in the middle of the floor, as Sena navigates around the clutter in black cords and her cobalt sweater with big covered buttons. She shoves stacks against walls, piles into corners. "I know," she says, "I'll make Irish coffees."

I see our Mom drinking from a juice glass painted with sunflowers. Drinking gin, then washing her glass clean with soap and near-scalding water. The glass sparkling, she places it on the window ledge behind the curtain spattered with violets and bluebells.

"Could you make me a cup of tea?"

"What?" Sena swivels around and studies my face.

"Do you have that almond stuff? Almond pleasure, sunset, almond –"

"No almond anything."

"Lapsang, then."

Sena brings our drinks and sits across from me, her back against a pine stool. Caught under one of its legs is a beautiful sweatercoat of my mother's, squares of angora and mohair, velvet and corduroy, sewn from scraps of our old clothes. She cut pieces from Dad's brown cords worn nearly translucent, a pilled angora sweater of mine, even a flannel pillowcase of forest green. It hurts to see it twisted and caught under the leg of the stool; only last Thanksgiving she wore it when we gathered at a restaurant near the hospital. I nudge Sena forward and carefully lift the sweater out from beneath the leg, laying it across my lap. Glancing around the apartment, I see other things of our mother's: her carved peacock letter opener inside Sena's junk drawer, her beechwood comb and brush, packets of old photos strewn about like playing cards. I run my hand across the sweater, feeling its many textures. Lifting it to my face, the fabric smells warm, of patchouli. I see a new hole, torn by the stool, and a helpless panic rushes through me. "You should take care of Mom's stuff."

Sena shrugs.

"Mind if I take this?" I drape the sweater over my arm and get up, surveying the debris.

"Go ahead." Sena folds her arms across her chest, then laces them beneath her knees. Rings are stacked on four fingers of both hands – antique gems, turquoise, agate – all cool stones.

I gather the letter opener, the brush and comb, the old photos, already getting dog-eared and coffee-stained. "We should make an album."

"Mom never bothered with pictures."

"You know, she wore this," I put my arms into the sweater and button it up, "when she was pregnant with you."

"Looks it," Sena says, laughing. "We could both fit in there now." Sena stretches out her legs and sips her Irish coffee, which still smells strong enough to warm me. "So. Was it fun being an only?"

"Sure." I sip my tea, as those seven years before Sena's birth sift back, when I had my mother to myself. She took me everywhere in a homemade sling she sewed from gauze bandages and a sheet. I went with her to her office at Eldridge High where she was a guidance counsellor. She bathed me in the bath with her. I slept tucked under her arm, so she could lift me onto her breast without waking up. She nursed me for two years, then I went on to lap-food. Apparently, I refused anything by jar or spoon; solid sustenance had to come, like the milk, directly from her. So I sat in my mother's lap as she mashed banana between her thumb and forefinger, and I nipped it off. I feel the gnawing in my stomach that won't go away now. "Sena, do you have any crackers or anything?"

She shrugs, then goes to look. "I'm planning something special," she calls out from the kitchen, "for your fortieth."

"No surprises, *please*."

Sena offers me a biscuit, then puts the plate down on a side table. "I need to see your book," she says, reaching for my bag. The heavy satchel slips through her fingers and thunks to the floor, its contents tumbling out.

"Shit. My life's in there." As I gather my belongings, Sena picks up my book and slowly leafs through it.

"My God," she says, barely moving her lips, her index finger marking a date; I'd folded back that page, noted monthly appointments in light pencil. Closing my eyes, pink rushes behind the lids. I see the tiny tadpole, smaller than a grain of rice. I didn't want Sena, anyone, to know what's still invisible. Once people know, it's all they'll see. My patients tell me this – their state takes up all the space.

Sena's fingers curl around my book, her hand trembling imperceptibly. The day I found out, I wrote September twenty-sixth on my palm, then erased the date with spit.

"Are you going to tell Zach?" Sena asks. "Might not be a good idea, if I know Zach –"

"Whoa! I haven't seen Zach for six months, Sena . . . unless his sperm are airborne."

"Iz, I'll go with you." Sena puts her hand gently on my shoulder.

I shrug her off. "Where?" The sharpness in my voice takes me by surprise.

"You've got to have crisis, Iz, this chaos swirling around you." Sena's face floods with colour. "Since Mom died –"

"Crisis swirling around *me?"* I hear my voice break, as I finish gathering my things and replace them in my satchel, along with Mom's letter opener and brush and comb. "Maybe this is a crisis for *you*."

"You can't see it," Sena says, standing, "because it's your element. You can't, you're not going to have this baby, Iz, I mean your life right now –"

I am alarmed by the look on my sister's face. Terror. Her grey eyes are wide and watery, her lower lip folded in, pinned by a tooth. She wraps her arms around herself, cold.

I take her firmly by the shoulders. "Look. I don't know what I'm going to do. I don't need your permission for anything. Or your opinion." Sena twists from my grasp.

I badly want to be alone, but as I put on my coat, I remember all those times I picked Sena up and enfolded her in my arms, when she was a baby and I was a child, and she'd fallen while holding onto the coffee table, crowing *Mamamamama*, jumping wildly up and down, ecstatic with the sound of her own voice and the power of her thighs, till her fingers slipped and she fell, hit her head, looking up at me for a stunned offended moment, as if to ask, *Izzie, am I hurt? Do I need to cry?* Later, she hurt herself with purpose, wore each new scar like a badge. Diving into a rocky river from a bridge. Returning to a burning building for her cat. It took everything I had just to keep her alive.

"Sena, I'm not going anywhere." I kiss my sister, a quick brush across her forehead, and head down the long flight of stairs. Although it's bitter cold, I walk.

Valentine's

Alana Calderón doesn't show for her six-week check-up, so I call. I can't tell much over the phone, though her voice is thick as she tells me she couldn't handle coming in. That's when I know I'll never see her again.

I send Justin a bouquet of green and purple balloons to cheer him up. He's pining for his old life, his lost practice – even the mad-dog craziness at the hospital – missing his hundreds and hundreds of children – the kids he can see for fifteen minutes, then leave. I haven't told him yet.

I get a card from him that says, *Remember . . . No Matter Where You Go, There You Are.* Telepathy.

Passover

Tonight, there's a warm wind blowing through my window. I peel off my clothes layer by layer and tilt toward the mirror. There's an unfamiliar roundness in my cheeks and chin. I have breasts for the first time, at forty, and trace my fingers over the blue web of veins shimmering through the skin. I know the inescapability of my Yes, to have this baby; the boundary it has drawn around my life, myself.

I look through flesh and blood and bone and see her forming. A beating heart I can't hear, arm and leg buds, the beginnings of fingers and toes, cartilage and bone. She's there and not there; so am I.

I switch off the light and lie naked in the dark. All at once, it comes. A bubble blooming, then bursting in the space of a breath. A winged fish streaming through sound waves. The dip of a kite, tugged sharp. A tiny parachute freefalling through space. The world tips away until the feeling stops, slips into nothing. I wait, listening. Summoning. I want to feel it again, but can't make it come.

I reach for the phone as pale watery light filters through my apartment. I'm taken aback by his pickup, his phlegmy, "Low-oh?"

"I'm pregnant."

The moment distends like a zero. I hear the phone crackle and spit, gaze out my window. The early morning light is dusky, as I stare up at the elevated sign for Manhattan Mini-Storage. Cobalt blue, electric white. Call S-T-O-R-A-G-E. A stick figure holds an empty box against the line of her torso about to enter a larger identical box. Then she's inside, holding her box within the box. A leadenness builds at the back of my throat.

"I want to be with you," Justin says, his voice low, his words uncharacteristically slow and distinct. "Now."

"Give me a minute." I feel frantic, need time alone. "Let's meet –"

"Squires."

We fill a thermos with coffee and get toasted muffins to go. Down Ninth, we pass Covenant House with its hundreds of tiny portholes, a great white ship frozen on shore. Some of the small round windows are lit golden, others black. When I met Justin, he was a consulting physician there. Many of the kids he took care of are dead or back on the street. He isn't sure if he did any good, maybe offered a temporary reprieve. As we pass by, I hear his achey laugh. He turns to me and says in Anthony Hopkins' English, *Whippet, am I a good man, or a bad man?* I remember trying to comfort him, years ago, after a boy he'd built some rapport with shot himself one bright morning in Times Square. That boy had a pull toward death no one could avert. The will to live was broken as surely as an arm or a leg. Death was more arresting.

We continue downtown and nearly have the streets to ourselves. At the Orange Cube at Liberty, we stop a moment and Justin gazes past me. I see a slight tremor at the corner of his lips, I have no idea what he's looking at. "So. You *are* flipping out."

He smiles, his tongue caught between his teeth. "Okay, but –"

"Don't get romantic on me. You've been through all this."

"It doesn't end."

I think of conception, pregnancy, labour, delivery, and parenthood in their unrelenting forward march, with or without you, ready or not, as we head down to Battery Park. Strolling along the Promenade, we watch the first sun glittering over the Hudson, more pink than gold. A wet wind blows over the river, whipping up tiny white-crested waves. Justin looks out toward the river, then at me. "You've been pretty elusive lately."

"I didn't want you talking me out of this."

Justin studies me, trying to discern my new shape beneath loose cotton blouse and grey leggings.

Encircling my satchel in both arms, I say, "I'm sixteen weeks," as leaves blow from dripping branches and cling to our clothes. "I got my amnio results. All's well, so far." I raise my right hand. "Never again will I tell another pregnant patient that it's just a pinch, feels like a blood test. It feels like a needle in your belly."

Justin's laugh is low and mischievous. "You're getting a *real* education."

I sling my bag over my shoulder and break away from him, walking toward the bank of binoculars. I plunk in a quarter and look through. Brown hairs slash across the lens. There's a blur of marbly green: the Statue of Liberty, a patch of torch. I lift my head. "This," I say, folding my hands across my belly, "isn't something I let myself want."

Justin tilts his head to one side, waiting, but I can't explain. Once I knew I was pregnant, I felt this longing surface, it was probably always there.

"It's funny," Justin says, his voice far away, speaking to himself. "I was certain, cocksure I wanted a big brood, five kids, as many –"

"As would come out?"

"Then we had Shoshanna . . . no time or energy for our old talks, just the to-do list." A ship creaks against the pilings; we watch a ferry pass. "I remember our first date. As parents." Justin shakes his head, laughing to himself. "We wanted to get to this Hitchcock festival, up in New Haven? Well, we got there. And crashed out in the front seat of the car."

"Didn't it get any easier?"

"Harder." Justin looks across the river, toward Jersey. "In different ways. You know, it's so easy to say, *I love kids.* Just one, that's another thing."

I think of my mother, splintered by our demands. Justin, the man who loved children, divorced before his one and only was a year old. I've seen it happen with lots of friends. "You simplified your life, Jus, now it's messed up."

"You could say that," he says, smiling.

I'm glad I've got the little dressing room off my bedroom, that'll be the nursery. Mom left me something, I can do this. My exhilaration speeds into panic as the promenade fills with mothers and children; nine months doesn't seem quite long enough.

We walk to the end of the boardwalk as a vendor swings open the quilted side of his snack truck. I buy another coffee in the park, despite Justin's disapproving look. Leaning against the lip of the fountain, I relish the quicksilver bolt of my second cup, thinking that when our child comes into the world, Shoshanna will be the same age I was when Sena was born.

Justin stretches his legs out on the grass surrounding the fountain. "Even after Shoshanna," he says, "when I'd stopped planning for kids, these names would float through my head. Just names I liked."

"Don't tell me," I say quickly, feeling my mouth tingle, tasting something sour and sweet.

Independence Day

From the Jersey Turnpike, I spot Cloudstreet, a grey cement block built low to the ground, windowless, temporary as barracks. The construction looks foundationless, plunked like a child's toy, on the Jersey flatland. "Why are they open?" I ask, turning to Justin in the passenger seat, then Sena in back. The place stretches out before us, the size of a football field with arched signs like goal posts, on either end.

"Because they never close," my sister assures me as I wedge the Volvo into one of the few remaining spaces, silky sun flowing over the bodies of hundreds of primary-coloured cars. Sadness squeezes the back of my throat, as I think of my mother pulling into the parking lot at the mall, Jones Beach, the circus; stopping the car, sometimes resting her head on the wheel.

Justin hops out, Sena a moment later, both moving quickly to my door to help me out. I swing my legs over, plant them flat on the burning asphalt and grasp Sena and Justin's hands for leverage. "One, two, three, okay, *up*."

One trimester to go and I've run out of clothes that fit. Today I'm in Justin's XXL t-shirt, a pair of terry mules, and a babushka to absorb sweat from scalp and neck. I can't stand anything banding my belly, so no no-nonsense maternity panties for me. It's ninety-six degrees.

I squint into the light, trying to find an entrance. "Why aren't these people at the beach? Why aren't *we* at the beach?"

Justin and Sena ignore me like a child who's whined the same complaint too many times. I shamble between them toward Cloudstreet, pressing against the heft of humidity.

Inside, refrigerated air blows down from side and ceiling vents. There's an information booth, several cafés, a ballroom. No, really, a Ball Room – a huge mattressed and padded space filled with red, yellow, green, and blue plastic balls – which the kids jump and roll around in. We follow pink and blue arrows to the southernmost wing, *Everything for Baby.*

Wedged between Justin and Sena, I walk slowly through sample nursery after sample nursery, surging with the crowd of pregnant women and their husbands, lovers, mothers, children. Many carry small note pads and studiously record descriptions and prices. Each room has a theme, a name. *White Angel* sports a shiny painted crib with a lace canopy tiered like a wedding cake, comforter, curtains and border to match. "What I want is a basket."

"You're not having a dog, Whippet," my sister says. "A bassinet is what you need. Jus, look at this one," Sena says, tugging him toward the dancing cherubs of *Jubilee,* as I wander off alone in search of food. Around the corner, I find a café and order a chocolate malt, savouring the satiny chill as it slinks back against my throat. Today, she lounges on my sciatic nerve, shooting hot needles through my spine, buttocks, and legs. She's growing huge, edging out space for bladder, stomach, lungs. I organize my life around the next bathroom, have trouble finding the next breath. I've gained forty pounds . . . so far. How can this be? When I complain to Dr Lucci, he prescribes more pasta. At this late date, I'm questioning my sentimental choice of a physician. Tonio Lucci was Dad's partner, his best friend.

For a while, I watch a mother at the next table. She looks calm in a blue sundress, blonde hair caught back low, six children surrounding her, all under seven, I'd guess. And she's on her own.

"Tell me," I say. "The real thing's got to be better," I pat my belly, "than this." Pregnancy has brought this out in me, speaking to strangers.

The woman has a secretive smile on her lips, sphinxian. "Depends when you ask me."

"So . . . planning any *more*?"

"I'm trying to get rid of the ones I have."

We both crack up, as she hugs her baby girl to her chest and wraps a shepherding arm around one of her boys. I'm beginning to see that motherhood is like this. Two halves to every question, an assertion and contradiction poised in gravity-defying balance.

It's painful to sit, so I walk, looking for a bathroom. Off a long dim hallway, I wander into a storeroom, a graveyard of unmatched pieces, all damaged or irregular. I spot a lovely crib of unfinished pine with a stencilling of vines and leaves on its headboard. There's a maple rocker with rounded arms and I sink into its quilted seat, propping my feet on a wicker stool. "Going this way," my mother would say to me in her ninth month with Sena, as I helped her turn in bed. I hated the creature inside as it pummeled and kicked, straining for freedom.

Inside a bassinet with torn bumpers, I reach for a dangling sausage arm and pull out a Humpty Dumpty doll with a jingle trapped in his belly. His black button eyes blink in the fluorescent light. He wears a red hat that sits like a tiddlywink on his head.

He is mine. Alive as Mom and Dad. He talks, can dance and laugh, makes a pillow for my head. What is he doing in Sena's crib?

I'm in her room, listening to her breathe. Her crib is cozy, the comforter soft and warm. I climb in. Sena moans as I rub her tummy. *You have to hold Humpty, hug him and hold him and never let him go.* I place my fat eggman in the crook of Sena's arm. She makes a whistling sound.

Mom is sad since Sena came, faraway. Dad is not the same. I watch him when he doesn't know I'm looking. He doesn't finish his sentences anymore. There's a trembling at the corner of his lips that makes his smile strange.

I stroke Sena's bald head, then place Humpty's belly over her face. *Hug him, hug him, never let him go.* I squash Humpty's belly against her eyes, nose and mouth, feeling her tiny arms flail, her legs kick, then flicker into a twitch. I press down harder, *hug him, hug him, never let him go.*

Let go. Let go!

Sena is pale, bluish, for a second before her gasp. Slowly, her cheeks warm. She screams as I climb out of her bed and take her into my arms, rocking her up and down, fast as I can. I'm shaking, can't stop.

Sena smiles at me with her whole face. Coos. Blows raspberries. She sticks her chubby fingers into my mouth till I bite them, then pulls them out. I nip again, our regular game. I love the sound of her chuckle, secret as bubbles bursting in her belly. Carrying her into my parents' room, I know: I can't tell them, anyone, *ever*. What I've done.

Holding Sena, I bend down and put my cheek against my mother's breast. She snores, air dragging in and out. I make little clicking sounds. Like magic, her sawing stops. I listen for my father's rasp – like something tearing – then put my hand on his chest to feel it rise and fall. I count each breath. His chest is warm – scratchy – a cage of bones. I lie down carefully between Mom and Dad, holding Sena tight, snailed inside the curve I make. I touch her soft dented spot, watch the tiny heart pulsing inside her head. Dad rasps, Mom snores, Sena whistles again. Lying awake, I feel myself grow big, scooping out into a cave. I hold them all inside me, warm and whole, miles beneath the earth.

Sukkot

Justin and I make love with purpose. As he strokes and tongues and kisses my belly, I feel deep sustained pulses, sensations never known to me before, and then a climax so powerful it seems bottomless. Minutes pass, and when I get up to go to the bathroom, waves of pleasure tug into a slow, rhythmic pull and release.

Three p.m. Alone at home. Blinds drawn. Contraction rings eddy under the skin. I watch them, counting the beats, the space between. I'm terrified. Why do I want to hold her back, inside?

Midnight. Painwaves. Crazy sea, the same ferocity, each wave with its own cleft, crest. An ache at the base of my spine, whipping into a vortex around front, squeezing in the pit of my belly, a burning vise. I rock and rock in my Cloudstreet chair, then sit in the tub, warm water lapping against belly, back.

Four a.m. Painwaves beyond imagining. A beat for breath. I call Justin, then move my chair into the shower. Let near-scalding water pound against my back.

Four forty-five a.m. I'm grateful for the wheelchair that meets me at the entrance. Surprise, surprise. Then I'm lying on the delivery table, feet up, feels wrong – I should be at the other end. Justin, Sena, Lucci, my labour nurse, Corinne. Too many people around me. Sena flashes photos, postcards: Isle of Skye, Portofino. I slap them away, hear breathsounds lacing into Debussy. "Turn that shit off!" Sena presses a cool cloth against my sweat-streaming head, Justin feeds me ice chips. An implosion. The bellyburst rupturing into an avalanche, green behind my eyes, inside my head. Rhythmic gushes between my legs, straw-coloured, flowing into green-brown. My insides turned out.

Peak atop peak atop peak. I'm hot, shivering. Corinne's face is close to mine, her mint scrubs spill against my cheek. I'm going *Huh, huh, huh.* She says, "Ride it, ride over the top of it."

A scalding sting from perineum to rectum. "Get the bitch out!"

"Stop cussing, Iz, Push!"

I sit up, holding onto Sena and Justin. One heel braced on Justin's shoulder, the other on Lucci's. I hold my breath, tuck chin to chest. Blood turns to fire. I bear down with everything I've got.

"Good!"

I reach down. A hard crescent, damp soft hair.

"Push! Hold it. Stop pushing – blow."

I feel her head squeeze out. Glance at Justin. He's mute, shell-shocked. I've got to see her.

"Give a little push, Iz. That's it."

Out she comes in a slithery rush. A blood-red scream goes on and on.

I feed her, both of us shrouded in the sudden quiet. Between her fingers and toes, in the soft crease of a thigh, are moist crusts of meconium. She has an inside-out smell.

I look at Justin. His smile is drawn out now like a long sound. We name her Arden for my mother, Ariadne.

They say you forget the pain. *I've* said that. I never will again. Never will forget for that's losing this forever. The green avalanche loosening, sliding free, my roar now hers.

THE HAVEN

Nia climbed out of the subway, shedding her sweater. Blinking in the light, she felt a hand on the back of her newly bared neck. The touch was gentle, familiar, and the depth of the voice surprised her, it too like a caress.

"V, you going back to the Haven?"

Nia wished she were V, wished she were going back to a place called the Haven.

A boy about sixteen looked down at her, his eyes emptying. The light hit them and they turned to glass, eyes of such a pale blue, they appeared crystalline. Cold and beautiful. "Sorry," he mumbled, tangling a hand in his blond curls before merging into the crowd crossing the street. Nia waited a minute, then followed.

She walked some distance from Seventh Avenue to a run-down section of Park Slope bordering Fort Greene, where the boy entered a large, shingled house badly in need of paint. Its soiled white downspouts ran along the front lawn; a porch lattice hung open in a loose flap revealing refuse, broken glass, and the innards of a foundation. Tiger lilies grew in tall, hunched clusters.

Nia lingered on the sidewalk under an elm. The house looked lost among the brown row houses: it was the colour of forest firs, shutters and trim painted black, with an extraordinary number of windows. Nia counted twenty in front, which caught the last of the light and glimmered gold.

Inside a screened-in porch, kids were gathering. They stood around a wooden table set for supper, laughing and talking like brothers and sisters. There must have been a dozen, no parents in sight.

Nia lost herself in the tinkling of glasses, the smell of garlic and butter wafting from open windows, the lighting of tall, wine-coloured candles. She stared at the candle light – it was so unexpected – till the bang of a screen door made her start.

A young woman approached Nia from a side door. She was short and tautly built, dressed all in black. *Diamonds are a girl's best friend* was scrawled above the picture of a baseball field on her shirt. The woman looked older than the other kids, probably late-twenties, about Nia's own age.

Nia folded her arms across her chest, though the June evening was mild. "I stopped to see –" She started again. The young woman waited, Nia made no move to leave.

"Supper," the woman said, motioning impatiently toward the house.

"Any openings?"

"I could put you on a waiting list. Do your parents know where you are?"

"I doubt it." Nia's smile flickered into a twitch at the corner of her lips as she followed the woman inside.

Of course there was confusion. It was a volunteer job Nia was after, not temporary shelter. Her interior landscape was so vivid, insistent, the pathway from inside to outside was paved with obstacles; she often didn't make herself clear. She got the job nonetheless, helping with meal prep on weekends at the youth shelter.

Within a month, Jez Garcia, the director who had found her spying on the lawn, told Nia that the kids had really taken to her. "You don't try too hard. You try, they torture you."

As Brooklyn blistered, Nia gave more time to the Haven. She organized day trips to swimming pools and amusement parks, planned outings to concerts in Prospect Park, dance performances at BAM; she joined the Haven's softball team and supervised menu planning. Once a meal was eaten, the table cleared, she found it hard to pick herself up and go, as if her limbs had grown heavy with an unfamiliar purpose and contentment.

It was a flammable August afternoon and the residents were sitting in a circle on the porch, a counsellor named Francis straining to get that week's Group off the ground. Behind his head was a carved wooden plaque designed by the first residents of the shelter: *People pay for what they do, and still more, for what they have allowed themselves to become. And they pay for it simply: by the lives they lead. James Baldwin*

That day's topic was "What Home Means." Nia sat in the one-armed rocker, bare feet propped on a footstool, a newspaper spread open on her lap, which she pretended to read. It was soothing to listen in, imagining what she would say if she were inside the circle. Nia's real home was a small coastal village in Argentina near Puerto Deseado. Of course she didn't remember it, didn't know the place at all. Her birth mother left her swaddled in a straw basket between the fruit and fish stalls at the open air market. Gisela Negrón, who owned the fish stall, cared for Nia for the first three months of life. Then she was adopted by an American couple, the Woods, and taken back to Lorain, Ohio. That was home for a while, but when Nia turned ten, her parents never returned from Rome, their plane exploding into a gold and orange fireball. . . . From the street came the tinny clang of one trash can emptying into another; a mother called her boy inside, "Ain't you gonna eat?"

Inside, Athena played with her hair. "Home don't mean nothing, it's a word." She had a wardrobe of wigs and extensions; that day's was strawberry blonde, cut short in a shag.

"A place you belong to," said Shamel, a heavy, soft-spoken boy with a mushroom haircut. He was always the first to co-operate, sometimes he took the lead.

"This is a jive topic," cut in V, tucking in her sheer blouse which showed a lace bra beneath.

"They all jive topics," Athena said. "'Dealing with our anger.' 'What we want to be if the world just give us a chance.' Shit."

"You tell us, St Francis. You going to Harvard. To the Divine school." That was V.

"You got talent, St Francis," chimed in Athena. "Don't be wasting it on us."

Francis laughed, an edgy show of good nature. He was tall and stooped with a roan-coloured beard, pale freckled skin. "You can carry a kind of home inside you," he said, tired blue eyes distant behind wire-rimmed glasses.

V sucked her teeth. Athena stared straight ahead, opened her mouth wide, and stuck her tongue out toward V, as they burst into song, "One boy. Boy for sale, he goin' cheap. . . ."

Francis laughed again, looking into his lap. The man worked by textbook script, asked the kids if they wanted to *share* – Nia knew she should be inside that circle – she glanced at Evan, he was watching her. Pulling the frayed, leather-bound notebook from his pocket that he carried with him everywhere, Evan slowly flipped through its pages. He'd written a play, *Chaingang,* which he was directing at the Haven; the first performance was scheduled for next weekend.

Athena feigned a yawn, V sighed. "The writer about to speak. Listen up."

"A haven – it's a refuge *from* home life," Evan said. The white, crescent-shaped scar at the corner of his lips emphasized his mouth like a word inside parentheses.

"Author, author," Athena said. "Who you quoting?"

"GB Shaw. Paraphrasing."

"We supposed to be talking about ourselves," Athena countered.

"Home to me is sister Stacia," Evan said. "That's why I had to get *out.* Where's home to you, Nia?" His silver lenses flashed at her. She was seen-through. No, maybe seen.

V pointed at Nia. "You always listening in. What, *you* writing a book, too?" She smiled at Nia, a quick flash, then folded in her lower lip, waiting.

"Where you live?" chimed in Athena.

"Where's home to you, Nia? Where you live? Tell us where you live!" They chanted at her and Nia's heart beat faster as she joined the circle, sitting on the arm of Lacy's chair, the youngest child at the Haven.

"There's nowhere I belong to," Nia said. "I moved from place to place so much, none of them got inside me."

Athena nodded, moving her chin in small circles. "I like the Haven," she said. "You don't have to bunch yourself up." She and Nia looked at each other in a moment of communion.

Shamel glanced at a giant purple watch he'd hung from his belt loop. There were plans to go to a Reggae festival in Bed Stuy. "We gonna miss Breeze in the Bed."

V said, "Athena, me and you leaving Group." Taking her cue, the others collapsed their chairs.

"Okay, okay," Francis conceded. "We'll quit while we're ahead."

An eight-piece band was playing when the group reached the park, the crowd pushing in toward the makeshift stage, kids and counsellors dancing and clapping, all but Evan who stood apart, his breathing laboured. Pulling an inhaler from his pocket, he drew in the vapour, as Nia lightly touched his wrist. "Let's get some air," she said, leading him away from the crowd.

"I want to show you where I live," Evan said, once he'd caught his breath. "I mean lived."

Nia checked it out with Francis, who gave the okay and told them to be back in an hour.

They pressed against the viscous heat with slow swimming motions. Nia held her arms out from her sides, not wanting any part of her to touch another part. She was a small, fine-boned woman, ordinarily contained in her movements: limbs held close to her body, gestures precise, even minimal. She had caramel skin, dark blue eyes, a prominent mole in the curve of her neck.

Black hair grazed her waist, but she swept it up carelessly with a tortoiseshell clasp. Her beauty made her self-conscious and she'd become an expert in camouflage.

As a child walking around Lorain, Ohio with her adoptive parents, people would look from Nia to Eugenia and Richard Wood and back again. Barely concealed puzzlement dissolved into complacent smiles, as if each perfect stranger shared a secret with the family. Nia and her parents hated those smiles. Later, at the Immaculate Conception Home, Nia felt drab and blurred, as if she'd lost her outline.

Evan pulled a knot of ringlets off his neck, securing a ponytail with a dirty rubber band. He walked with his feet set wide apart, shoulders swinging, hands sweeping and slicing the thick air. He was an actor in a one-man show, glancing at Nia now and then with the vague smile that was a permanent part of his facial features, a smile that had little connection to his thoughts or moods. His smile disturbed her – it was like a hand covering a face – Nia's own habit as a child. Now she wanted to peel Evan's smile away as her friend Camille had drawn Nia's hand from her face and said, "Nia, look at me."

They turned onto a side street and Evan pointed out a brown brick building resembling a fortress, with an iron gate flanking its steps. "You know, I go to Ellery," he said.

Nia nodded, an imperceptible motion of her head. She found she learned more if she refrained from questions, but she had to hold herself back. Ellery was a special school for troubled kids.

"That's where I got the inspiration for *Chaingang*. My hero's Lonnie. Wants to be a HardHed like his idol, Soca: thick gold chains, double HH's hanging inside the collarbone? Soca gives his chain to Black-Eyed Susan. She wears it double round her ankle. But the chick loses it in the street, where Lonnie finds it. See, he's going to give it back to Soca – win him over – but Soca spots Lonnie first. Shoots the sucker for it. That's the irony that makes the story turn. You know, 'cause you're a writer."

Nia snorted. She was a staffer on *Primary Care* and had a knack for translating complicated medical concepts into English, not a skill she valued – it had nothing to do with her. Nia thought of recent projects: *Shedding Light on Photosensitivity* or *Pyelonephritis: Practical Pearls* and sighed. "Recipes."

"You're good at those." His smile widened, then contracted. "For my plays, I take stuff from life then blow it up into drama. My mind's always spinning – man, it's a kaleidoscope!" Evan squeezed his head between both hands. "One day, I go home to pick up this book I need. My *Roget's*, right? Sometimes I'm looking for a word, the one and only right word, like the one and only right person? And when I find it, it's like I rejoice!"

Nia smiled at him as if he were on a lighted stage. He'd been harder to know than the other kids despite his bravado . . . no, because of it.

They joined the thick crowds on Myrtle Avenue. "See, I had to cast kids who knew the story," Evan went on, "like they wouldn't be acting even when the lights went down."

Nia knew Athena had gone to Ellery. "That's why you picked Athena for Susan," she said.

Evan stopped speaking, his chin toward Nia. "Nobody knows that."

Nia instinctively covered her face with one hand and looked away. One afternoon, Jez had left her in charge for an hour. The kids were doing a variety of chores and Nia went from room to room, helping out, checking on them. Things were running smoothly, so smoothly Nia was at loose ends and felt a pull toward Jez's office, her desk. She sat in the swivel chair and slid from desk to bookcase to phone. Sliding open the file drawer, Nia drew out the stack of records. As a volunteer, she wasn't allowed access to files, but wanted more background, a context for each individual kid. She had an insatiable need to *know*.

Her fingers went straight to K for Knight, but Evan's file was out, and the air punched out of her chest. Next Nia found Jez's records, discovered she'd been a heroin addict, a resident twelve years before. Athena had gone on a binge smashing Christmas display windows along Fifth Avenue which sent her to Ellery; now she was doing okay in regular school. V had a history of crack use and prostitution. Shamel's parents had committed a joint suicide; he was raised by his grandmother, currently in the hospital for a third hip replacement. Nia gathered facts about everyone at the Haven, as if reaping an abundant crop.

It began after her adoptive parents' death. Everyone, *anyone* knew her history, the facts of Nia's life spread out around her, exposed, like the private contents of a spilled purse. No one imagined privacy might be a need like hunger or thirst. That's when the urge began to rifle through closed drawers and files, pockets and purses, to open sealed letters and packages, to expose, the need gnawing as hunger, a raw pull.

"Show me your building," she said, "where you and Stacia live."

They passed a dump ringed by barbed wire, piled with spare tires, slag heaps, and rancid garbage. "It's like smelling your own insides," Evan said, turning into one of the concrete courtyards of the Tompkins Houses. "Nia, think of this as a field trip, a little field trip of my life."

Brown brick oblongs stretched in an unvarying block-long series, windows boarded up, others shattered or missing their panes. Kids had scrawled their names life-size in paint-box colours: GARNET** DARNELL! CHEETAH$$$ JASMINE?? Laundry hung motionless on lines, heads peered up from stoops, down from window frames and fire-escapes, while hydrants spewed water into the street, kids splashing in the geysers and spraying the slow-passing cars.

Evan pointed to a top floor window in the project. On the fire escape was an oasis: red geraniums in big clay pots, gold and orange nasturtiums in earth-toned troughs.

"It's lovely," Nia said.

"Stacia's good with flora."

"Not fauna?"

“She’s twenty-one. Not exactly what you’d call together. After Mom died, she got worse. The morning Jez got me into the Haven, Stace was having her breakfast beer, right? Demonstrating how Halpen strokes her neck.” Evan rubbed the left side of his throat, moving his right hand in lazy figure-eights, his neck impossibly twisted. ‘He kisses so smooth,’ she said, and when I pulled away, she left her mark.” He pointed to the moon-shaped scar at the corner of his mouth. “Stacia’s got talons.” His thumb and forefinger formed a three-inch span.

Nia looked at him, but he was in his own world, laughing hard, single-syllable bursts detonating in the heat. “You don’t have to put up with that,” she said softly, glancing back at the flower garden on the fire-escape. “Won’t she see you hanging around?”

“Stacia, *home*? She’s still with Halpen or Grey Pepper or sloshing Screwdrivers at Tahira’s.”

They left the projects and passed by a Gaseteria, then a block of darkened, barred up stores. Ashkan, Everything 99 cents Everyday, Wanda’s Weaves, Waves, Cuts & Curls. “That’s Stacia’s shop,” Evan said. “She’s talented with a scissors.”

On Broadway, the heat pressed against them and Nia felt they might choke on the very air they were trying to breathe: an electronic clock thermometer said it was 4:32 and 100 degrees. Nia stopped an old man selling snow cones from a wooden cart.

Sucking the sweet fruity liquid from the ice, they passed under the El whose tracks spanned the width of the street, and all at once, it was cooler, a twilit world. Shards of sun glittered through the roof of the tracks, breezes tunneling down the street. They’d been plunged underground, the subway their ceiling, the roar of the train overhead like a thundering sky. Evan reached over and swept a stray tendril from Nia’s eyes, and her hair tumbled down thick and hot around her face. Nia felt for her barrette, Evan scanned the Avenue.

“We’d better get back,” she said, “they’ll be waiting.”

That night, Nia heard knocks on her door. His face was round and flattened in the peephole as if seen through a fish-eye lens. Nia pulled her robe tighter and opened the door halfway, standing behind it. A dozen of her scrapbooks were out, many of them open. She glanced behind her at the silent intercom, then her watch.

"I came in with some visitors," Evan said, reading her face. He had changed clothes since that afternoon. A freshly washed t-shirt hung loosely from his shoulders; cut-offs emphasized the paleness of his skin.

Evan reached into his back pocket and held something in his right hand, his fingers curled around it. His left fist was bunched up too, like a child with a treasure.

Nia gave him a puzzled look and waited till he opened his palm.

"I went back later," he said, "to find it," handing her the tortoise-shell barrette.

Nia laughed uncomfortably. "You know you shouldn't be here." She looked at her watch again.

Evan stepped past her into the apartment. "Sure," he said.

Her building smelled of damp, smoke, and solitude; the tiny studio was her cave.

"Old geezer in the foyer was laying out baseball cards," Evan said, stooping dramatically, "babbling about Lucy and Desi. Old hag comes out of the ground floor apartment, shrieking 'Frankie.' A whale waddles in with a parrot on her shoulder, bird's cackling 'Gertrude,' a bald chick right behind, pulling three dogs on a leash, ugly black wrinkled mugs."

"My open-air sanatorium," Nia said.

"Hey, I'm inspired! Why don't you save *them*?" Evan said abruptly. "It'd be neighbourly."

"Evan, you have to leave." Nia opened the front door wider.

"I need to talk to you."

"I'll be at the Haven on Saturday." She swept a hand through the open door, motioning him out.

"I can talk to you easier than Jez," he said.

Nia knew she should make him leave. Instead she asked, "Why?"

"My time's up soon," he said, as if he hadn't heard her.

Nia had the same qualms she'd felt in Jez's office when she discovered Evan's file missing. Later, she found out files were reviewed by the board before a resident was discharged. Once a kid left the Haven, volunteers were not to contact them for at least a year: that was one of the rules in the thick Conduct Code Jez had given her. The current group had woven together in a tight mesh, the fabric would unravel if anything changed . . . but that was the point, to change. To get better and leave.

"Why didn't you bring this up before?" Nia asked.

"You have a way of knowing things."

Nia looked away from him toward the blinded window and gathered up her scrapbooks, which nearly covered the floor. She'd been going through old ones, while sliding in photos and pasting down mementoes for her latest. She worked on them nearly every night; it soothed and absorbed her and put her life out in front of her where she could see and touch it. Where all her losses were just the links of a story, where everything flowed and made sense, even looked pretty.

"Stacia's on her best behaviour," Evan said, watching Nia stack albums at the back of the bottom bookshelf, before lining the front with volumes.

"Before I came to the Haven," he went on, "I'd tiptoe around her, for dinner, eat a sandwich in my room. Sometimes, *that* set her off." Evan gave Nia a sidelong glance and went to the bookcase.

"I know it's hard to believe, me being such a wuss." He laughed, then looked sad. Squatting, he pulled out Nia's copy of Greek myths, leafing through the illustrations. "If only my Mom was around."

Nia turned to face him, her back against the bookcase. Several scrapbooks were still open on the floor. "You can't live by if onlies," she said. It came out all wrong, like something Francis would say.

"Mom lived for us kids," Evan said, replacing the myths on the bottom shelf and scanning the spines of Nia's other books. "She worked as a nurse in a loony bin. Got involved with one of the patients. *Stacia* was the result. Had me, then left with us for another job, another state. We were living in Pittsburgh with our mom when he tracked us down." Evan looked at the floor, his large hands kneading empty space. He shook his head, then glanced at Nia, as if he was asking for something. "Mom changed our name, we were always moving, running."

"Did you know your dad?" She'd never known hers and didn't let herself wonder about him; there was nothing to go on. It was only when she saw girls with fathers that she got a jolt, wondering what it could be like, having one still.

"Not at all. After he died, I mean, I went to the mental hospital where he'd been on and off. Mom was dead by then. The nurses, aides, the other patients told me all about him. They said he liked to play Hearts, always gave little gifts to everybody." Evan closed his lips, his smile transformed into remorse.

Nia nodded slowly. She'd tried to know her adoptive parents after their deaths, too, to really find out who they were. Working on the scrapbooks her mother had started let Nia inside Eugenia's skin.

"You know what I like?" Evan said, his eyes steady. "You never say, I know how you feel."

"Because I don't." Nia retrieved another scrapbook and replaced it on the shelf.

"I really want it to work out," Evan said quietly, "with Stacia. She's visiting, trying to get on the wagon." He turned and went to the window. "I'm worried it's not going to last."

Nia shook her head slowly. She'd never let herself invest much in the people who took her in after her adoptive parents' death. Adults were people who deposited her at bus stops and train stations. She knew Evan sensed her resistance. He said, "Stacia's family. We're what's left." He opened the window blinds and looked out onto the street. "It's unfair," he said. "You know everything about me. You're a total blank."

Nia stared at his back, an ache in her chest. "That's untrue."

Evan leaned against the window, legs crossed before him. "I bet you grew up in a mansion, big white pillars around the porch, whole army of slaves."

Nia laughed, waving him away. "You're way off, Evan Knight."

When Nia spoke of her past, her voice was flat, eyes unfocused. People offered reflex shock and pity, or thought she was making up a story. The story of her life *was* like a fairytale. Recited so many times, it had lost its meaning.

Evan left the window, circling around her. He knelt on the floor before an open scrapbook, studying a photograph of Nia's foster mother standing in front of her stall, rows of fish gleaming in their troughs. Nia looked over his shoulder.

In the picture, her foster mother is not young, though tall and sturdy. She has dark, leathered skin, mute eyes. Blunt hair threaded with grey. Firm arms hold the swaddled baby out before her, an offering, though she is unsmiling, not even attempting to smile at the Midwestern couple who wield the camera.

Evan laughed, looking at Nia's infant expression: one finger poised at the corner of pursed lips, bald head tilted to the left, as if she were pondering some philosophical question. "Old sage," he said.

"That's what my Mom called me."

Evan turned the page to a picture of Nia's family in Ohio. Richard, Eugenia, and Nia sit in their "Florida Room," her father stretched out on the chaise lounge, her mother reading in a wicker armchair, Nia folded into the sill. Evan asked her about her family and Nia laid out the facts in her usual way.

"Thanks for the Cliff Notes," he said. "This is your life, Nia Wood." His eyes swept over her scrapbooks. "So . . . I get it. You *do* think you're like us." He nodded quickly.

She shook her head. "I never said that."

Evan stood, brushing himself off. "Why you doing this?"

It was impossible for Nia to answer. For a while, she'd lost her focus. Cranking out articles for *Primary Care*, the world seemed flat and drained of colour, but when she started working at the Haven, she felt herself come alive. Nia could never tell him how she'd float along in a good mood, everything right with her world, then realize all the while she was thinking of him. Seeing his face. "Look, do I have to justify myself to you?"

"Maybe," he said, as he walked out the door.

The Tuesday evening after Labour Day, Nia was at the donut shop sipping black coffee, glancing up each time the door opened with a jingle and windswept rain splattered against the milky glass. The rain had brought a greenish dark, an unseasonable chill. Nia was alone at the counter, wondering how Evan was doing when he slid onto the stool beside her with a suddenness that left her breathless. His hands trembled as he laid down his suitcase, then shucked off his knapsack, letting it drop to the floor.

"What's happened?" Nia pulled a clump of starchy napkins from the dispenser and gently wiped his face. She threw her coat around his shoulders. "You're going to get sick."

"Stacia's threatening me. Says she's going to make my life miserable."

Nia ordered Evan a coffee. "She's started in?"

He nodded, ladling four heaping teaspoons of sugar into his coffee. Cradling the cup between laced fingers, he let the steam warm his face.

"You speak to Francis?" asked Nia.

"Haven't even moved all my stuff yet. Wouldn't you know it?" Evan leaned his elbow on the counter, chin cupped in his palm. "My bed's already filled."

Nia looked into his face, at the scar where Stacia had scratched him. It was blanched, even whiter than his skin.

Evan snapped open his suitcase and lifted out a metal box. He handed it to Nia who placed it carefully on her lap as if it contained jewels. Its weight was a strange comfort, the lock a disappointment.

"I get so down around her," Evan said. "Guess I'll hang here tonight." He motioned the waiter and ordered a refill.

"Do you have any friends? I mean, someone you could stay with?"

"Sure. At the Haven."

"Look," Nia said, as she pushed her cup away, "there's not much room, but –"

His face glowed as if she'd turned on a hidden light beneath the skin.

Nia heated vegetable soup, made toast and tea, then settled across from Evan at the rickety card table outside the kitchenette, where she ate and worked and listened to the radio through nightly bouts of insomnia, mostly jazz. She clicked on the dial while soup simmered and tea brewed.

As she watched Evan eat, Nia smiled. He bent over his soup, gripped the spoon in a fist, and ate with ravenous absorption. She took pleasure in the crunch of toast and click of his spoon against the bowl. When Evan finished, Nia handed him the sleeping bag she'd pulled down from the closet and pointed out a place by the window.

Crouching, Evan peeled off his wet clothes, unfurled the roll and slid inside of it in one motion, his body barely changing its configuration. "Thanks," he whispered, "for everything."

When Nia came out of the bathroom, she heard the steady sounds of Evan's breathing. It was cool in the apartment, rainwashed breezes sweeping through the window. Unable to undress, unable to think about sleep, Nia sat in her usual chair at the card table, barely moving, making herself small so as not to wake him.

It was still night when Nia heard the strangled cry. She'd dozed at the table, and for a moment, felt it was her caught in the web of the nightmare. Realizing it was Evan she went to him.

He was curled, knees to chest. She touched his shoulder, said his name, and Evan's eyes flew open; he stared blankly at her, his pupils unnaturally wide.

"She's standing next to a butcher block filled with knives," Evan said, his voice nearly a whisper. "Serrated, paring, straight-edged. But the knives are like . . . *redundant.* She's stroking my back. 'There,' she keeps saying, like to a child who's fallen. 'There, there.' Each time she touches me, a layer of skin peels back, from my head down to my feet. Air stings. I'm shedding skins, getting thinner, transparent to the light."

Evan trembled and Nia shut the window. She stooped down and stroked his hair, but he jerked his head away. With one hand, he unzipped the side of the sleeping bag and threw off the top layer. His skin was blue-white, like mother-of-pearl.

"Make me come."

His face wore that smile and Nia wanted to slap it away. "Is something funny? Or is that a permanent part of your facial scenery?"

"I'm deranged. Ever been deranged?"

"Yes."

Evan covered himself with the flannel robe and Nia sat on the floor, crossing her legs lotus-style, then her arms.

He cupped her face in his palm, stroking along the underside of her jaw until she leaned into his touch, unconscious as a cat pressing against a bare leg. His hand glided down her neck, and settled at her shoulder near the wrap collar of her robe. She heard a soft murmuring of numbers, "one, two, three. . . ." as his thumb and first finger gathered collars – robe, flannel shirt, t-shirt – as if he were counting pages in a sheaf, shirts stacked in a drawer. His touch was so light yet methodical, it made her shiver. "A many-layered woman."

Nia shrugged, thinking of her mother's entries in her scrapbook, the words written in different coloured pens, like an intimate letter. *You hated being naked, screamed with every diaper change and sponge bath. The neighbours thought we were killing you. Air bristling against bare skin made your blood go cold.*

Evan drew her robe back off her shoulders and let it fall to the floor. "It's too warm," he said, "for all this." She unbuttoned her flannel shirt and pulled her T-shirt over her head, wanting to peel down to a core, for once, whole.

The rain had stopped, the breeze stilled, but the air held the moisture in every pore, suspended. It would be a dark, cloudy day. Evan covered her with his body and lifted her against him, long arms crossed around her back, and in the dark, his face lost its contour. "It's okay," he said, echoing a voice inside her own head, as she felt an unbearable weight in her abdomen, pressing down through her thighs. "It's okay," they both said again and again.

Nia spotted the sister right away, working a young girl's hair into a stiff prow and jungle of curls, a style identical to her own. She was dressed in a black lace bodysuit, short-shorts slung low across narrow hips. Nia had to see the eyes, but they were lowered.

"I've got a trim with Stacia," Nia said casually to the manicurist who sat by the door with rusty instruments soaking in cloudy water. She nodded toward the sister's station. Her hair was the same colour as Evan's, honey-blonde.

"She'll be with you in a minute. Coffee?"

Nia shook her head and settled in at the cushioned bench up front, watching the sister. She applied gobs of gel, minute-long streams of spray. Her makeup was frightening, violet lips and lids. Nia waited. Finally, the manicurist said, "Stacia's on the phone."

Thrown, Nia turned toward the back and saw a slim shadow leaning against the doorway, the phone cord twined around her legs.

A moment later, Stacia was in front of her. "Nia?" She motioned to her station in back. The slight ungainliness and stoop of her narrow shoulders took Nia by surprise, as she followed her. Stacia was tall and painfully thin with unusually long hands and feet. Her brown hair fell in soft waves to her chin.

As she sat in the swivel chair, Stacia's long fingers combing through her hair, Nia looked at their two faces in the wall-length mirror.

"What are we doing?" Stacia smiled at Nia in the mirror.

"An inch maybe?"

Stacia gathered Nia's hair in one hand and turned up the ends. "When was the last time you had a trim?"

"Can't remember."

Stacia laughed, a light quick sound. "You've got about five different lengths, bad ends. Let me even you out."

Nia nodded slowly.

"You'll still have yards of hair."

They moved to the sink. Stacia gently lowered Nia's head into the warm stream and Nia felt Evan's hands cradling her head, his fingers threading through her hair. "Why are you doing this to him?" Nia demanded.

"Excuse me?" Stacia's comb stopped near the crown.

"I know what's going on at home."

"Who *are* you?"

"A volunteer," Nia said. "The one he told the truth."

"The *truth*?"

"About your addiction; I know how Evan got that scar on his face."

Stacia stared at Nia, then slumped into the empty chair beside her. She shook her head hard. "I can't go through another round of this," she said.

"Neither can Evan. I'm going to help him get back on his feet."

"*You* are." Stacia laughed, a harsh rasp. "You don't get it, do you?" Her hands were up, fingers fanned between helplessness and fury. "Evan makes up stories."

Nia didn't speak for a minute or so. "You had a drinking problem."

"And my hair is hot pink."

Nia felt the blood drain away from her skin, leaving her cold and pale. "Wait a minute – your dad, he was in a mental hopsital, right?"

"Yeah." Stacia looked away.

"And your Mom moved from place to place all the time?"

Stacy's eyes were wary. "That's true."

"And Evan never met him –"

Stacia nodded.

Lies, truth, woven into tapestry. "I don't know where Evan'll go, what he'll do," Nia said.

Stacia fingered the pendant at her throat, a Fatima hand suspended from a black satin ribbon. "He'll come home."

Nia felt strange as she entered the Haven later that afternoon. She heard the front door bang hollowly behind her and walked through the screened-in porch, feeling odd and out of place. She found them in the living room. Stacia packed the last of Evan's things into boxes. They spoke in murmuring phrases, a private shorthand.

Nia stared at Evan, willing him to look at her, and then was startled by his gaze, as if his eyes had magically changed form. They swept down and through her, fluid and tremulous as water. She thought of him entering her the night before. The slats of the window blinds had let in the glow of the street lamp. Evan lay above her supported by his arms, his body slashed in black and white. A zebraman.

He plunged and reached, said her name, asked it like a question and the word sounded strange in her own ears, gone, a third person both of them were trying to find. Nia wished he'd hit bottom, but she was without edges; he fell into her.

Now Nia looked for him. Through the window, she saw Evan and his sister pass by the elm, as they headed home. Nia left the Haven for good and walked without stopping, until her limbs ached and her throat parched and she found herself on a street where she'd never been before.

SHRINE

When I was a young father, two kids were murdered in our small, sleepy town. No one mentions it anymore, but their faces stay with me. See, I loved those kids like my own and was involved, not in the murder, but in how things got unravelled.

Rocky Hill was a quiet place. Nothing much happened and it could get dull or too peaceful after a while. The dullness was mostly feeling closed in and too safe, surrounded by too many of the same kinds of people.

I met my wife Leigh here. It was early spring and I was driving down Mount Lucas Highway toward home. The sky turned a funny purplish green; I heard rumbling, a clap of thunder, and then rain pounded down, lightning bursting across the sky. There was a splintering crack – I lurched to a stop – then a whooshing crash like a wave breaking on shore, as a huge oak smashed across the road. Me and the driver going opposite got out of our cars and walked around the dead tree. We stood there, looking at each other, then the tree, its branches stretching across the double yellow lines, shivering in the wind and rain like some lost, tentacled sea monster.

Leigh was a tall, full-bodied woman with a smooth, easy walk, more like she was floating toward me. Her light brown hair blew in the wind and whipped across her wide cheeks, as she smiled at me – her brown eyes a match for her hair – and got into my car. She slid close and I felt the warmth of her body through the wet of the storm, her cheek cool against mine, her skin a little rough. I could have sat in that car forever, a more private place than a room somehow, as traffic stopped in both directions and help came in a whirl of flashing red lights and sirens.

Within a month, we were married. Leigh got pregnant almost right away with our first boy, Grove. It's hard for me to remember those early weeks when it was just the two of us, the closest to paradise I've known: part of another life, in another time, belonging to a different man.

We lived in a two-family house and I worked nights in a bagel bakery, while Leigh got a job as a nanny in the ritzier town next door. Soon our second was on the way. Leigh missed Grove and ached for the baby who we called Brady. Of course she was bitter about leaving ours to look after someone else's, but what it takes to survive doesn't always make sense.

We shared our two-family with the Dowds, Paul and Thea: yard and basement, keys to each other's houses, we made the separate halves back into one. Paul and Thea also had a couple of kids – Melissa and Nicky – a near-match in ages with ours. The year of the deaths, our Grove and their Melissa were three-and-half, the younger boys, two.

Paul was a shy, quiet type, an electrician. He hated the word, but I have to say it: sweet. It was in his smile, which was slow and kind, his eyes which looked at you steady, but there was something else about Paul. He was a lonely, driven guy, more serious than anybody I've known. I'm not saying Paul didn't enjoy life or laugh at a good joke, but behind that, he was super-sensitive, didn't like to give an inch, especially when he'd been drinking. Thea had a lighter edge, always with the ready come-back, quick as a fox.

Most days, I'd get home at the crack of dawn and sleep till noon, then fix lunch. Those long afternoons when I was home and Leigh at work, I spent time with all four kids. I had a special thing for Mel because my secret wish was for a girl. Mel had a gravelly voice; I'd hear her saying, Uglybugs, more story, her skinny legs slung over mine, an arm around my back. Ladymite was our main character and we talked out her adventures, day after day, a story with no beginning and no end. Nicky was gentler than my boys, happiest in his play kitchen brewing cup after cup of coffee in his own special way.

The nights were a strange time when different ways came up between us and the Dowds. Each evening, when ours were in bed, Leigh and I sat together at the butcher block having coffee. That's when the Dowds' signals came through the walls. Incense or scented candles were lit, their strong, musky odour drifting over. Eucalyptus. I liked that smell, but it made me sad.

The next thing that flowed through was the sound of jazz playing, sax and bass. Then the other sounds came. Thea was loud: a caterwauling scream, like she was dying from pleasure, and I saw her raking her nails down Paul's back, biting his neck, drawing blood for sure. Paul was quieter, coaching Thea low and insistent, like some athletic trainer or something.

Drinking our strong coffee, mine light, Leigh's black, we'd look at each other with half-smiles. One or the other would make a joke. Then Leigh or I'd get up quick, do something, anything, so as not to think. I had to leave for work soon, anyhow.

I noticed the change in Paul first. He started getting bad headaches, clusters he called them, with a sudden pain so bad, Paul cried out with it. He took painkillers and drank along with them. Furtive and edgy, now all he had for Thea were questions, this scared, suspicious look on his face. A detective out for clues to prove what he's already firmed up in his own mind.

"Whaddya give them for lunch?" I heard him say once, straight home from work, looking sideways at Thea.

She smiled, but not in her usual way; this was a sneer. Flipping her dark red curls over one shoulder, she goes, "Popcorn sandwiches."

"Salt? Nicky can't take salt."

"No, cyanide."

Another time, we were having one of our barbecues. Paul swirled the ice in his whiskey and said to Thea, "There's this lifeboat. You gotta save me or the kids."

"C'mon," I said, "quit."

"And to change the subject," Leigh chimed in. "Hotdog or hamburger, Paulie?"

Paul kept on with the same question, every which way. Thea had been drinking too, in a crazy kind of self-defense, and the sad thing was, when drinking, she got like him.

"No contest, baby," she went, huddling her two children close.

I saw the light turn in Paul's eyes as he shoved Thea so she nearly fell against the flaming coals. My Grove caught her. Nicky said, "Mommy, come inside."

The next day while Paul was at work, a woman showed up at the house. All through that spring and summer, she hung around Thea. She was older than us, maybe late-thirties, her features as strong and large as Thea's were small. This woman had a handsome face that would look good on a woman or a man. Her hair was a coarse black that went every which way. A part zig-zagged across her scalp, that wild hair greased close to her skull and braided messy. Her lips were thick, topped by a faint moustache, but she had nice eyes, a dark clear grey with the longest lashes I'd seen on an adult. I knew she wasn't from around here. Thea liked to take continuing classes and I figured she must have met her at one of those.

Jade. That was her name. Something she might have dreamed up for herself when she decided she was different. She was partial to the stone, wearing some jade-type ring on every finger of her big, sun-browned hands.

Nearly every day that spring, she and Thea made long fancy lunches in the kitchen, omelettes with ingredients you wouldn't want to waste in eggs, like salmon or spinach. As I played with the kids, delicious smells drifted into the yard; I heard their glasses clink, their private-joke laughter.

After lunch, Jade and Thea worked on their murals, drinking white wine or mimosas all afternoon. Those two cut out designs from coloured paper, magazine scraps, shapes from foil and whatnot, then pasted them on long pieces of other paper, covering the whole business with a couple coats of varnish. They would work at this for hours, all spread out on the kitchen table, with the mess from lunch moved to counters or the sink, drinking all the while.

There was so much in those pictures, so many bits and pieces, you just couldn't put two things together if you tried.

Once Jade left, I cleaned up, running hot water over egg crusts, sponging down cigarette butts mashed into blobs and smears of jam. I'd find small, coloured boxes in the garbage pail – Jade liked to give Thea presents – a silver lighter from Tiffany's engraved with a saying or poem, a pendant that held a perfume inside called Poison. I don't know where the woman got her money or balls from.

The day it happened, Thea flew out of the house looking . . . different, that's the only word I know for it. The morning was hot, air so sticky you wished you could peel it right off your skin. Not fit to breathe. Thea had on perfume sweet enough to make me cough and was all dressed up to kill: short tight skirt and one of those billowy tops that look so good on small women. She fed her kids quick, then went with them to wait at the edge of the driveway. Soon Jade's shiny red Jaguar pulled up and they all took off.

Around one o'clock, I heard Paul's old jeep Cherokee crunch into the drive. I was out in the yard playing with my kids, a game called Walking the Wire, where we balanced on the curb like it was a tightrope. "Where are they?" he asked.

I shrugged.

Paul shot into the empty house, then prowled around the yard.

I brought out a couple beers, a bowl of chips, Paul's favourite death-by-salsa. The air buzzed with the heat as much as the locusts, but I set out two chairs on the deck in a patch of shade from the maple. I sat down and stretched out my legs. Finally, Paul came over and we watched the boys looking for lucky rocks in the millions of grey gravel stones in the driveway.

Light sucked out of the sky, it turned lavender and watery, like colour painted on with a brush. The heat stuck around. Leigh called to say she'd be very late, so I phoned in at the bagel bakery. When it was almost twilight, the Jaguar pulled up.

There was a moment of quiet, when Paul looked at Jade, at Thea, at his two kids, and they stared back at him. "Hey, Mellie,"

Paul called out, his arms open, knees bent. His little girl stayed put, then ran straight back to the yard.

"Hey buddy, c'mere!" Paul went to the driveway and lifted Nicky into his arms, but Nicky shouted, "No!" wrenching away and hollering till Paul put him down.

I glanced back at the Jaguar, where Thea and Jade were unloading packages from the trunk: big plastic bags from the toy store, white boxes from the bakery. They made trips in and out, Paul following their footsteps and voices, not looking, not saying a word.

Jumping up, I clicked on the yard light, just for something to do. Moths flickered around the yellow bulb, clinging to the light, while Paul and I watched the kids play. Now and then, one of mine or his called out for me. I had a feeling then, though I couldn't have said it, that the people he loved most were slipping away from him, that he had no sure way to draw them back.

Thea popped her head out back and Paul leapt up, had her by the arm.

"Where've you been?"

Thea tried to shake him off. "Out."

"No? Really. Fucking where?"

I put my hand on Paul's arm, as Jade came out and stood by Thea. Then I squeezed Paul's arm hard and Thea broke free, and she and Jade ran into the bedroom. Paul and I heard the lock slide shut.

Inside, Paul stood staring at the blank white door, then lifted his fist, only to drop it. There was another silence. Paul was a man who didn't say anything unless he had something to say, a guy who didn't make a move till he had somewhere to go. Maybe five minutes went by, then Paul went down to the basement.

Total blackout.

Paul walked straight out of the house, sure in the dark, as a blind man. I heard him drive away in his jeep, and the quiet that had started when Paul entered the room gathered around us. Finally, that tall, dark-haired woman left, her safari jacket tied around her waist.

I got a flashlight and headed down to the basement, Brady in my arms, Grove right behind. Paul had removed a wire leading to the fuse box. Back in the kitchen, I got on the phone with Paul's work partner, Jamie, hoping he'd be able to talk me through the fix, but Thea was terror-stricken. "No!" she shouted. "Leave it."

Meanwhile, Jamie was still talking, giving me a blow by blow, which I'd already missed half of. I got back to him, but Thea disconnected the phone.

She went around the house gathering candles, checking the locks. If we'd lived in separate houses, she and the kids could've stayed with us. None of us had family nearby.

When Leigh got home, she and Thea set up more candles and a couple of hurricane lanterns. Leigh kept Thea company, comforting her and the kids, putting out all their favourite foods: peanut butter on cheese crackers, coconut snowballs . . . if you hadn't known what went on before, you'd have thought it was a party. I left for work.

Around four in the morning, I pulled out a tray of burnt raisin bagels, char falling off the crust. That's when I got the call from my older boy, Grove. His voice was shaking; he could barely get words out. Said something about fire and our house. I heard a deep voice talking to him in the background, then a man got on the line, the chief of the rescue team. He told me Paul Dowd set himself on fire, set his kids on fire, then someone else was speaking to me in a low, firm voice, a woman this time, the head nurse at the hospital. She said Leigh was okay, that she was watching over Brady and Mrs Dowd in the intensive care unit.

What I hadn't seen lodged in my gut, retched up in pieces. Paul dousing himself in kerosene. The burnt-oil smell in Mel and Nicky's room, getting inside their breath, under their skin, into their dreams. The catch of Paul's match on flint, a scratch, almost delicate like. The breathy pop of flames, exploding. Paul running, a human fireball. Straight for the bed Mel and Nicky shared when they were scared of being alone the whole night through. Paul squeezing himself in between, pulling his children in.

Nicky's keening, Mel's moans, deep in her throat, the two sounds, one high, one low, twist up together. The heat first outside – something to run from – then all around, inside, where you can't get away but take the fire with you. Burning wood, plastic, cotton, wool skin blood flesh bone.

Mel's eyes, wide. Green. Reflecting light. Eyes swallowing her face, Nicky's squeezed shut. His mouth, quivering, face falling with his crying, returning to Nicky's face, then back again. What I didn't see retches up. Paul again. Put pictures in an order. Douses himself in kerosene, lies down between, pulls Mel and Nicky in. And then I hold onto this: Mel, Mel and Nicky both believing their Daddy's saving them from the fire, holding them so tight against his chest . . . but my blood turns acid, not believing, a burning inside my veins.

Mel and Nicky were dead. Thea and my Brady, fighting for their lives. Grove and Leigh, nearly whole.

Brady pulled through. He'd live his life with bad scars; anyone who looked at him would know he'd been to hell and back. Thea, no one would recognize. Looking at her, I searched for the face I once knew. For the rest of us, the scars were mostly inside, where you couldn't see them.

Leigh and I moved to a new house, a cottage all our own. We were superstitious about two-families, even if it meant company and more space. Leigh left her job as a nanny and started waitressing at Friday's so we could be together days, and spend time with the kids. We hired a sitter and hoped life would get normal again.

For a while I was numb, except for what I could feel through my senses, the dry heat of the ovens at the factory, the smell of moist dough in huge vats, the squidgy feel of it between my fingers, the lingering odour of garlic, onion, and oil, the hot spray of my dawn showers.

Yet each and every day, I saw Mel and Nicky – heard their voices – but then their faces would melt into the faces of other kids, the voices went quiet, and I felt that raw burning in my veins bad enough to make me crazy. I'd rush home to my own boys, Grove and Brady, but when they were near me, I felt more strange than close, like they weren't my own, but somebody else's. Kids I could never really know, never be able to love or protect enough.

That first week in the cottage, I misplaced my keys, lost my wallet, left my watch somewhere. Even got lost driving home. Meandering through the back roads, I remembered a bitter cold fall day, not long after my mom died, when I was still a kid. Through the open window of our latest "new" house, I smelled pine and rotting leaves and saw my dad, home too early. Pushing my train through its tunnel, I kept my head down. Dad home this time, the sun still up, meant he'd lost another job. An iron hand squeezed from inside my chest as I crouched in the stairwell.

Dad lurched in, calling my name. He reached for a quart of Jack Daniels and drank down two hits straight, then slid the whole bottle into his pocket with an angry grin. Looking straight at me, weary and world-beat, he whispered, "Gotcha."

I whistled, had just learned how from my dad, on my eighth birthday. My trains clanked as I gathered them all into my arms. Then I started upstairs, still whistling, Dad's footsteps right behind. I was afraid to go into my bedroom, it spooked me, so I hung around at the top of the steps. On the landing, I set up my brand new bridge, holding the red caboose in my other hand as Dad lunged for it, toppling head over heels down the staircase. The sound of him, a cannonade. Then silence, as he rose up on hands and knees.

I took off. Not the stairs, out my bedroom window, shimmying down the exposed drainpipe to the yard and running deep into the woods that stretched for miles behind our house.

My feet numbed and bare hands burned with cold. I had nothing to eat, no shelter but the pines. I was too cold to lie down, even to sit, so I walked first in one direction, then another. Soon the sky got dusky. A curve in the path, bend of a bough, ledge of rock, I knew each like I knew my own hand, but when I got up close, they turned strange. All wrong. I set out a different way. Zig-zagging through the woods, it got darker and colder, and the fear inside froze me through. I sat down on a stump and cried, something I hadn't done since my mom got sick. When the salt-wash cleared, I felt better. Cleansed somehow, from the inside-out. I dug myself a burrow and crawled in, covering myself with leaves and earth. I found my way back with first light; no one had come to look.

Dad and I moved around even more after that. By the time I turned twelve, we'd lived in thirteen different houses. Nothing stuck in terms of people or things, we packed up that fast. Papers you think of having for life, things that make for written proof of who you are – birth certificate, marriage license – were left behind or were just plain missing. I learned from different people, but there was nobody particular I held onto. Just took a little bit, got it to stick, then moved on.

When you're here and then there, you've got to get the groove of a place and fit yourself in. I learned that knack. Yet there was this swelling sadness inside, waiting for something to wrap itself around, so it'd make some sense. At sixteen, I left home for good and saw my father next only as he lay in his coffin. Going through his things, I found my parents' marriage license, dated a year after my birth. Weeping, my aunt told me the truth: the father who I vowed I'd never be like wasn't my real dad after all. The shock made me feel loose and trapped as a pinball in a machine.

At the factory, I mixed raisins into the onion bagels, sprinkled garlic on the Super Cinnamons. In the cottage, I was restless. On days when I was meant to be with Leigh and my boys, I gravitated back to the old house instead, this black burnt-out shell. I walked through to the space where Mel and Nicky's room had been, now earth and cinder. I'd waited so long to put down roots, to be settled in one place, here. A place I couldn't give up or leave alone. That's when I got the idea of putting up the shrine.

I took our old shoeboxes of photos to the bagel factory. On my break, I sat at the floury counter and leafed through, searching for a picture of Mel and Nicky, but I only had photos of the Dowd kids with my own. Back home, I took my boys' play scissors and cut their faces out of one of the pictures, till I had Mel and Nicky alone. In it, Mel holds Nicky on her lap, in the same position I once held her. He has one of his famous cups of coffee in his lap and he's smiling his puffed cheek smile, a squirrel with a nut. Mel has her chin tucked into her chest and looks up at the camera out of the tops of her eyes, a fighter. I slid the picture under glass to keep it safe from the elements.

Back at the old lot, I erected a stake out of two crossed pieces of wood, then attached the picture to it and plunged the stake into the ashpit that had been the kids' bedroom. Under the picture, I put a bouquet of Mel's favourite flowers, daisies, vowing to myself I'd come back every week with a fresh bunch, no matter how hard it was to get them. Around the flowers, I put the stuffed red lobster, Oscar, that Paul and Thea got on their Maine honeymoon. It was too painful for Thea to have around now. Anyway, she'd moved in with Jade and Jade didn't like anything stuffed. At the five-and-dime, I got myself a looseleaf notebook and a plastic case to protect it. On the cover, I wrote, "Ladymite." Every day, I went back to the shrine, continuing the story Mel and I had started, so it would still have no end.

"It's wasted energy," Leigh told me, "come home," but the best I could do was to shuttle back and forth.

Other people came, flocked to the shrine, that summer, fall, and winter, to leave their own flowers and letters and mementoes for the kids. Like the punk who tried to rip pages out of my notebook, the old loon who tore the heads off the daisies and ate them. Each day, I had to be there to prevent the break-out of fights among the mourners. I tried to explain this to Leigh; she just didn't get it.

The autumn day this old woman ate the daisies, another lady called Shirley shoved her and said, "Don't you have no respect?" The old lady shoved back. Soon the two were on the ground, tousling like wrestlers in the dirt. The younger one gave the old lady a one-two punch and the daisy-eating geezer dropped down nearly dead. I revived her.

The boy who kept messing up my notebook infuriated me; that book meant a whole lot. So one day that September, when Leigh had plans with the boys, I camped out at the shrine. The guy found me in a light, edgy sleep and threw kerosene on the notebook. It exploded into flames; my words soared up in smoke. I chased the guy, but he had a knife, so I backed off.

The next day, I started another notebook: I had the story in my mind, in memory. When the guy came, I told him I'd keep starting new notebooks till he turned cold in his grave. By October, I was sleeping at the site. I was so tired, I missed work once in a while, and got canned.

I tried to take my boys with me to remember their friends, but Leigh fought me tooth and nail on that one. She looked almost ugly as she cried and yelled, her lips pulled back over her teeth like a she-wolf, the lines around her eyes and mouth deepening, breathing through her mouth with a stale breath I hadn't smelled before. That's when I asked myself questions, like why people have kids in the first place, why I loved Leigh, if I ever really loved her at all. Then she hauled back and cracked me hard across the face, like she could see right inside my head. I grabbed her by the shoulders and shook her till my fingers made red dents in her arms.

When I checked in at the cottage the next day, Leigh and my boys were gone. Vanished. Yeah, there was a note. Not at home – or I should say, not at the cottage – at what had become my home: the shrine.

> Chip,
> Are you blind, stupid, or both? I lost the baby, surely a
> girl, the doctors tell me. Already I was five months along.
> Goodbye and go to hell!
> Me and the boys

No word as to where she'd taken off to, but I figured it must be to Thea's. Did I go there? No. Not right away. And by the time I did, it was past-time. Too late.

Driving away from Thea's alone, I remembered a morning in spring before it all happened. I came home and spotted Paul and Thea on our front stoop. The dawn was just beginning to blue and I sat in my car and watched them. My best friends looked like a photo, not quite real – I mean – not quite them. The way people don't look like their real selves in pictures. Or maybe the truth is, we never really look at the people who are around us so much, they're up too close. The way you don't notice furniture that's in a room you've lived in for years, or how your own teeth line up in your mouth.

Thea and Paul were talking. Paul's head was bowed, listening close. They were eating from a container, Thea spooning some up, then feeding Paul. Brady's rice pudding. He'd woken up and Leigh was exhausted, so Paul fed Brady and resettled him, like his own son. Thea was wrapped up in Paul's blue chambray shirt, one of his ties holding it closed around her waist. Every part of them that could be touching, was. I wanted to be them, the two of them, together.

About eight months after the fire, I was at the old place at daybreak. As Sunday morning's light burned away wisps of fog, I saw the familiar husk of the house: the most living thing there, my shrine. I looked at the picture of the dead kids, Mel and Nicky, behind glass, and saw my own two boys, realizing how rarely I'd touched them. Rearing back with my hammer, I smashed the glass covering the picture of Mel and Nicky, as if I could finally reach my own two sons. Shards fell into the pile of flowers, stuffed animals and sorrowful letters, left by dozens who flocked to see where a father set his own on fire, while holding them tight to his chest.

TUNNEL HILL

Nessa

I watched Davis move about my kitchen. He didn't ask where to find things, just reached for them: spices, a slatted wooden spoon. Steam curled from the saucepan as he stirred mulled cider, the smell of cinnamon and tart apples warming the room. He sat beside me at the table and we talked about what fall might bring.

As Davis kissed me, so quiet there in the kitchen, I heard only the buzz of the stove light. It cast blue on the side of his face, his hair, planes of straight shiny silver splayed about his slightly rounded shoulders. I'd been alone so long – alone together with my son Aram – eleven years, just the two of us.

I heard a *thunk*, the splash of something spilt. Aram stood by the upturned trash pail, garbage sloshing in a trail toward Davis and me: a swamp pool of garlic, a chicken wreck clotted with oatmeal and sticky yellow fat like wax. I pushed back against Davis's chest and got to my feet. I was down on the floor, scooping up garbage and dumping it into the pail so it splashed up my arms. Then I ran the tap hard, scalding my palms; with clean wet hands, I pulled Aram to me, although he struggled. He looked small to me then, a softness still in his arms, thighs, and belly.

I felt Davis at my side, the shadow of his hand slanting across the wall and stretched out to Aram, as he said, "I'm Davis, another person in the world."

Aram pulled back, sliding his hands into his pockets. I saw a new tear in his pajamas where the skin of his shoulder showed through; it made me flinch, as though the skin itself were torn. Tugging at the sleeve, Aram covered the bruise-like birthmark on his left shoulder-blade, then turned down the hall. Since he was little, he'd been self-conscious about that portwine mark and kept it hidden.

Cold wind blew through the kitchen window, late summer turning into fall. Early in the summer, I'd met Davis Carroll on a short break, visiting my Aunt Ruth down in South Carolina. It was my first time away from Aram in all these years, and when I returned home to my boy, Davis was my secret.

Davis was gone before Aram and I were up. Making coffee, I spotted his tiny crabbed hand, a footnote at the bottom of my shopping list: *Don't make me skulk.*

He went straight home, I suppose, sketched, ate, changed for his shift. Nights, Davis collected tolls on the George Washington Bridge; days, he drew cartoons and slept. Since we'd met, I raced up to his loft in Washington Heights late mornings, between harp practice, lessons, and rehearsals, while Aram was at school. Sometimes I found Davis asleep on the couch, one long arm dangling to the floor, a pillow clutched between his legs. I liked to stand by, silent, until he sensed me there and awoke. Most mornings, the windows were open, a mild breeze with river smell on its underside, the Hudson swept into tiny waves like crinkled foil. The breeze ruffled his hair like a hand, lifting it from his neck. I would always be home by three, ready with Aram's snack.

The day after Aram saw the two of us in the kitchen, he didn't come home from school. It was a warm afternoon, without sun, and I followed the course of the meadow-stream behind our house that widened into Wanaque Pond. Aram sat on the muddy shore, pushing floating leaves with bare feet. Stoneworts, cattails, and water shield grew in the shallows. Strong-scented cedars filled the high ground and hazel alders grew thickly on shore; their leaves gave off a sweet, gummy smell.

Aram was in denim cut-offs, his skin honey-coloured, peeling across his nose and forearms. By his side was the pigskin shoulder bag I'd given him to carry his collecting gear. Even at eleven he had a crick in his neck from carrying that bag everywhere; he walked with a slow, loping stride, leaning forward to offset its weight.

Around his waist was a leather belt with loops for specimen vials and the waterscope he'd made himself by sealing a piece of glass into a bottomless bucket.

I touched his shoulder; he didn't jump, just leaned into my palm and said, "Look, Nana," holding up a turtle. The creature had a ruddy throat and a single yellow spot on each plate of its shell; as Aram held it, the turtle's legs paddled, then drew in. Aram placed it back on shore and the turtle glanced at him before swimming out to the dark water.

Aram stood, leading me a yard or so down shore, pointing to the place where the spotted turtle had dug a hole, deposited her eggs, and covered them again with sand, where they'd be incubated by the sun.

"Thought we'd do something tomorrow," I said.

Aram looked up at me, expectant.

"The three of us."

Turning from me, Aram stooped over his nets and sieves, where he'd collected anabaena – like a string of jade-coloured beads – and snails with pink, spired shells. He came to the pond every day, observing creatures and plants, collecting some for closer inspection at home: there was a regular flow between the pond and his room, which itself had a strong, brackish smell. At the moment, he had a Woodhouse toad, a red salamander and marbled newt, a pair of mud turtles. . . .

Aram ran both hands through his hair, then moved to a flat rock and dangled his legs into the water. Scrambling off the rock, he cupped his hand around a pair of mayflies with transparent wings and feathery, dun-coloured gills, feeling them flutter against his palms. After a while, he set them free through slowly spreading fingers. One grazed the pond, leaving thread-thin trails; the other stayed well above the water. Some of them would live only a few hours, mating in flight, countless millions in a nuptial swarming.

Watching them, I thought of Joshua, Aram's father, doing to Aram what he'd done to me: descending, taking flight. Fathering in bursts. Once, Josh told me that being a father from a distance felt like hanging onto a ledge. He couldn't climb inside, could just hold on for all he was worth. Or let go. Josh hadn't seen Aram for two years now. He still travelled the world taking pictures, covering some war or another for the news weekly, *Newtimes.* Once in a while, a postcard came from some corner of the globe, enough to keep Aram suspended, longing.

I crouched at the shore, digging my nails into the warm, mulchy sand, remembering when Aram turned five, how Josh gave him an aquarium filled with exotic, jewel-coloured fish. Aram knew the fish shouldn't be handled like his frogs, salamanders, and turtles, but couldn't stop himself: the fish died within weeks.

"Any ideas for tomorrow?" I tried to keep my voice neutral, but felt it go shaky.

"Freedomland?" Aram asked. "We didn't go yet."

We liked to get there off season when the place was nearly deserted. I nodded quickly, trying to picture the three of us there – no way.

"Where's Kristin?" I asked. Aram methodically tied his sweatshirt around his waist and gathered his gear, not answering. She was his one friend, a thin girl with blonde hair long enough to sit on, pale green eyes, and a face that must once have been pretty. Now there were scars on her left cheek, neck, and upper arms. When they caught the light, they looked almost metallic. The popular girls called her Lichen.

"Special place," he finally said, his smile a sudden streak. I relaxed a little, for that smile hadn't changed much since he was a baby, a constancy that soothed me, reminding me who I was. I dug a shell from the wet sand, rinsing it in pond water. It was an iridescent green, thin as paper.

That Sunday, I drove crosswise through the near empty parking lot at Freedomland, Aram wedged between Davis and me, his father's old Leica strung around his neck. Rain drizzled against the windshield. I parked, leaving the key in the ignition, my hands on the wheel. "Forget it?"

"No, no," Aram and Davis spoke nearly in sync.

We bought tickets and Aram chose the Tunnel of Love, where we wouldn't get wet. Only four other people were in line: a solitary man and three young girls from Aram's school. He glanced at them, then looked away. I knew at once these were the tormentors. Girls with long, white colt's legs, blonde hair cut short on one side, and thread-thin chains around their ankles that flickered when they moved.

Our boat was red. Aram climbed up front, sweeping his hand with a flourish across the long back seat. Davis rocked the creaky boat as he lumbered in. For a second, I saw him through Aram's eyes, a little ridiculous in faded drawstring pants, loose at the ankles, and orange sneakers without socks or laces. I slid in beside him, leaving ample room between us.

We floated through the tunnel, rocking side to side. No one spoke, and the darkness felt good, warmer than outside. Oily water lapped against the sides of the boat. Aram looked up and I followed his gaze, as stars sparked different coloured fires above our heads. Scenes floated by, the River of Rapture, which rippled red, the Lake of Lust, blue-black, Passion's Fire, which blazed up in molten tongues of red, orange, and gold to the accompaniment of firecrackers and explosive music, all horns and percussion.

As we rounded a bend, I saw Aram fingering his father's old camera; it gleamed like a gun. "Please, *don't*."

Davis went, "Going to immortalize us?"

Aram lifted the camera to his eye, and I reached forward, touching his shoulder. "Look at me. We have something to tell you."

We lurched out into cloudy light and the attendant handed us a silver chalice wrapped in plastic. An odd favour. I imagined it filled with store-bought ambrosia, a love potion, sickly sweet, Pepto-Bismol pink. I passed the empty cup to Davis. Aram aimed and shot.

Aram

He's locked himself in, Nana's saying. Which I didn't do. Like that could keep her out of my room. Nana's into being there. But not. Last week, she climbed in a window when she got scared about me. Nana's a goof about heights . . . like she can fly? I was setting up a new tank for my baby gecko. It took hours because the tank's got to be just right or they die from the new environment. Touch and go.

My bedroom window's steamed up and I write my name in it over and over till I can see clear through. Don't want to. There's his blue clunker. Surprise, surprise. Him and Nana unloading boxes – whatever's left – makes me think of stuff I've dug up lately. Dufus doesn't travel light, not at all. Coffee mug in the sink, sketchbooks stuck into our car seat, pens sitting on the side of the tub. Yeah, the tub. All kinds of picture guides on prickly plants. I mean, everywhere. One guide on Nana's night-table, her hair ribbon stuck in as a bookmark.

The front door slams. Nana calls up, *Want to help?* I stay put like I'm frozen here.

Snow sandblasts my window. Outside, the sky's a grey puffy face, blue holes for eyes. I stare at it so long, it's like I'm falling. But up.

Snow's coming down pretty hard – only it's just Halloween – we'll be buried under by Christmas maybe. Dream on. Tonight I'll go out real late, when both of them are out cold. Don't need to dress up, just be me, right? That's what they tell me. Nana, all the time.

She walks by my closed door. X-ray eyes see her taking more of his stuff into the spare. Downstairs, he's lugging cartons, a couple in each arm. *Splat.* Down he goes, kneeling in the wet. The guy's a total klutz. I mean, whenever I see him, he's banging into a door, spilling his drink – bourbon and beer – even for breakfast once.

Can stop whenever he wants to. Sure. Could win weirdest-looking. Skin so white, like he doesn't see sun or breathe regular air. Makes me think of monsterman at *World of Wax* – big square head, giant hands to crush and eat metal like Popeye. His junk's spilling out all over, rolling onto the lawn. So what's he got? Divide it into two groups: cooking, cacti. No, make that three. Don't forget pens and crayons for his drawing occasions. Now I see pans, wood spoons, wire things. More cactus plants in pots. He picks those up first, scooping up dirt, smoothing it down, like he's covering sleeping babies. Or something.

This morning Nana blew me air kisses, said, *You sleep.*

Aram, you like sweet potato fries, Aram? He's balancing her, wearing my name out. All the time.

I leave my room and go into the spare. When I was little, Nana read to me here, rocking, looking out on Inwood Place. We watched the trains go by, wheels clattering so loud I got scared sometimes. Saw one barrelling right through our house – making it a tunnel – flashing fast, like light, only more so, could carve the insides out of anything with that velocity. Well, in my eye's mind that train propelled us through the air, then against the tracks, squished us underneath. Nana said no, never could. I believed her.

We ate supper in here, too. Things Nana fixed quick: clam chowder and toast, macaroni and olives, chicken and potato salad with onions, browned to a crisp. Stuff she doesn't make anymore. When I got bigger, I read to Nana. She likes Andersen's Tales, "The Ugly Duckling" is her absolute favourite. Because she thinks what's inside counts. She sees past skin and what features a person has and gets other people to. But with Nana, it's not just an expression she pulls out of the closet and puts on or anything.

The rocker's piled high with his junk – cartoons, pads, pens. Surprise. More cacti! Boxes and cartons wrapped around with shiny brown tape. Presents for me, I guess.

I throw everything onto the floor. Let his papers fly! Then I cut open a carton with my pocketknife. It makes a cool sound. Who cares? So he hears.

On top is a snap-shut case, for glasses maybe. I spring it open. Inside is a pen made of different coloured wood. It's cool. I could use it for field notes, plans and stuff. I snap the clip under my nail. It bends, won't break, no matter what. Underneath, there's some writing in curvy script, each letter spinning into a pinwheel.

For Davis, ad infinitum. A shaky heart scratched in.

Can hearts fly, up in sky, to where I'll be? Can hearts beat, when they fall, down on ground? Beats me.

This morning, I saw a heart fly out of a squirrel. Nana, you hear me?

Kristin and I stole a gun that shoots copper pellets. We went through Adder's Wood out to Tunnel Hill. Kristin saw him first, the squirrel we feed. He scooted down the trunk of an oak, his bony old head darting. Kristin breathed through her mouth, laid the gun down in the dirt. "Isn't he pretty?" she said, as I picked the gun up. Kristin opened her palm and I smelled the roast peanuts.

The squirrel had fat cheeks, skinny black fingers, all shriveled up. His eyes didn't blink. Even if I clapped in his face. So I ran behind Kristin, saw spider threads in the sun all of a sudden disappear. My sign. Fur turned silver as his hair. Kristin fed the squirrel one nut, then another, like Nana feeds him, hand to mouth. I saw him – I mean the squirrel – getting fat, moving slow. Had to lift the gun, gaze through its sight. No big puzzle or anything.

Kristin pounced on me from behind as the shot went off. I bit down on dirt, Kristin on top of me. Her hair fell across my eyes, smelling bitter, because she doesn't wash it much. I squeezed my eyes tight, saw the squirrel's heart burst free, soaring up into the sky, like a pink bird.

I slide the pen into my pajama pocket. Downstairs, I hear the buzz of the grinder, coffee smell floats up. When I was two, Nana gave me coffee cream, a drop of espresso in my milk. Even black, I liked it. Her drink.

On the sill is *Webster's.* I flip through the *I*s, trying to remember that weird word. Don't know what language it's in, maybe a secret one, theirs. *Ad in fum.*

Ad infinitum. L. to infinity. endlessly; forever; without limit.

I pull sketches from his carton, tied up tight with leather twine. Now I sit on our rocker, teasing that knot loose, flipping through. There's a drawing of a slimy black thing with red stripes, one down its middle, two down each side. It's got a frog's face, turtle's shell, lizard's tail, a snake's tongue. Looks sort of human anyhow – maybe because it stands up – has a brain in its eyes. The skin's throw-up green, warty, with black, brown, and red spots. Its mouth is big, the eyes bug out.

Amphibiman!

You can tell about people from their hands, you know. Davis has big ones, cut off from his body. Like heavy objects he's carrying around. I see them taking off, flying around like bats. Only white. They're super white, whiter even than the rest of him, except maybe his butt – don't want to think about that. He hides his hands – behind his back, in his pockets – or they're busy, doodling. When he comes into my room, he stands in the doorway, asks lots of questions, cool pen in hand. Points to my gecko in his cage. *What does he eat?*

Yesterday, I grabbed that pen, slid little gecko into his palm and said, "Check him out." His eyes closed halfway; he shivered like he was cold.

In his sketches, Amphibiman has adventures. He climbs rocks, trees; can jump, swim, even fly. Amphibiman digs inside the ground, into termite mounds; he comes out in rainfalls. When big guys prey on him, he swells up to ten times his size, giving off a poison stink. Which can kill. He doesn't croak, bark or speak – the guy sings! He lives forever. *Ad infinitum.*

I'm *him.*

But. Everything's messed up with Dufus around. I mean, different. The light, sounds, even the smell of things. He walks spasticated, making the floor squeak. I see mice slithering around his big old feet. Up close, he smells like cigarettes and sandpaper soap. In the carton is a bar of soap. I gouge it under my nails, makes me cry, my nose runs.

Shit. He's coming up. I slide the drawings under my pajama top and the corners scratch pretty bad. Who cares? I got to have them.

The door's opening. He stands there, blocking my light. Out of my way, Dufus. He looks, turns away, a scratched-up pan under one arm, two cactus plants in the other. One has brown pricklers, the other's a blown-up sand dollar. I run my finger over the woolly spots, then prick its spines. I don't bleed. Like there's nothing to come out. Sure, it fits. He'd stock up on something there was no way to kill.

"You got a lot of junk, you know." I toss the soap at his feet. He doesn't pick it up.

"Snow should keep up a while." He rubs his lower lip with his thumb, making it bulge out. "Aram. You always swipe people's stuff, Aram?" See.

I hear Nana call him downstairs. He heels, a dog to his master's whistle.

In my room, I watch the snow, see him licking her neck when I want to see only white, licking and licking, till she melts.

Kristin gave me Simeon today; we brought Rattus back from Tunnel Hill. Once we had their tanks ready, we climbed inside my sleeping bag. I rubbed Krissy's face, even touched her chest under her shirt. Her skin's real smooth, much smoother than her face. No buds, nothing yet.

Sliding the drawings out from under my shirt, I twist them into a roll. Everyone's hungry, waiting. For *me*. Amphibiman. Relax. Nothing to it.

I started culturing this summer, after I saw Nana with Dufus. Mealworms kept in a shallow box with a layer of oatmeal covered cloth, one or two chunks of apple (changed every couple days). I got the crickets going in old egg boxes. Started a colony of flies with banana skins in a corner of our garden; soon it was teeming. Swept a net through trees, bushes, grass, and caught the most beautiful grasshoppers. I stored them in jars. Then I got dozens of moths going with light-traps: a white sheet hung up on the porch with a real bright light on it.

I open one terrarium, then another, lifting out my gecko, my big old frog, my garter snake. For a long time, they just stand there, don't know what's up. Rattus and Simmy stay put, snug; those guys really like their beds. Wood shavings, nice-smelling cedar. Who wouldn't?

I take my little grasshopper with the blue head and orange eyes, feeling his legs tickle, his tail flap against my palm. He's cool. Then I cup my gecko in the other hand, his body brown and black, his eyes slanted, rimmed around with gold. Wow, he's gorgeous. His eyes get big, his mouth opens wide. I slip in the grasshopper's head first, pushing his body down the gecko's throat. It shimmers going down.

Man. I wonder what it feels like. Maybe good.

Reaching for my frog, I feel her heartbeat a while. She has huge ears. Brown skin, a mask over her eyes. She makes a whistling chirp in my hand. That's her swansong. I hold out my baby gecko – here, take him. The frog's tongue lashes out like a whip and reels my gecko in, swallowing him whole. Wow. Where's he gone *now?*

The frog stands still, full, as the garter snake slithers toward her. He's brown and green, with yellow side-stripes. His tongue flickers, each side of his jaw moves; it's so cool. His teeth are small and hooked. They grab on, fastening around the frog's head, all the way back to her eyes. I can't look, can't stop looking. She's going down. I mean, in. To the same place the others are. The frog's legs swim in the air, her body jumps, going nowhere.

It takes my garter a long time. Then I see the outline of the frog's body, inside, its muscles still pulsing for life. She's in a better place too. *I* know.

I wrap the snake around my neck; he twists, writhes around. He'll make a good dinner for Rattus and Simmy – you know, they can't eat him alive.

With my pocketknife, I slash off his head. The snake's body twines around itself. I grit my teeth, slice him once, twice, three times. Each bit twists, turning over and over. Holy shit! Looks like rope. *He* can't feel anything, not at all.

I want Rattus and Simmy to have him. To be so full. Then everyone will be somewhere. Inside each other, not nowhere. They're in a place where I can't see them. But still, there. I know I can get back to them, if I want. You open the biggest one, then the next. Till you get to the littlest. You're there.

I squeeze my eyes shut, see Rattus and Simmy, my garter too. There's the frog. My gecko. The gorgeous grasshopper. He's the baby, all orange and blue. I see the willow at Tunnel Hill, its branches reach up, calling me back. *To reach the Tunnel of Conclusions, crawl through. You. You!*

I look out my window. Now I'll sleep. I want to. That's all. My mind white as the snow out there. I see me inside a flake, part of a drift, frozen perfect under the ice. At that place below the ice, where it's so cold, it's not cold anymore.

Nessa

I went up to Aram with dinner Halloween night. He was crouched in the corner of his room, elbows propped on the sheepskin rug, his hands cradling a small animal with soft grey and white fur. He looked like he'd just woken up. Seeing the leopard spots on his old pajamas made me think of Halloween. "Going out?"

He shrugged, his eyes blank.

I nodded toward the window. "Not too late." Outside, snow fell thickly, clinging to the glass, softening the skeletal outlines of the trees. "They're saying it's a record. Don't know if we'll get anybody." I put the tray down on the floor. "Please, love, eat." Davis had brought frozen trays of his own dishes for these first nights: lasagna, baked ziti, veal and peppers. "There's minestrone soup. Garlic bread." My voice broke. The smell of the soup and bread rose into the room, another odour beneath them, like rotting fruit and wilting flowers.

The creature stretched in Aram's hands, nosing the food; Aram lifted him against his chest. Downstairs, I heard the clang of pots and pans, the tinkling of glassware, as Davis put away his cooking equipment, adding to my sparse supply. The small animal looked up at Aram, then buried its pink nose in his hair. A new hamster. "Where'd you get *that*?"

"Krissy," he said, matter-of-fact.

I didn't want to look at it, the way Aram was with the thing. Glancing about the room, I saw Aram's twin bed was gone, his cages and terrariums, empty, all but one. I forced myself to slow down, look again. Cages and terrariums filled only with greens, bark mulch, and rocks: uninhabited landscapes. One large aquarium with a second hamster whirling about on a wooden wheel.

Downstairs, the doorbell rang, our first trick-or-treaters. Although he'd moved in all day, Davis still stopped at the store and made up treat bags for the kids.

Watching Aram gaze into the back yard, through trees, I wondered what he saw. Sometimes his imagination stretched so far, it scared me. Waving my arm to encompass the room, I said, "And the others?"

"Home, right?"

I pictured the pond, quiet in the cold, only a few animals stirring under the forming ice. I'd always liked going into Aram's room; his absorption in pondlife comforted me, it was so ordinary, I guess. When did I stop paying attention?

Aram pushed the tray away, turning his face aside. The smell of the hot steaming food mixed with the smell of his room, made me queasy. I shoved the tray into the hall with my foot. Stooping down, I took Aram's chin in my hand. *I'm never going to leave you*, I wanted to say, as I stroked his face, which was streaked with dirt. He cringed.

I watched him burrow his cheek in the creature's fur. My stomach dipped when I saw: a rat.

Aram whispered to it, murmuring Simmy again and again. Then he let out a shrill whistle and the rat twitched its pale ears. A shudder ran through me, as if its tail had brushed my skin. "You can't keep it."

Aram nuzzled his nose and eyes in the rat's fur. Then he held the creature out a ways, staring into its eyes, kissing the wet black nose. "They carry disease," I said, my voice high and strained.

"They're *clean* animals. They wash themselves from head to toe six times a day. Nana, really."

"Really."

"It's *true*."

Downstairs, I heard Davis humming the piece I'd played the day we met: *Fantaisie Op. 124*, by Camille Saint-Saens. He could remember any piece, even if he'd heard it just once. Yet he didn't play, just listened.

As I'd played that evening at Keowee's supper club where I was visiting my Aunt Ruth, I glanced through the arched doorway of the parlour and saw a solitary drinker in a corner of the bar. He sat with one leg bent, his ankle resting on his other knee. His head was bowed, chin tilted toward my music. Between his large hands were two drinks: a shot of bourbon, a beer chaser. I looked his way, without meaning to. He didn't look up.

Later, I stretched out at the lake. Low clouds darkened the shallows while the deepest parts glowed amber. I threw my terry robe onto the picnic bench and walked in, my scalp prickling as the water closed over my head.

When I got out, a man was sitting on shore, building a castle. The small string of lights that lit the path back to the compound clicked on. I took my terry robe from the bench, dried my face with it, then my hair. On the picnic table was an old cigar box. Laid out around it was a collection of things: a worn leather binder, a crystal egg, small animals carved of soapstone. Maybe his special things.

The man stood up and tripped, wrecking the castle he'd built, then came toward me, as if he'd always been aware of my presence. I turned my head as he drew the robe away from my face and hair, opening it, and wrapped it around my shoulders. His huge hand held the ends together like a shawl.

"Never heard it close-up," he said, referring, I guess, to my harp music, as though continuing a conversation we'd started before.

There was a halting quality to his speech, as to all his movements, which made me wait and take notice of each word, its component syllables, the small motions that made up a gesture. Everything took time and trouble, but seemed unguarded, which left him unprotected in a way most people weren't. That effort and struggle about everything.

A rattling sound, like clawed feet in dry leaves, jolted me back to Aram's room. I saw with horror that the other rat was straining to be let out of its cage. "You can't bring just anything into *this* house!"

"*You* do." Aram's eyes were grave. They looked more alert now, charcoal grey, with flecks of gold in the iris.

"Baby, I've got students coming in and out. And –"

"Him."

I glanced away, listening to the sounds of Davis moving about downstairs. The bell rang again: more kids, dressed in costumes. I wondered what they were. "I want your bed back here. Tonight."

Aram shook his head.

"What'll you do with them?" I forced myself to look. The rat Aram was holding had a hooded coat: white body, dark head and shoulders. It began to groom itself, licking fur and paws, rubbing its face. The flexible wrists and pink fleshy claws, were so much like a human hand and fingers, my skin broke out in bumps.

"Come," I said, tugging Aram by the hand, an urgency to get him out of this room, back into the world. "We'll make a fire."

Davis

Aram watches my feet, keeps an eye on my every move. He's got a stack of papers under one arm, a roll, his other hand cupping the opening. Give me a clue now. What you gonna do?

He pulls up his pajama bottoms – elastic's shot – then slides that tube around front, balancing it on his knees, folding both hands over either end of the roll. To hell with clues. I'm gonna watch.

Aram lays the fire. The kid's practiced, an expert. I'm impressed because I'm no good at that. What's weird is, he ignores his Mom, not giving her so much as a sideward glance. Looks over at *me*, says "Hey, Davis." Yeah, I'm suspicious.

I go over. Hell. I'm tired of trying, trying too hard, trying not to try. Got to watch, though. Ness stands by her boy, a little behind. When Aram slides in the Duraflame log, I'm surprised, I feel cheated somehow. The fire which was licking real slow at the wood starts crackling and spitting. Ness sees it first. On her face is this look, more hurt than surprised. Wedged into the tepee like another sliver of kindling is the pen she gave me, her first gift. Nicest thing I own – faceted barrel, each section a different colour of wood – purple heartwood, honey-coloured maple, mahogany. Ness gave it to me the night I first showed her my work, the whole portfolio. I draw with that pen every day, I love the feel of it. Yeah, it's lucky. What can I say?

I've got Aram by the scruff of the neck. Above the fire is a tearing sound. Aram falls back, a flap of leopard skin hanging away from his shoulder. I'm not ready for his weight, the feel of him, soft and firm, a bone at the back of his neck like a damn crabapple.

He gets up on all fours, rocks back on his heels. I'm facing the fire, watching the cartoons I've worked on for what – oh, six months – burn, the pen roll to the side of the log. It's charred, intact. "You fucking terror." It just comes out, under my breath.

Aram crosses his legs like a guru, then shoots me this look, his lips stretched wide, his eyes watering. A tearing smile. Just messes me up, makes me more fucking mad.

Ness keeps an equal distance from me, from her boy. The heat of the fire's drawn wet from her eyes. "*You* get upstairs."

For a second, I'm not sure if she means me. Or him.

A log topples out of the hearth. Before I know what's happening, Aram circles around his mother and shoves his hand toward the fire. I lunge, grabbing him under the arms, yanking him away.

"Fuck off!" he yells, kicking backward against my shins. I watch the pen twist, curl in on itself, burning to cinder.

Ness runs into the bathroom, hustling Aram along. I follow, hanging back. Again, I'm watching. She spreads A&D on Aram's hand and I see him flinch. When she's done, she closes her eyes for a second, and the thought's just there. *We're not a family*, my mind reading hers.

Aram

I'm sure it's Nana, the knock's that light; she always knows when I can't sleep. I've got no idea what time it is.

The door squeaks open. No shit. Dufus. Hunched over, like he's being chased. His back's bent, must be from the weight of that big old head, like the bones bent when he grew or something.

When he sees Simmy on my lap, he edges the walls. She's dark up front, silky white behind, a cool black stripe running down her back.

"Where'd you get *that*?"

"You open your eyes, they're there."

Dufus' laugh hacks into a cough, his face all shiny. In the aquarium, Rattus scoots up the ladder I built, then crawls through his cardboard tunnel. He's all one colour, his grey coat almost blue. I watch him splashing around in the pool.

"You got a whole amusement park here." He scrapes a paint drip from the window frame like it's wrecking my decor.

"Freedomland."

Dufus rolls in his bottom lip. For a second, there's a flash of gross teeth. I mean, yellow. What do you expect? The guy smokes a pack-and-a-half of Camels a day. "I drew him for you," he says.

"Am-phib-i-man," I go, hacking the name into pieces.

He comes all the way in, sits too close to me on my sheepskin rug. I smell his stale cigarette breath covered with those lemon mints he sucks. Dufus turns my hand over, laying it against his palm. So concerned, right? I yank it back. Shit, it throbs.

"Every day . . . you know that pen's –"

"Nothing."

"Things have got life in them."

I push Simmy, short, quick, into his face. "Here's life. Hey. Hold her." He shrinks backs, his mouth twitching. I put Simmy down on his leg and watch his body freeze. Simmy scoots up to his crotch, then down the other side. I pick her back up. She's cool.

"My dad made friends with a rat," he says. His voice gets so low, I can barely hear him. Like he's telling me a secret. Dufus stoops on the rug, so he can make a quick escape? I pet Simmy till she stretches under my touch.

"A roof rat, it was. Real skinny, an acrobat. My dad taught it to fly."

"What do you mean, *fly*?" I figure, this guy makes stuff up.

"Dad liked this peanut butter candy. Peter Rat flew from the floor to my dad's cot for a piece. Worked every time."

"Rattus can jump eight feet, scale these four walls." I point him out in the tank – he's sucking on his water bottle – blissed. "I'll show you."

He shrugs, stands up quick.

I laugh, easing Rattus from his bottle, one-handed, holding Simmy against my chest. Dufus leans against the wall near the door, arms folded, while I put Rattus down all wet – I mean dripping – where his hands cross. Dufus shakes his head, the guy can't believe what's happening. Sliding his hands free, he holds Rattus underneath, cupping his other hand on top, both of them shaking. Rattus slithers out and zips up one arm, hiding in his sweater.

I laugh so hard, I'm crying. Real tears. When I can see clear, Dufus is sitting right there on my sheepskin. He touches Rattus' whiskers with the tip of his finger, then jolts back. Zapped. I sit down, stroke his whiskers on the other side. They feel real good, all waxy and bristling. Rattus stands on Dufus' thigh, while he feeds him a peanut from the sack I've got on the floor. Rattus scarfs it down, shell and all.

I didn't think you'd touch him. I want to say this out loud, but end up just thinking it to myself. "I'm going to put them together soon. They smell when they're ready."

"What you gonna do with all those babies?"

"If you fool with them, she'll eat them. They can't even pee on their own newborn."

He smiles, lips sealed.

I hold Simmy out for him to stroke. "Look at her, up close." Each hair's striped grey-blue next the skin, yellow in the middle, black up front. She's gorgeous. I hold Simmy and Rattus, one in each hand, balancing them on my lap. They stand on their haunches, face to face, licking each other's fur. Wish Nana could see. After, I put them in one cage. "So. What was with your dad?"

He shrugs. "A thief, basically. You know, castaway."

"What?"

Davis gets up and walks to the window. He just stands there, like he's forgotten how to talk. I get like that, around him. He stares out at the snow, tranced, and before I know it, I'm into it too.

Davis

Standing in his room, I think of my dad – don't know why but I do – maybe it's the kid's Leica, his dad's, hanging there on the wall. The map of the world next to it, silver stars where his dad's been and gone. My dad's gone, can't take that in somehow. I see him in a grey fedora and string tie, me in hat and tie just like him. That's weird. All I've got to hold onto.

I buried him this summer and went off to Keowee to escape. I mean not to think, all I did of course. Then I met Ness, not that she stopped me from thinking or anything.

I brought Dad's old cigar box down to the lake. He'd carved animals from soapstone, a bird I couldn't name, a squirrel, even a fox. There was a leather book in there too. Not a diary or anything. Dad actually wrote down these phrases to live by. *Feel the fear, do it anyway.* Not that *that* stopped him! Cliches mostly, but with some truth behind them, I guess. I like the crystal egg he kept letters under. Summons, more likely.

"Hey."

I look up and see Aram staring at me, like he's waiting.

"Your dad?"

"Didn't know him."

"How come?"

All of a sudden, I feel bad. The kid sounds so eager, it makes me turn around and go over to him by the cage. Aram's face never looked like this, his eyes searching for something, like I could fit my life into one talk. Explain it or something.

"My dad. Did time at Riker's Island. Lowdie Correctional. Oregon State Penitentiary after that."

"*Prison?*"

"Yeah." He's too impressed.

Aram taps my shoulder, first time. "What he'd *do?*"

"Grifted, schemed. Some pretty elaborate ones from what I can gather." Aram's eyes get this gleam, like the glitter in my mom's whenever she talked about Dad. She had these terms for him – infernal, malevolent – big, complicated words she never came out with most of the time. To me, they had a dark smell – poisonous – like he wasn't a man, more of a contagious disease.

Aram looks out at the snow, then checks the rats in their cage. "When I was old enough, I looked for him. For two years, I searched. Checked out homeless shelters, even death notices." I take out a pack of Camels, all crushed, just two left.

"Finally, I got a tip from a friend he'd lived with. Dad answered my ad in the *Newark Herald*. A real fluke, because he'd placed an ad himself. To fix air conditioners and heating systems."

Aram slides his fingers through the bars of the cage, reaching to pet the different-coloured rat.

"So. I walk over, past barred windows, guard dogs." I light up my cigarette. "Delis with guns behind the counters."

"Hey."

I give Aram a drag, knowing Ness'll kill me. He grips that cigarette between his thumb and first finger, squeezing the life out of it. Doesn't want to give it back. "My dad lived in a rooming house above a poolhall. I climbed five storeys to this tiny room." I tap out my last and light up.

"It was a dingy place, sour liquor, piss. For the next ten years we got together. Once a month maybe. Dad was a custodian then. And like I said, he did fix-up. Mr Mechanical, customers called him."

"My dad's a photographer, for *Newtimes*. He travels around the world. Now he's in Istanbul, want me to show you on the map?" There's that look again, hard to take, I nod real slow.

Aram shakes his head. "Skip it. So what happened to Peter Rat?"

"Poisoned by my dad's landlady. Dad died the next day. It was like his only, his last fucking friend."

Aram goes to the cage and takes out the pair of them. He slides the blue one into one pajama pocket, the coloured into the other. He looks calm, feeling them curl up against him.

I ruffle his hair, then realize my hand's still wet from the rat's fur. "Hey, sorry."

Aram pulls a bunch of his hair around front and inhales, like he's never smelled anything so good.

Nessa

When I didn't hear Aram's movements in the morning, his calling out my name, when I saw his room was empty, the rats' cages bare, when I realized he wasn't in the yard, the colours of last night's fire flashed through my mind, exploding with the shock.

I ran next door to Kristin's in my robe and the family thought I was a burglar. He hadn't been by, they didn't know anything, nothing at all.

Davis held out his arms to me when I got back, my hands shaking out the match I tried to light for my cigarette. He handed me a piece of scrap paper torn from Aram's field notes, scrawled in his loose, large hand.

Nana, to visit the tunnel of conclusions, you crawl through.

"We talked, real late," Davis said. "What was weird, we connected. I told him about this place I had as a kid, you know, secret. An abandoned oarhouse on Lake Ottumwa. Aram told me he had a place, too. Said a little about it – ever pass through Shellrock?"

I shook my head.

"There's a newsstand stays open late, the guy's always got coffee going."

I took Davis by the shoulders, nearly shook him.

"Once there was a railroad through there, direct to the City. Now there's just this tunnel, a tunnel to nowhere. C'mon, let's go."

I shook my head hard, knowing I had to go alone.

Davis took a scrap of paper from the pad near the phone and drew me a map, then brought me a flashlight from his toolbox.

It was still snowing when I left, a warm wet snow from an iron sky. I parked my car in back of the newsstand, following the derelict railroad bed along the ridge of the mountain, passing through a patch of woods, which came out onto an abandoned, godforsaken place.

A fence separated a lot from the steep bank, a horrible cyclone fence of braided diamond-shaped wire with barbs on top. At the bottom of the slope was scrabble, broken bottles, heels of shoes, an ugly slant down to nothing where people threw whatever it was they didn't want. There was a narrow space where the fence separated from the ground; I pulled it higher and crawled through, scratching my back against the sharp wires. I followed tracks – filling fast with snow – up the bank a ways and into the mouth of the tunnel.

Blackness closed in around me; for a second I panicked, feeling buried alive. The smell was dank and putrid, sharpened by the cold. I stood for a minute, afraid, as my eyes adjusted to different shades of dark.

I clicked on the flashlight. The top of the tunnel arched over my head. Graffiti sprayed above me, the floor glistening wet. A few yards into the tunnel, the ground was sunken into foul-smelling sewage water, getting deeper the further in I went. At first, I felt nothing, protected by my boots, then the water seeped into their toes, soaking my socks. I gasped, breathing through my mouth. With each step, my blood throbbed; finally I got numb, or didn't notice it anymore. I ran, splashing through the putrid flood, which inched over the tops of my boots, soaking my pants to the knees. I called out for Aram, screamed his name, again and again.

I slogged through maybe 250 feet of the tunnel. Then I saw my son, curled up like an animal, circled by the white beam of my flashlight. Aram shivered, his face streaked with brown; his lips formed a word I couldn't make out.

I went to lift him, but Aram was pretty big, heavy too. After several tries, I managed to ease him onto my back, holding his hands against my chest, as I slushed back through the tunnel. In the lot was a delivery truck, the driver sipping coffee, a newspaper spread out on his lap. I asked for a ride to the hospital, so I could look after Aram on the way. He found an old army blanket in the bed of the truck and handed it to me.

I laid Aram across my lap, swaddling him in the blanket. There were firm, cold white spots on his face, ears, and hands. I carefully took off his boots and socks. His feet were cold, clammy, and numb. Putting his face against my neck, I slid his hands under my arms, his feet against my bare abdomen.

The ER nurse told me it was a good sign Aram was shivering, fortunately he'd been wearing some layers. I sat with Aram while the nurse injected a drug called Reserpine into an artery at the top of his thigh. Then I helped her lower him into a tub of warm water.

It was agonizing for Aram as he went from numb to blotchy red and swollen, then warm again. The tears streamed down his face, though he made no sound.

For several days, the nurse kept his hands and feet dry, open to the air, and as sterile as possible. He drank cocoa, sipped soup, and we talked in drifts, when he had the strength. We returned home three days later.

As we approached the house, I saw Davis' van in the drive, a light on in his studio. I struggled with the key, my hands unsteady. When I tried the door, it was unlocked; Davis had left it open for us.

Through the screened-in porch I spotted his two remaining cacti: the Old Man of Mexico, with its white beard, and the Queen of the Night. Living with us, he had to tend them with special lights, heaters, and fertilizers – they were not doing well. The others were thriving at a local greenhouse where Davis visited them like family.

The kitchen was very warm, soup bubbling over a low flame. I drew the stool out from the corner, the one that was Aram's freedom as a toddler – enabling him to change darkness into light, to reach for his own food, even talk on the phone. Collapsing on its top step, I pulled Aram into me. He stretched out his legs within mine, as I closed my eyes, thinking of last summer, my first time away from him, the weekend I met Davis Carroll, aching for Aram one moment, breathing in my release, the perfect quiet, the next, the split beat of my heart thumping out that rhythm, ache/breath, ache/breath.

Our first time together, Davis made love with a slow concentrated attention, cradling my head in his arms, the way I cradled Aram's after a bad dream. I slept curled on my side, Davis crescented around me, his face burrowed into my hair, fists drawn to my chest. Davis awoke the next morning, his face flushed with sleep. When he left, I slid into the warm dented space that still held his scent.

Upstairs, I heard Davis now, his slow cautious tread, as though testing the ground with each step. Aram heard it, too, and got up.

In the dining room, the white bowls gleamed. Warm air filled my parched throat. Each breath hurt.

SOUL NAME

Josefov, Prague

Pinkas Synagogue is warm and smells of must. Devorah Paresch stands motionless inside the gallery for women, letting her eyes adjust to the brownish dark. She's alone, looking for her name on the walls. Names, thousands and thousands, their letters less than one inch high stretch from floor to ceiling, walling her in. Dev finds the rows of *Ps*, eleven Paresch's – murdered and lost grandparents, aunts, uncles, cousins – then traces her fingertips over the etched letters of her own name and the aunt she never knew, her mother's younger sister, and the letters go strange, twist into foreign marks, stitching through her fingers in black thread.

She has seen only one picture, worn soft as cotton, with a white, lettuced edge. Two girls sit close together on a hard wood bench. Dressed in black frocks for shul. Her mother, Malka, stares straight into the lens, heat in her eyes. She is full-figured, staunch-backed. Devorah sits sideways, curved around her older sister, her cheek nestled into the hollow of Malka's shoulder, as if to absorb her strength. Devorah wraps her arm around Malka's back, her other hand curls between Malka's two, which are folded squarely in her lap. So unlike Malka's, Devorah's eyes look light, translucent, the slender lips down-turned and wary.

Dev lifts her hand from the wall. As she moves to leave the shul, she hears her mother call her name in a deep and stubborn voice and looks up, spooked, (why can't she find herself within those sounds) and there is the look in her mother's eyes, a searching that turns tender or flashes into fury: *I'm talking to you.*

Outside, Dev's eyes sting, watering in the sun. She cuts through the line of elderly men and women, some talking in Yiddish as they wait for a hot, kosher lunch. Dev wanders the city, missing Malka – they were to make this trip together, but her mother wasn't well – and Dev imagines them now, arms linked, as she follows the course of the Vltava alone. As a girl, Malka cast her sins into the river from Cechuv Bridge each Yom Kippur; once she jumped into the water on a girlfriend's dare and Dev feels the rising leap of her mother's blood, the tumbling thrill of the fall, as she stares into the cold current. Walking away from the river, Dev climbs the wooded slopes of Petrin hill, another of Malka's girlhood haunts. The park's tree-lined gardens are deserted now, dotted with empty chateaux, pavilions, and a stooped Hercules, his arms broken to stumps.

Roaming, Dev walks in one direction, then another, losing her bearing, which is more menacing than being lost because then at least she'd have a destination. She walks until her legs ache and feet numb with cold. The late winter dark comes all at once and she hurries back to her hotel.

At the front desk, Dev finds a message from her mother's best friend, Eppie Leskov. Malka has suffered another heart attack, her second in two months. Dev packs her suitcase and leaves on the next plane for home.

Equinox, New York City

Malka can't find the door. She glances down at the small business card she's taken from Dev's night-table: *Equinox*, in glossy white letters on a field of pool blue. The correct address. In front of her is a wall of glass. Inside, a uniformed guard talks on the telephone. A young woman carrying a knapsack clips past, jostling Malka's shoulder and the wall parts, whooshing open, then closed. A trick door. Magic. One must step on the lucky spot. Malka slowly approaches the door, but it remains impenetrable. She stands within an inch of it, feeling stupid, knowing if she advances further, she'll bump her nose against the glass like a fish inside an aquarium. At last, the guard comes out and takes her arm, leaving Malka relieved, then anxious – is it so obvious she needs help? The attendant at the front desk is busy and does not see her.

Only a month and Dev is back. Already they fight, fight about everything, about nothing, and last night Malka said terrible things to her only child, things she cannot take back. Or forget. *You are not my daughter!*

Always they make up, but this time, no. Dev left early for her waitress job without saying goodbye. She had another audition. After an audition is her swim to relax. Since Dev came home to care for her, Malka keeps a copy of her daughter's schedule tacked to the fridge door with a bright apple magnet, so she can find her any minute of the day.

That morning, Malka's friend Eppie appeared in the doorway shortly after Dev left for the city. "A boom, I hear and worry," she said, out of breath from her climb upstairs. "Like thunder, but a clear night we had."

"Dev's not right, she's back," Malka snapped. "A glass tea with lemon?"

Eppie nodded. She was a small woman, light and quick, with a cap of straight silver hair and girlish bangs. As they walked into the kitchen where the kettle was whistling, Malka admired her friend's lilac dress, bordered at the neck and wrists in cream-coloured lace. Cool colours soothed her now – white, powder blue, mint green – though she didn't feel right in them herself.

"I make everything what is her favourite and she picks around the food on her plate." Malka lowered the blue flame. "In the night, she is with terrors. Always now smoking in a chain."

"Maybe she's worried about her mother," Eppie said.

Malka clicked her tongue, then went into the living room, carrying the tea on a tray with linen napkins. The two women settled on Malka's tapestry couch and took off their shoes; Malka put her feet up, Eppie tucked hers under her. "Lately, Dev is always with one question or another," Malka said, stirring sugar into her tea.

"So," Eppie sipped slowly from her steaming glass, "look in her face and talk."

"I'm not in much of a mood."

A shadow passed across Eppie's grey eyes. "She has the life whole out before her," she said, speaking too fast. "All the men and boys look on her when she's passing." She ruffled her bangs with a delicate hand. "A beauty, your Dev."

Malka sighed. "Don't let's talk about it."

Now, waiting in the lobby of the health club, Malka cannot get enough air to fill a breath. She glances quickly around the lobby: teal carpet, empty white walls, a hush heightened by the soft whir of the air conditioner. Behind the formica desk is a young man, half-naked. Malka often sees bare-chested men strolling on the boardwalk, bobbing in the surf, toasting their fleshy backs in the sun, but this chest is different: hairless, smooth, and seamed as flesh-toned plastic. *The man, he looks like he is operated by remote control*, she imagines telling Eppie later, to feel less strange now.

"You must find for me Dev. Devorah Paresch," Malka says, her hands curled around the lip of the desk. "At once now I speak with her."

The attendant goes to a wall of white pigeonholes. He pulls out one laminated card, then another, refiling them slowly on purpose. "She's a member here?" He looks over Malka's head. His hair is close-cropped, drained of colour, his eyes drained of light.

Malka nods impatiently, her head circling. "Can you make maybe a page?"

The man doesn't appear to hear her; he clicks on a computer, which grumbles to life. Malka leans across the desk as lines of chemical green names roll upward on the screen. "We don't have a record of her."

After the war, when Malka returned to what had once been her home, there was no record of her, though she stood living and breathing. "Ninety days membership she won. A drawing at *The*

Ballroom." Malka thrusts the blue business card with its white letters across the desk into the young man's palm, then turns, rushing down the long carpeted corridor into the elevator. On each floor, more people get on. They are all young, dressed in bright stretchy underwear on top of their clothes. Dead eyes, face front. The elevator gusts, rising floor by floor.

Malka gets off at the roof, following painted arrows to the pool. Inside the white-tiled space, she stands by a row of empty bleachers, searching for Dev among the swimmers. When her daughter is upset, it spirals. She gets careless of herself.

"Hey!" the lifeguard calls out, "you can't come in here in street clothes." Malka watches the water, glittering with movement, impossibly blue. The room is warm, damp with steam, and she is dizzy. The guard walks to a corner door near the shallow end of the pool. "Here," he says, swinging it open for her.

Inside the women's locker room, Malka stands next to an abandoned blow dryer, feeling the useless blast of air. A few yards away, in front of an open locker, is Dev. She is bent over, her long dark hair trailing the floor as she towels it dry. Malka feels such relief that she just stands and watches her daughter for a moment. Such beautiful hair, a rich dark brown, glinting copper, the highlights the colour Malka's hair had once been. The thought occurs to her, *just go, now home,* as Dev flips upright, her hair cascading over thin shoulders, beads of water glistening in the mass of curls.

"Mama, what's wrong?"

Malka shrugs, wishing she'd escaped. "Worried thoughts I had. How did it go, the audition?"

Dev shrugs, palms up. "What am I going to do with you?"

"What play?" Malka asks lightly, sinking onto the uncomfortable wood bench that bisects two rows of lockers.

"*Separation.*"

"That one, I don't know." Last night she'd said: *When are you going to start your life? Mama,* her daughter said, slender hands shaking, *this is my life.*

"*Off, off* again. I think I may have gotten it."

Malka crosses the fingers of her left hand, then knocks her curled fist against the bench.

"Is it late?" Dev asks.

Resting, Malka fingers the silver pocketwatch that hangs from a braided chain around her neck. She opens the cover, glancing at the time. "Just three." One of Dev's quirks is that she refuses to wear a watch. Ever. A watch binds, closing you in, as if asking the time every minute is any better.

"I'm taking you to lunch, Mama. Wait a minute. Tea." And there is her daughter's half-smile that never looks quite happy or at ease.

Malka clicks the case of her pocketwatch closed. It is large and heavy, suited to a tall, hardy man. The silver case is adorned with a crest, her father's initials, *SNP*, Saul Noah Paresch, engraved inside its cover. During the war, Malka's family left it along with other valuables with their Christian friends in Prague, Sylva and Pavel Kroner. It was a miracle the watch was preserved, sent to Malka in Brighton after the war.

Of course it didn't run. The crystal was cracked, the silver case marked with gashes. Malka's cousin Rachel told her about Elias Laundau's shop on Coney Island Avenue. Malka had trouble finding it that August day, the air heavy with late-summer stillness. And then: there it was. Just a cage, really, wedged between *Everybody's Business Legal Immigration Center* and *The Black Sea Bookstore*. Malka saw gold and silver rings glimmering through the iron bars. Inside, a slender man sat on a stool, a loupe in his eye. When he looked up, Malka was startled by his eyes, light and clear as a pale sky. He had a sand-coloured moustache. As he stood, she saw he was very tall, fine-boned, with a quiet elegance about him, a calm which drew her. Elias cleaned the watch and put in a new mainspring and crystal. After, he shined the case, which retained its dents – as if someone had bitten into the silver – reminding Malka how to open and close the case by depressing the stem, how to wind the watch with its tiny silver key. Elias converted the watchchain into a pendant and gave it back to Malka, no charge. She baked him a poppy seed cake.

Within months, they married. The new couple honeymooned in Montreal, where Elias had family. A cousin on Jeanne Mance, near Nat's Grocery. Browsing together past the old-fashioned scale, the bins of fruits and vegetables, the worn paperbacks and salvaged toaster ovens, the paintings, crooked and unframed, Malka found a brass kettle she still uses, and Elias a pair of brown leather boots that actually fit. Elias took Malka to lunch at Schwartz's, held the door for her as they passed through a curtain of smoked meat. The smell was Heaven and Malka saw the framed tribute, *When I die, I want to to to Schwartz's.* Malka loved the Main, the familiar hum of Yiddish, the strangeness of French street names, Cadieux, Esplanade, and Marie-Anne. She even liked the purity of the Montreal winter, icicles the size of umbrella stems, the crystalline cold, the excuse to be cozy, not for a day or a week because you were sick, but for half the year! Besides, you could talk about the weather and never be boring. Malka remembered sitting by the wood-burning stove with Elias, drinking sweet milky tea, in fuzzy slippers and fleece robes, dreaming, gazing out the window at the whirl of white, snowflakes fluttering like butterflies.

Fourteen years ago, Elias died of emphysema. Dev was thirteen. Now, still, the ticking of the pocketwatch he fixed is Malka's comfort, her companion.

Watching Dev dress, Malka is disturbed by her thinness: the bones and new hollows in her face, the deep cleft at the base of her neck, her shoulder blades like wings. "Let's go to Wolf's," she suggests, imagining filling Dev with hot, salty soup, an overstuffed liverwurst sandwich, babka for dessert. Dev smiles at her, dressed in loose, low-slung jeans, a soiled white shirt and old leather jacket, and Malka sees a gentle mockery in the barest wavering of her lips.

As they pass by the front desk, a young woman calls out, "Dawn!" her voice ringing with groundless cheer. "Ms. Paris –" Malka looks around, confused, as the woman steps out from behind the desk and hands Dev a white and blue laminated membership card.

On the train home, they don't speak. Tea has been forgotten, the good feeling between them punctured. Malka looks up at the posters lining the wall of the train, settling on *Poetry in Motion*, something by Elizabeth Bishop about a burning boy. She's not sure she understands it, but the repetitive rhythm, like a child's nursery rhyme, makes her unexpectedly sad. While Dev is studying the script of *Separation*, Malka takes the small plastic card from her daughter's hand. In the center is a photograph. The skin, flour-fine, subject to hives and rashes. The broad forehead, straight brows, narrow dark eyes, and thin mouth. And underneath the picture, this name, Dawn Paris, and her daughter's signature. "Who is Dawn Paris?" Malka asks, looking into her daughter's face.

Dev looks away, then pries the card out of Malka's hand. As Dev looks at her, Malka watches her daughter's dark blue eyes grow wary and amused, a common look of hers that withholds so much. She is separate, outlined in black ink. Mysterious.

"Who is Devorah Paresch?" Dev asks.

"Dev was beautiful. Brave. With a life too tragic." Malka does not hear her own words, just the pauses between them. It's what she's always told her daughter, a refrain.

Dev looks up at the ceiling, then into her lap. A dismissive click comes from her mouth, her tongue up against her front teeth and Malka thinks *this Dawn Paris is not a person, is a time and place, not a place, a postcard in red, orange, and fake gold*. Even after marrying Elias, Malka wanted a living Paresch in the world. She kept her name and they gave it to their daughter. "In the city, you are then everywhere Dawn Paris? A *goyische* name."

Dev shakes her head. "I never –"

Malka waves away her words. Except for this lost-and-found name, Malka cannot fault Dev. She is observant, even devout. As a girl, Malka attended shul with her family on Shabbes, but since the war, she has had to be seriously coaxed back. Once in a while, Dev lures her to shul and the two go together on the high holy days. Mostly, Malka steers clear of organized faith, of groups. Going to temple, praying in chorus, these are ceremonial acts. Faith is between her and God. "Why?" Malka presses.

Dev rolls in her lips until they disappear. "Forget it. No . . . I wanted to see what it would feel like to be . . . *light.*" Dev's small smile twists askew, sagging at one corner.

"And Dev Paresch can't feel like you say. Light. And what is anyway *light*?"

Dev gazes past Malka, out the window of the train toward the streak of stations. "Light? Shit. Not the new version." Dev's laugh is harsh, sand in her throat, and Malka's skin tightens; her hand is back, slapping her daughter's face.

Malka's palm stings as she watches Dev rise slowly from the seat and walk, head bowed, through the sliding doors into the next car. She pushes herself to her feet and tries to follow, but can't open the sliding doors. Dev is standing on the other side between cars, the wind whipping her hair around her face. Malka looks around, asks for help. A young woman gives Malka her arm, offering her seat. Malka holds fast to the overhead strap, as a transit policeman taps her on the back and she points into the space between cars. With one hand, Dev opens her script; with the other she threads her fingers again and again through her knotted, tangled hair. Malka watches her daughter's face, concentrated on the printed lines; in a minute, she'll try again that heavy door.

Boxes, Brighton Beach

The next morning, Dev opens the window to feel the day. It is cool and blowy, a tentative sun and long streaks of cloud. She's unnerved by the row of six bottles, green and amber glass, lined up on the fire escape; Malka has returned to her old ritual, an early warning sign in case of burglars. Through sleep-drenched eyes, Dev reads Malka's note scribbled in light pencil on the inside cover of a matchbook, *Downstairs, lovey,* in the shaky print of a child just learning her letters. Dev glances at the nighttable clock, already past eleven. She's slept again like a stone, the dead-to-the-world sleep of being home.

She misses her studio in Chelsea: the sun-warmed brick, the skylight. Every few weeks, she climbs a ladder to the roof and washes the glass herself with scalding water and lemon. Today, she'd have been up early and walked down to the piers with a thermos of coffee and steamed milk. She'd sit there all morning, Benjamin might come by.

He was in her place, now, watering the spider plant, feeding the goldfish, sleeping under the cream-coloured duvet and looking out the window onto the desolation of Tenth Avenue. Her best and oldest friend. He'd grown up in the apartment next door. They'd acted out their own plays in her room, kissed on this bed, which is made up now exactly as it was then, with forest green flannel sheets and the earth-toned afghan. It leaves Dev displaced: odd and out of time.

The walls are still papered in black and white collage, the *papier maché* layers, an unfolding of Dev's tastes over the years: Rita, then Marilyn, and finally Betty. Dev remembers her mother saying to her father, "Into her mind, she gets one thing," suspicious of Dev's single-mindedness about the theatre, disturbed by single-mindedness itself – *a girl she should be well-rounded* – and her father smiling calmly, letting her be.

The chipped white bureau still displays the soft fabric dollhouses Malka made for her: a bear family, a zoo, the circus, and her favourite, the farm, with its red barn tumbled onto its side.

Dev wraps a velour robe around her, sets a pot of coffee to brew, and wanders from room to room. The rest of the apartment is sparse now, temporary, and Dev can't get used to it. Malka's piano is gone. Up until her last attack, she gave lessons and sat down herself occasionally (less and less these last years) to play. Dev can still hear the Brahms *Liebeslieder Waltz* her parents played together each night after dinner, glancing back and forth at each other, as the lilting music filled the house.

Dev pours herself coffee, straying into Malka's workroom, fashioned from a walk-in closet, relieved to see it still crowded with life. The table of unfinished pine is stacked with raw wood boxes: oblong, square, heart-shaped. On the wall, baskets hang from pegs, each filled with colourful trimmings and adornments: bits of fabric, semi-precious stones, paste jewels, silk flowers, shellacked pictures Malka has cut from magazines.

From the center of the work table, Dev picks up an oblong box finished to a rich maple, its top tray divided into small compartments. Beside the box, Malka has spilt out a small pile of semi-precious stones. A turquoise, gold-veined Eilat stone is set aside, and Dev realizes, this box is for her.

In Malka's room, Dev finds her mother's hospital suitcase, still packed, shoved partway under the bed. She puts away her mother's things, sets *Grapes of Wrath* on her night table, tucks *Midstream* into the magazine rack, thinking, it's always been the other way: Malka setting her things right, smoothing unfinished edges.

On the bureau, Malka has left out a pair of amber earrings, as if she planned to wear them, then changed her mind. Or simply forgot. Dev slides out the deep bottom drawer of her mother's jewelry case. Inside, drawstring bags of worn felt are filled with pieces Malka rarely wears: a string of pearls, onyx and opal rings, a wristwatch decorated with diamond chips. Dev slides her fingers into one of the drawstring bags, curious, and something sharp pierces her finger. She presses her lips around the cut, then upturns the bag. A small shard of red glass spills onto the bureau. Remnant of an earring, maybe. Or one of her mother's ornaments. Dev carefully picks up the piece of glass and holds it to the light. It is crescent-shaped, the colour of red wine, and has a slashing grain like a piece of hard candy.

Dev hears Malka's heavy tread on the upper stairs, then the jangling of keys, and slips the shard of garnet-coloured glass into her pocket. A moment later Malka enters the room, her hair loosely waved around her broad shoulders, a mesh of grey and copper and gold. "You've cut yourself," she says at once.

Dev looks down at her finger, the blood beading, as Malka binds a tissue around it, then goes to the bathroom for a bandage. As Malka unwraps her shawl to bandage Dev's cut, Dev tests herself. She cannot remember the pale blue numbers on her mother's arm or their order, nor can she think of which arm bears the tattoo.

"You'll live, I think," Malka says, smiling.

Dev reaches into her pocket and holds out the piece of glass to her mother, glinting on her palm. Malka drops the shard into its drawstring bag and slides the sack into her pocket. "Lunch I'll fix," she says, matter-of-factly.

"No, Mama, we'll walk. For your heart."

Glass and Stone

Malka's feet ache so she slips into woolen mules that flap at her heels with each step. She and Dev head away from the beach toward Brighton Avenue, her daughter's arm threaded lightly through hers. The noise and crowds thicken around them, the street suddenly darkening.

"Mama, I can't –" Dev holds out her hands as the El roars by, clattering overhead.

"What you can't?" Malka asks, leaning into her daughter. Though it is cool, the air is thick with so many people breathing and talking. A babel of horns, drivers shouting. The old man in front of New Deal Chow Mein beating out his fury on five upturned trash pails. Malka's green mesh shopping bag swings empty from her wrist and the sounds of the street envelop her: the familiar tangle of Czech, Russian, Chinese, Spanish, and Korean, the interrupted scales and minor chords plunked out by the dirty bearded boy in front of Hirsch's Knishes, with his torn duffel and thermos, his steel guitar and keyboard, the tumult of his own rock songs pummelling through his head. Malka listens for the distant keening of gulls, the muted shush of the waves. They are there too, like any other late winter afternoon with Dev home from school, errands, then dinner with Elias at six, the three of them, a family. . . . "We go first to the deli," Malka says, savouring her anticipation, almost like being carbonated. She has not felt this in so long.

"How do you hear yourself think?" Dev asks as they pass under the green awning, jewel-coloured fruits and vegetables arranged in bins, protected from the cold by a thick plastic tarp.

"I don't want always to hear." Malka peels the husks back from several ears of corn with resolute rips, then examines the colour and regularity of the kernels. "You have been too long away," she adds, thinking of Dev's neighbourhood in Chelsea, the wind-blown streets, quiet and forsaken, paper scraps like white leaves shaking in the trees. Next, they go to Variety where Malka picks up thread, a new egg beater, and an alarm clock with a face that glows green in the dark. She insists on buying Dev a tortoise-shell headband, like the one she wore as a child, sweeping her daughter's hair straight back from her brow, as Dev gently pushes her away.

They walk on to Coney Island Avenue past Hello Gorgeous Beauty, where Malka used to get her hair done. The sight of the huge For Sale or Lease sign out front dissolves her open-ended expectation and she says, "Enough," as they turn back toward the beach. Again they pass the boy on keyboard and his halting minor melodies filter through the cacophony of the street – they are all Malka hears for a moment. Dev, glancing at her mother, says, "Mama, you miss your piano."

"No, no." It is a relief to have it gone. Donated to the Youth Group at Beth Israel. Not to have to push away the longing to play, a daily ache, like missing a loved one who is there, but not there. And the space, this open space, is a new clearing in her mind. Malka finds she wants more to be alone in her workroom making boxes, or just to sit with a wandering mind by her bedroom window. The El rushes past with its metallic clanking and Malka watches the checkerboard of light and shadow pass along the pavement and across storefronts, feeling the motion of the train in her feet, shuddering involuntarily at the white and black boxes. Once she lived inside a box where slept five women, each inside the other's legs. Linked together, they could lie down and rest a little. Malka sat with her back against the wall, legs spread, her younger sister Devorah inside her legs, her bald head resting on Malka's stomach. Quiet without room to talk or move, it seemed to her that each was attached to the other, in links, a chain they made. . . .

"Come, Mama," her daughter says, tugging her arm, offering to carry the mesh bag that Malka holds onto more tightly, the swinging weight of her shopping, small and solid, holding her down to earth, this day. Soon they reach the sea and stroll for a while on the boardwalk. Dev slips her thin arm again through Malka's and Malka holds her daughter's hand at her hip. Malka stops in front of Cafe Volna, her breath coming raggedly, a weight in her blood. "Let's sit," she says.

"Do you want to try a new place?"

Malka shakes her head. "Here they know me." Lately, she wants her usual, nothing new. They sit outside facing the sea, close enough to feel the spray. The day is confused, a scuffling of sun and shadow; the sea glitters into blinding points of light, then all at once darkens into blue-black. "Where else, Dev, do you have sun and clouds, wind, maybe a little rain, all in the same hour of one day?" Malka stares at the sea. She lights a cigarette, inhaling deeply.

Dev clips the cigarette from her mother's fingers, stubbing it out. "Yesterday, you lit a second while the first one was smoldering."

This strikes Malka as absurd, and she laughs low in her throat, relieved that Dev resists the urge to smoke herself. Sun glints through the clouds streaming in long bands across the pavement; Malka slips her feet from her mules, sliding them back and forth in its warmth.

Olga brings their coffee in lidded cardboard cups. Malka, then Dev, tears a half-moon from the lid, as if they are travelling. Malka feels in her pocket for the shard of garnet glass. She'd forgotten it, buried in her jewelry case where she'd left it years ago, when she and Elias first took the apartment on Brighton 4, and she'd been forced to decide herself: *what to save, what to let go*. Strange to have Dev dig it up like buried treasure. "Do you always go, Dev, snooping?"

Her daughter pours milk into her coffee, absorbed in its billowing cloud shapes. Dev's bowed head, her silence, tries Malka's patience, and she spills the glass shard onto the tabletop where it catches the light.

Dev looks up, and Malka says, "Something I save."

"You, Mama, are not a saver."

Malka laughs, but the urgent expression in Dev's eyes holds her and bursts of words come up in a rush. "We work clearing the compound for a new barracks for women. Cold and always with a drizzle. The construction site open without protection from an element." Malka pushes the sugar bowl away, resting her arms on the table. "Moving and lifting rubble in piles, we set ourselves a game. To see what maybe we find in the dreck." Malka twines her soiled napkin around her fingers. "There was the steel twisted and torn, edges of glass from what was windows. Sometimes I spot something and take. Or Dev sees. A scrap cloth to cover the head. A leaf maybe to eat. One day sorting, I see something round, reddish in the dirt. Nothing we were allowed to take, so my heart was beating too fast. A small glass jar, to put inside maybe homemade jam." Malka takes a deep breath, her hand resting on her chest. "Quick, I dig out. The jar I slip inside the sleeve of my dress, under my arm. Soon to go inside the barracks."

Malka watches her daughter lift the shard of red glass from the table. She cannot make out the expression on Dev's face, her features are still. "Later, they bring the grey soup in metal cans. No bowls, or even spoons. So the women they slurp out of dirty palms. Until I take out my glass jar and we pass from hand to hand. Dev pretends we sip wine."

Malka glances again at her daughter; Dev's eyes look like they are burning and Malka feels a little of her old strength. "The day comes. Men on top of tanks into the compound, so I take my red glass jar and smash, but cannot leave every piece. . . ." Malka's hair tangles in a skein. Her shawl ripples loose around her shoulders until her daughter pulls it more snugly around her.

"And Dev?"

Malka tries to gather a full breath, but it stops short of full, short of empty. "She was very –"

"No Mama, start again. Start all over again."

Malka cradles her coffee between both hands. She thinks of *Dawn Paris*, this newborn stranger, a blank, or is it a space needing to be filled. Dev looks at her, waiting. Malka sighs. "As girls, we fight. Later, we come to be everything . . . but before, I tease her." Malka shakes her head, biting her lip. "I call her sometimes names."

Dev tilts her head, "I'm sorry, Mama, I thought she was beautiful and brave and . . . *what* names?"

Unnerved, Malka says, "From polio, she walked with one step short, one longer." Always Papa's special. Malka remembers her father, husky with square-veined arms and eyes so pale, clear, and blue, her sister Dev imagined she could look through them all the way inside of him. Eyes like Elias Landau.

Olga appears with a steaming pot and refills their cups. Malka tries to sip her coffee, which is too hot yet to drink, as her daughter scrapes the oilcloth with her spoon. "Tell me about Dev."

"I say she is a mechanic." Malka folds her hands on the table remembering them all together in Terezin, marching toward the SS officer who is making the selection. He asks sometimes questions, then directs right, left, and she sees to the left are children and the older and ones with something wrong. Mama puts on her and Dev's makeup. She hears Papa say he is a businessman and goes left, and Mama, a piano teacher, also left, then Dev comes up, standing straight to hide the limp. "A mechanic, I say she is," Malka repeats.

"What?"

"The officer points to the van what is standing a few yards distant, another guard working under the hood with a box tools. He shouts to Dev, 'Show me how you check the master cylinder.'

"And up Dev goes to the van and opens the top of this cylinder, like she learns from Papa who tinkers with cars." Malka remembers her hands trembling, looking from Dev to Mama and Papa, who are loading onto vans, her head shaking, *no, no, no,* as Dev looks to her. "She wipes with a cloth clean the cylinder," Malka says, as if to herself. "Then inside the lid she looks. 'The fluid is low,' she whispers, her voice just a thread. Then Dev pushes up the rubber cups and puts back the lid.

"To change the spark plugs, he tells her. Dev asks him for the tools. She looks for the thick wires in rows, takes then the cable and twists. To pull out straight the plug. Her hands are strong, she never makes a damage. Dev blows away the dirt and through the change she goes, while he is making other selections. When Dev is done, he starts the truck to prove inside everything still works. Dev and I go right." Malka breathes in deep. She sits for a while watching the sea, the tide going out, the remains of her coffee tepid, and from far away she hears her daughter ask, "Mama, what happened to Dev?"

Malka remembers that Dev stopped eating, then speaking. Her face, which Malka could always read, closed shut. The next time in the line-up, dresses in left hand, run fast in a circle. Around the compound, tall chimneys spewing black smoke.

"Mama."

Malka feels her daughter's hand on her arm. "I make white my mind, go once around, then again, Dev behind me. Together running in the circle, the circle breaking here, again there, into right or left, the left with the older prisoners, the smaller, and the sick. Swinging baton motioned me right, then Dev also right, but she jerks from the circle into the charged wire, onto the ground she drops, her head in dirt where was the things we find."

Dev puts her arm around her mother's shoulder and Malka feels its warmth, but her daughter's arm is so light, like a willow resting on her, and Malka thinks, *You can't make someone to live, even if you give them life.* She glances at Dev's other hand resting lightly on the table, the nails bitten to ragged stumps, the cuticles raw and peeling, and says to herself, *If you could just let alone.*

Shabbes

Later that afternoon, Dev sits across from her mother at the kitchen table, the jar of thick pink polish by her side, rubbing the tarnished candlesticks with a soft cloth until they gleam. Malka peels husks back from the corn and sets a pot to boil. Reaching up, she clicks on the radio that sits on the kitchen windowsill, rolling the dial through snatches of talk, music, static. "I'm looking for news," she says, flicking the button to AM. "Also weather." Malka settles on an *all-news-all-the-time* station. She braids the bread and seasons the chicken while Dev goes into the dining room to set the table. The radio dim in her ears, Dev sets out her mother's best silver, lingering over the white linen napkins, rolling them into their filigreed rings. It is a relief to be active, preparing, not to have to talk or even to listen.

Growing up, her mother hardly ever spoke to her about the war. Mostly she spoke around it, in carefully prepared anecdotes. An eerie voice invaded her natural one, her tone formal and distant. Official. The strange staccato rhythm put Dev on edge, though she learned little of her mother's experience from these stories or their gaps, which left her heavy and formless.

Dev joins Malka in the kitchen and together they peel and wash vegetables for salad. Taking the lettuce from her mother, Dev pats it dry with paper towel, then puts it in the spinner; she winds the crank faster and faster till it whirls on its own. Next, Malka mixes the lettuce with peppers and scallions in the large wooden bowl. "You, I will call now only Devi," she says softly.

Her mother clasps her hands together and Dev thinks of the creased, scalloped-edged photograph of the two sisters, imagining the warm weight of her aunt's arm around her mother's back, the curve of Dev's cheek against Malka's shoulder, the small hard hand, its knot of knuckles sharp against Malka's folded palms. For the first time, she can truly visualize a body.

The apartment grows warm with the smell of roasting chicken and rising bread. There is time yet before sundown and Malka is weary. Dev coaxes her as she would a child to go down for a nap.

Malka lays in bed, drained. Wondering if she has done right. *On a grave, we put a stone, the dead we can not make more heavy, but with Devi, never did I want to make more weight.*

As the light fades, Dev goes to wake Malka. Her mother lies in bed on her back, one arm folded across her chest, the other at her side holding her pocketwatch in her right hand. Dev calls to her. She gently shakes her shoulder.

Dev moves to take the watch, can't, not wanting to unravel the chain twined through her mother's fingers. She goes to the window and opens it. On the fire escape, the bottles have blown over, rolling in the wind. Outside is the near-empty beach, baggy clouds hanging overhead. Two old men on a wood bench move chess pieces across the board balanced between their knees, a young woman in a red kerchief strolls on the boardwalk, a boy buries another child in the sand. Dev listens for the sound of Malka's voice, her words, the grit in her throat that comes with her flashes of anger, but hears only the silence hollowing out, as if Malka's voice alone held up the house and, empty of its sound, the brown brick box will crash, like a breaking wave, into the sea.

Dev sweeps Malka's hair back from her brow. She closes her mother's eyes. And begins to say Kaddish.

(For Brana Hochova, in loving memory.)

WHAT REMAINS

Settling into his Olds for the long, snowy drive from Montreal to Pennsylvania, Dr Sol Stein hears his wife Evelyn's voice echo inside his head: *What a shame.* Sol dislikes this expression, especially when it refers to his shameful secret, that he has never met his own father, Nathaniel Stein, though Nathaniel is alive and living in North America. Driving South on Route 15, Sol gets the call on his cell from his father's case worker that Nathaniel Stein is dead. Passed in his sleep, felt no pain. The connection is bad and Art Koenig's baleful voice is breaking up, but it doesn't matter. Sol gets the facts.

His father had a pretty long life. He lived to seventy-three, not bad considering that Nathaniel Stein was mentally ill and had suffered several heart attacks.

Sol doesn't know what he feels and thinks. Truth is he doesn't feel much of anything. How can you have feelings toward a father you never knew, in fact never met? But he keeps driving because now he has to go to the VA hospital in Westchester to collect his father's belongings and to arrange for the funeral and burial. There's no one else to do it, nothing else to be done: Sol is an only child and all of Nathaniel's other relatives cut him off years ago.

Sol started out early that March morning to avoid traffic and make good time, left the house before six, hoped to pull into the VA by late afternoon; there would still be some blueish winter light to see by. Travelling alone was so different than with his wife and boys, no one to talk to, no one to placate with snacks, no one to play *I spy with my little eye. . . .* Sol is always surrounded by people needing him and believes this solitude will be bracing, give him time to think, to collect his thoughts (funny expression, that, as if one could delicately gather thoughts like pick-up sticks or shells on the beach, sorting and saving). His thoughts about his father are too hard to locate, let alone collect. His mother told Sol once that his father was a collector. Sol was about Daniel's age, seven or so, and wanted to collect stamps. His Mom bought him a red leatherette album at the post office in Lachine and signed him up for a stamp club which sent Sol a colourful newsletter in French and English, as well as new stamps for his album each month. Sol loved poring over the newsletter and pasting in the stamps. Sometimes, he liked to place them in his own pattern, not in the specific dotted space where they were supposed to go. He asked his mother what his father had collected, but she didn't want to talk about him, it was rare that she said anything at all. Sol was intrigued, storing away this tidbit, collecting it, hoping to add more to the near empty treasure box where a few lone facts rattled around.

En route, Sol stops in at a Québec diner and orders poutine (heart attack in a bowl, a doctor should know better), but he craves the greasy fries drowning in brown gravy, fatty white cheese curds spattered on top, washed down with his breakfast coffee. Out here in the Québec countryside, you can get poutine anywhere, anytime. A half-hour later, he pulls in at a gas station to check the oil, fill up on washer fluid, and stocks up on Camels and Diet Cokes at the adjacent dépanneur. He thinks to call Evelyn, but decides to do it from the road, and some miles later, sees that his cell is not in its usual place, clipped to his belt near his groin, a little to the right of his pager where he can frequently check it and have it at the ready. The cell's lost, missing, left behind . . . but where?

Losing his cell would tickle Ev who calls the mobile, Dick. *Is it turned on? Antenna up? Lights blinking? Sure it's working? Is Dick still . . . there?*

Evelyn hated Dick because it was always on. Dr Sol Stein had the unusual arrangement with at least a dozen of his long-term patients that they could call him any time – day or night. And they did. He needed to be available. And he was . . . which bugged the hell out of Ev . . . but he and Ev had a good marriage, seventeen years now and they still made love twice a week, Dick or no Dick: if they were interrupted, well, they picked up where they'd left off. Ev would not be amused by the timing of Dick's loss: she was the one who had encouraged Sol since she'd first met him to contact his father, to visit him, get to know him . . . before it was too late. Those words cracked like shots, reverberating inside Sol's chest, their echo a dull ache so chronic Sol had become accustomed to doing whatever he had to do, as if the pressure and pain were not there.

He had tried to visit his father twice before. Two attempts, both aborted. A third try today. Today was to be the day, before it was too late. Each prior attempt was triggered by an urgent, incoherent letter from Nathaniel, full of love and longing, but also spattered with bizarre ramblings, delusions, non sequiturs, and what sounded like hallucinations. Once, while Sol was a freshman at McGill University, he made the trip to New York City via Amtrak, then rented a car and drove to the VA hospital in Westchester, Pennsylvania. He was on the grounds, sitting across a desk pocked with cigarette stains and coffee rings, face to face with a humourless bearded fellow with sad brown eyes and deep bulging pockets of fat beneath them. This was his father's case worker whose name at that time was Schlomo Lipshitz. Although Sol had saved up for this trip, missed a major Physics exam to make it, and travelled from dawn till dark, Schlomo urged Sol *not* to see Nathaniel. He warned that visiting Nathaniel "at this point in time could catalyze dire consequences," for Nathaniel, and he threatened, Sol as well. When Schlomo said the word "dire," his bushy black unibrow pressed down into his low forehead and his dark eyes hardened into onyx, glittering like threats. Sol wonders now, as he drives south, why he didn't challenge Schlomo or at least press him to elaborate or explain, what exactly did he mean by dire? How was his father? What was he doing? Who was he? Why didn't he hang around, try the next day? Why did he shoot up from that chair and gun back to Montreal, breathing in the burning cold as if it were his last breath?

Then there was the second attempt at Evelyn's urging. She was hugely pregnant with their second child, Jonah, while caring for their two-year-old Daniel. Ev was to accompany Sol, they had a sitter booked for Danny, but at the last minute, the sitter cancelled and Ev stayed home with Danny, along with her heartburn and sciatica, while Sol made the trip alone. Slowing down to change to the right lane on 15, Sol tries to remember what aborted that second attempt. Once again, he managed to make it to the VA hospital, parked his car, and glanced around at the otherworldly quiet, fortress-like brick buildings, the not unattractive deserted grounds, which could have been a college campus. He felt his heart clawing inside his chest like an animal trying to get out of a trap, and found that he could not breathe. Panic. He sweated it out, then turned around to go home. Later, he told Ev he'd had a premonition, he was sure she was going into labour and he could not miss being there for the birth of their second son. She didn't call him on it and delivered Jonah two weeks later.

More time passed. Life intervened, or supervened, the visit was on Sol's back burner. He would get to it. He would do it! Before it was too late.

Sol nears the Canadian-American border, reaches in his chest pocket for his passport, and thinks what he will tell people after this epochal visit, how he didn't see his father until Nathaniel Stein was dead.

As the Customs Officer scrutinizes Sol's passport, asks him to open the trunk, and is examining its contents, Sol thinks how incredible it is that he never met Nathaniel face-to-face or spoke to him directly on the telephone. He has only heard terrifying stories about him from his mother, Sarah, who told Sol when he was just a boy, twelve in fact, that Nathaniel had raped her, which resulted in Sol's birth, even though she and Nat were warned by her doctor that she should never have children. Sol's mother also told him that she had been running away from Nathaniel Stein ever since, dragging Sol from L.A. to Mexico City and then London, finally up north to Canada, to get away from him. If he had been on to them, she would have continued up the North Way to Inuit Country and beyond. Sol wasn't sure whether his mother's stories were true (his mother was a frightened woman, some said paranoid) but it didn't matter, for the stories were burned into Sol's soul as if from a branding iron. Of course, Sol had seen a few pictures of Nathaniel Stein over the years, photos he couldn't verify were actually of his father.

The Customs Official asks Sol the usual questions about why he is going to the U.S., how long he plans to stay, if he is bringing anything with him, and Sol answers mechanically. When he explains about his father's death, the man gives his condolences and Sol thanks him. Then the Customs Official says, "Good luck, Dr Stein," and, "Have a nice day."

Sol pops open a Diet Coke and looks about him at the long expanse of white farms, the clumps of cold cows and the occasional black bull, the winter-warped trees and ash-grey sky, everything blanched of colour. Actually, Sol loves winter, but not for the usual reasons. They have six months of it from November through April, though this year it snowed in early October. It is mid-March now, Sol has no craving for spring. Most people talk of winter sports – downhill, cross-country, raquetting, snowboarding – yabble, yabble, yabble – the white silence, unearthly quiet and calm, this is what suits Sol. Now, he is grateful for the length of the drive, but the lost mobile distracts him; for sure he has missed countless calls from his longtime patients, not to mention Ev and the boys. In ten minutes, he stops at a gas station and calls his own number from the pay phone.

There are five rings.

"Oui, allô?"

A male voice, deep and throaty, clotted with years of smoke, maybe whiskey. "Good, you found it. Is this the dépanneur in Napierville?"

"You have already huit messages."

"Just eight?"

"Sept from Madame Weiner."

"Rona or Harriet? I've got two Mrs Weiners."

"She is wanting to know, can she combine . . . what is it? Tylenol numer trois with her bladder medication?"

"Okay, that's Rona."

"Look, I am needing to wait on my customers. Can you come and get this cellular?"

"Who is the eighth call from, if you don't mind my asking?"

"Okay. I write this down. A Monsieur Levy. He has been up, he says, for three nights and is seeing sounds. Also new colours and the shapes of jungle animals, these come black behind his eyes. What to do?"

"Shit. If he calls back, tell him to take the medication I gave him on Thursday. No, tell him to call Dr Aucoin at once. And to call Monique at our office, she can squeeze him in on Monday. I'll be back in the office then."

Outside the greasy window of the pay phone, Sol sees snow falling, white whirling flakes, soft, petal-like.

"So, are you coming to retrieve this cellular?"

"I'm sorry, what's your name?"

"Guy. Monsieur, I mean docteur, can you get this telephone?"

"Guy," Sol says, "I'm in a bit of a personal crisis right now. I won't be able to retrieve the cell till tomorrow, maybe the next day. How late are you open?"

"Vingt-quatre heures."

"Great. It'll probably be tomorrow."

"But what is it I do for these people calling?"

"Tell them Dr Luc Aucoin is covering for me. Tell them I'll be back in the office on Monday. Tell them to hold on. Tell them everything's going to be all right. Tell them . . . anything you want!"

Sol hears a deep sigh unfurl from Guy's lips. "Guy, everything's going to be all right."

"Au revoir," Guy says. "Until tomorrow."

It is a strange, new feeling for Sol not to have his cell on hand. It makes him anxious and edgy, but there is a novel sensation of openness, possibility.

Driving again, Sol pulls a map out of the glove compartment, glancing down at it to make sure he's going right, can't afford to get lost today. The feeling of freedom is short-lived. He does not feel good about missing a day at the hospital or his office because too many people need him all the time. He puts in a seventy-plus-hour-week, and despite that effort and personal sacrifice, and the effort and sacrifice of every other FP he knows, thousands of patients can't find a family doctor to care for them when they need one. Sol's medical secretary Monique turns away twenty to twenty-five new people a week seeking an FP. Though Sol likes to squeeze his patients in as soon as possible and never have them wait more than a couple of weeks for an appointment, these days the waiting time can stretch into a month or more. Sol hates to turn people away; often Monique does the dirty work: "Call your CLSC to see if they know anyone available in the community. Ask all your friends for names of doctors. Call all the hospitals and talk to the family-medicine departments. Keep trying."

Still, Sol thinks, he wouldn't trade it for anything. Nor would he consider relocating to the States, like so many of his med school peers: his life is in Montreal.

Sol glances at his watch. It's just noon – making good time, too good – he wants to drive through, toward, to travel, but not to get there. Meeting, knowing after a death is too new-agey, crazy, and FPs were not supposed to be nuts; it might be an asset in a psychiatrist to be a little kooky, but not in an overworked, forty-eight-year-old family practitioner with two-thousand patients who relied on him for their life and well-being.

Sol's long legs cramp, and he exits the highway. Following signs towards food and gas, he sees there is an Appleby's, and realizes suddenly how hungry he is. He takes his time eating and reading, then leisurely smokes a cigarette down to the filter. In the phone booth, Sol holds the smoke deep in his chest, then dials his own cell number. Guy picks up on the first ring.

"Oui, bonjour!"

"It's Sol."

"Oh, really?"

Guy's thick, smoky voice is a comfort, the sound makes Sol think of cognac, warm and amber, burning sweetly as it goes down.

"Okay. Look. Sorry, did my wife call?"

"Now which one is the wife exactly?"

"Ev. Did Ev leave a message?"

"Let me check all the time my notes. Hold this a minute. No Ev. You do have –"

"Never mind. I'll check in later. I'm in a hurry."

"You doctors, it is always a hurry, no?

"I'm off today."

"Some people have all this luck. Off to where?" He laughs, "Dr Sol, are you running away?"

"Actually, the opposite. My Dad died. I'm going to collect his belongings, plan the burial and funeral."

"Oh, je suis désolé!"

"Ça va. Ça ne fait rien."

"Sol! Of course this matters. This is your Papa. You have only one."

"Right. Listen, Guy. I've got to get back on the road."

"Of course. May your father he rest in peace."

"Merci, Guy. Au revoir."

"Bye. Safe trip!"

Sol gets back in the car, starts another cigarette and heads toward 287 South. It is still snowing soppy wet flakes that melt the instant they hit the ground. Falling, they look more grey than white, a New Jersey snow, not a Montreal one. Sol thinks of his boys, Daniel and Jonah. He promised to take them ice-fishing on the Lachine Canal when he gets back home. He grew up overlooking the five-foot-deep, nine-mile-long canal. As a boy, he had no idea what a father did, what a father was good for. They just got by, his Mom working days in a beauty shop and nights at a local greasy spoon. It was a rough neighbourhood, though bikers, roller-bladers, walkers, and boaters flooded the area in summer. He thinks of that sign from the town's administration: *Persons of good education and morals are invited to this park.*

With his own boys, Sol learned how to be a father without knowing what a father was, and he was still learning. There are traditions Sol wants to share with his boys, like jumping sheep. Sol veers left to avoid a Mustang, which speeds up and passes in an unsignalled lane change, almost clipping Sol's car. He's explained jumping sheep to Daniel and Jonah several times, but this year, they're going to do it. Father and sons. For three seasons of the year, locals meet at the Waterfront to jump over sheep – Québecois for whitecaps: les moutons. For forty bucks you climb aboard Jack Kowalski's custom white-water boat for a tour of the Lachine rapids. You suit up in waterproof gear, except in the height of summer when you can wear a swimsuit under your life-jacket. Sol misses his boys, thinks he should call Ev soon.

He reaches the New Jersey Turnpike South, drives for a bit, and stops at another rest stop for a stretch and more coffee. This time Guy picks up before the first ring finishes.

"Ça va, Sol?"

"Ça va."

"Ev is not calling. Want me to make a call to explain?"

"Guy, I appreciate the thought –"

"D'accord. You are arrived?"

"Not yet." Sol lights a cigarette. "You know, I never met him."

"Who did you never met?"

"My father."

A long silence stretches out between them, the line crackles.

"How is this happening?"

"He was not right. In the head."

"So what is that to be a reason? Who do you know, Sol, who is right in the head?"

"Touché. But really. He was sick, dangerous." Sol takes a drag from his cigarette and sips coffee from the small opening in the lid of the container.

"How do know if you are not meeting him?"

Sol glances outside the phone booth, sees a woman with three children waiting. She mouthes the words, *You going to be much longer?*

"Got to go, Guy. Someone needs the phone."

"Parfait. You do call me later."

"Perfect."

Sol hangs around, buys another coffee, lights a second cigarette while the first is still smoldering and, when the woman is finished with the telephone, he dials home. He's got to speak to Ev, to the boys. Ev doesn't even know his father died. When he gets to the last digit, his hand is trembling, he looks out the window, he better get on the road, doesn't want to arrive after dark. Anyway, how can he tell Ev that Nathaniel is dead, and it is *too late*. He swallows his longing to hear the sound of his boys' voices, to talk to Ev, stubs out his cigarettes, and heads back out to the car, the coffee warming his hands. He follows the New Jersey Turnpike South to 95 and roars right through to Pennsylvania.

By three-thirty, Sol reaches Westchester, the afternoon light filtering through a pearl-grey sky. The air is cool and moist, but there is no rain. Sol recognizes the area, but finds himself circling around the perimeter of the hospital. He can't find the entrance to this fortress. He heads down one path, then another, a rat in a maze, his pores leaking sweat and he's got that live animal feeling again in his chest, the one that did him in the last time. He reaches toward his groin, shit, locates a sad little Main Street strip with a pharmacy, coffee shop, and dingy bar, and heads into the coffee shop. The phone booth is empty. He hurries inside the cubicle, squeezes the door tight and tries to breathe the stale air. Now, he's got to call Ev. Or should he call Guy and see who's tried to reach him all day, find out how the patients are doing, or should he get in touch with Art Koenig before the man goes home for the day, tell him where he is and get some damn directions *before it's too late*. Once again he dials his home number, the boys should be home now and Ev would have laid off for the day, she can't really work with the boys at home, the phone rings once, twice, where are they, maybe Java U for a snack and then he hangs up. He can't call Ev, he realizes, until he's seen his father, the body, until he is standing next to it, recognizing Nathaniel, being there, he can't call en route in some state of suspended animation because then it will be *too late*, the in-betweeness of not being there, where at any point he could still turn around and go home. Now he is hit with an uncharacteristic case of indecisiveness, Art or Guy, Guy or Art. Art because he could leave for the day and Sol doesn't have Art's cell number and doesn't have his own cell, so once he leaves this booth he will be out of reach, but Guy because for sure Ev has called by now and maybe the reason she is not picking up is that there is some emergency with Danny or Jonah, something's happened, an accident –

"Guy! It's me."

"What do you think I expect, Jesus Christ returned from the resurrection?"

"Did my wife call?"

"And the wife her name is –? I get your different women mixed together."

"Ev. Evelyn."

"She did call. And together we are laughing."

"Laughing? What do you mean, laughing?"

"About Dick."

"Goddamn it."

"Now, Dr Sol. I'll pardon your Français, but –"

"Are my boys okay? Did you ask about my boys? Jonah and Daniel?"

"Me. I did not have to ask anything, I hear them yelling like wild creatures in the background."

"Both? Could you hear both boys? Jonah, he's five. And Daniel, he's seven. How do you know it was both?"

"Because your wife had to yell at the both so she could hear me."

"Whew. Guy, you're the best."

"Not exactly, but merci. Did you see your father . . . yet?"

"No, I'm still getting there. I'm sort of lost."

"Me, I don't understand this."

"No, Guy. Really lost. I don't know how to get into the damn hospital. I'm circling around and can't get in. It's like a Kafka novel or something."

"A what?"

"Never mind. Guy, can I ask you something?"

"Oui."

"Do you have a father?"

"Everyone has a father. He is being right here. Taking over the cash while you are always calling me to be talking."

"Wow. How old is your Dad?"

"Quatre-vingt-trois. Eighty-three. And he is living to be cent ans. This I am sure. Sol, you want to be speaking with him so I can get back to my clients? He is not speaking Anglais."

"No, no. Got to get where I'm going. Won't be long now."

"Bonne idée."

Sol hangs up, then rifles in his coat pockets for Art Koenig's number at the VA, picturing him as tall and stooped, with a long rabbinical beard, yellowish-brown eyes like egg yolks. Why do these social workers always have beards?

"Koenig."

This time the voice is staccato, manly, a busy executive with business waiting.

"Sol Stein here."

"Oh, Dr Stein, I was getting worried about you. With this weather and all."

"Weather never affects me. I'm from the City of Weather."

"Up in Canada, for sure. Where are you, Dr Stein?"

"Call me Sol. On . . . Elm. At Phoebe's. Can't find a way to get *into* the place."

"Okay. Here's what you do."

Sol hears the first few, take a left here, pass the light, then static camouflages Art's voice, he weaves in and out.

"Can't hear you," Sols says. "Bad connection."

"Listen. Stay right there. I'll come get you."

Now Art sounds like he's talking a patient through a bad time.

"Thanks."

Sol stays inside the phone booth for a long while but makes no more calls. When he comes out, a well-scrubbed kid with a blond ponytail and green eyes like bottle glass is looking around for him. He's a tall, lanky fellow with athletic shoulders and big feet and looks like he should work in a ski shop or health food store. Handsome, no beard.

"Sol?"

Sol takes Art's extended hand and Art holds on. "I'm sorry," he says, and Sol is immediately grateful that Art has not appended, "for your loss." And then to Sol's amazement. "We all loved Nat. He sure kept us on our toes."

"Nat?" Sol asks, as they head out of the diner.

"He preferred Nat," Art says matter-of-factly, as they walk down the snowy street toward their cars.

"Before we go see him," Sol finds himself saying, "can you tell me one more thing. . . ."

"Sure," Art says, "shoot."

"*Any* thing. One more thing," Sol says. He stands before a dirty white van with the name of the VA hospital painted on in forest green, a few of the letters missing; maybe his Dad went on field trips in this van.

Art puts a firm hand on Sol's shoulder. "Want to ride over together? Then I can run you back to your car on my way home."

"Great." Sol opens the front door which makes a rusty whine, and climbs into the torn front seat. When Art turns on the ignition, the radio blares out a mournful girlish voice singing over and over, *You must rinse him. Rinse it all away. You must rinse him.* Obsessive and seductive, she gets into Sol's head, under his skin. "Who's that?"

"Vanesssa Carlton. *Be Not Nobody.*

"What?"

"Nat liked her, too. Liked the title of her CD."

"Tell me another thing."

Art switched into drive and pulled out onto the road. "Gooseberries. Nat loved gooseberries."

"Yeah? Never tasted 'em"

"You're in for a treat, then. Your father grew them in a little garden. I'll show you where it is, though of course it's frozen over now. He and Selma picked the berries, made jam and pies."

"Selma?"

Art stops at a light. "Nat's significant other, his lady love."

"Wow."

"You'll meet her, too. Oh, there's a jar of jam Nat left for you, plus other stuff. And some instructions."

"I've never had gooseberry jam."

"You said." Art lifts his hand from the wheel and kisses bunched fingers with a smack. "Sweet and sour."

Sol looks up as Art inserts a card into a gatehouse lock, and they rumble onto the grounds of the hospital, the sky midnight blue.

The grounds are lit up, the brick buildings darkened with age, the grounds frozen under winter. It is silent, deserted, and Sol wonders how he ever saw the place as a college campus; it was missing the buzz of life, of people criss-crossing the paths with purpose.

"Why did you tell me not to visit my father?" Sol says suddenly, his words clipped, bitter.

"Not me," Art answers softly. "I would never say that. Not ever." He looks straight at Sol. "Whatever Nat's state is, I mean, *was*, I think it's better, would have been better, to see him. For you two to have seen each other. I think you both could have handled it."

Art takes Sol into his office, a small windowed room with a photograph of a Bernese Mountain dog on the desk. "That's Booh," he says. "The love of *my* life." The men laugh, as Art grabs some keys. "I don't want to rush you, but I think we should go see him first."

Art lets them into the morgue that's attached to the VA hospital. A small, spectacled woman is attending in a crisp white coat, and Art says, "This is Dr Stein, Sol Stein, Nat's son. Dr Stein, Dr Murphy."

Sol nods and the woman barely moves her lips, "I'm sorry for your loss."

Sol approaches a stone slab, a body covered over with a white sheet. He is used to this meat locker cold, he knows the smell of a dead person's insides. Without asking, he lifts the sheet and pulls it all the way down, so the body of his father, Nathaniel Stein, lays exposed.

"So . . . this is him," he says, glancing at Art for a moment, unable to meet the younger man's eyes. Art nods, and Sol thinks, I wouldn't even know the difference, couldn't pick him out myself. Art lingers about a yard away from Nathaniel, while Dr Murphy stands guard by the door.

Sol says, "Could I have a few moments. . . . " and before he can finish, he hears the two shush out of the room, the slammed door reverberating in his ears.

His father is, was, taller than him, about six-three, Sol thinks. Barrel-chested with a paunchy stomach and long, soft-looking arms and legs, his penis pale and curled into itself, testicles wrinkled as figs, drooping low. His face is clean-shaven and he has a thick head of silver-white hair, worn long and shaggy over his ears. Though Nat's skin is turning waxy and yellowish, Sol can see he was dark-featured but fair-skinned. His eyes are open. Large dark brown eyes.

Sol places his fingers on his father's lids and closes them. They are moth-wing soft, filmy. He glances at the face again, one lid lifted a slit where Sol sees a gleam of eye-white.

Sol stares, as a voice in his head says, *Your father, this is your father, your own father, your only father.* Insistent, obsessive, but still disconnected, unreal. He knows, but he can't feel, can't feel anything.

Sol thinks of Ev's favourite television series, *Six Feet Under*. She's addicted. For her birthday, he bought her the boxed set which comes in a black case that swings open like a casket. He's watched a few of the episodes with her. In the show, dead people *always* come back to life: sit up, talk, walk around, console, admonish, confide, keep company. They dance! Fight. They debate their living counterparts and wrestle with unresolved issues. It is all about death, only death, always death, yet death affords insight, even opportunity. In one episode they watched, the character, Nate Fisher, discovered secrets about his father after his father's death and had a chance to talk to him, something he was never able to do while the man was living. Sol wants his father to stir, speak, but sees only that eerie gleam of eye white.

Dead body. Sol knows the routine from the hospital. In a swift, cruel motion, he snaps the white sheet over his father's body and leaves the morgue, walking at a clip back to Art's office, before the young man can catch up with him.

In the office, Art says, "Have a seat. I'll make some coffee, we can talk about arrangements. Unless you need to –"

"No."

Art nods and pours fresh water into the machine, shakes coffee from a Bustelo can into the basket, using a folded paper towel as a filter, not measuring the grounds. In a corner is a small fridge and Art takes out a pint of half-and-half, shakes it, smells it. "We're in business," he says.

The smell of the coffee is comforting to Sol and he gratefully takes the steaming yellow mug from Art, shaking his head before Art pours in any cream or sugar. Art pulls open metal drawers in his desk until he finds a card. "This is a local vet," he offers. "A funeral director."

Sol pockets the card without looking at it.

"I told Quentin you might be calling."

"Is there a place I could stay overnight?" Sol asks, "I'll make the arrangements first thing."

Art picks up the phone. "I'll book you a room at the Holiday Inn," he says. "They've got a pool," he shrugs, "and a decent breakfast."

Sol nods, tapping his fingers on Art's desk while he makes the reservation.

After he hangs up, he says, "Can you show me where –" Sol stumbles over the words, "my father lived?" Father will never seem right. Neither will Nat, he thinks.

"Sure. You can take your coffee along."

Carrying their steaming mugs, Art takes Sol to one of the men's dormitories with about two dozen metal cots, twelve squeezed in on each side. It looks to Sol like an orphanage with no orphans, and he imagines the men snoring, shifting and crying out in their sleep. "He started out here," Art says, "then he moved to Maple Grove, and before he died, he was living in Forest. He had a smaller, more private room, just one roommate. When Gus died, Nat had the place to himself for a bit. He sure liked that. He snuck Selma in and. . . ."

"So. Where is everybody?" Sol asks. He doesn't want to hear about his phantom father's sex life, that's for sure.

"Dinner. They eat at five sharp."

"Oh, dinner."

"Want to see Maple Grove . . . or Forest?"

"Forest, I guess. That's where all his stuff is, eh?"

"That's it."

Crunching through the snow, the night crystalline, a riot of stars overhead, Sol follows Art to a small stone cottage and unlatches the heavy front door.

"Hey, wait a minute," Sol says. "I thought he lived in a half-way house on the property."

"Forest is a half-way house. We've got six cottages."

Sol follows Art inside, the cottage is overheated and stale.

"Everything is as Nat left it," says Art. "For you to –"

Sol holds up his hand to stop Art. One bed is stripped, the other one, his father's, rumpled with bedclothes, as if Nathaniel had just risen. Pale blue sheets, a pilling mustard-coloured blanket, stained and torn in places, and a pretty patchwork quilt, something one might expect at a bed and breakfast. On the sheets, Sol sees a spill of coins and his eyes burn, filling till they ache. He hasn't cried since he was a boy, decades ago when he cried easily and it washed him clean as rain. He didn't even cry when his mother died or when they almost lost Daniel to salmonella. Sol doesn't know what he feels now, not loss of a loved one – loss of a father he never had, never would have, *ever* – the waiting and wondering *when* were over. He was here, there would be no new memories, just a lost lifetime of old ones he'd have to learn second hand . . . or was it the sad solitude of his father's life in this shut-in, shut-away place with no one he could call family? No tears come and Sol's eyes smart as he looks around the room, trying to shake free uncomfortable thoughts.

"You okay?" Art asks, putting a hand on Sol's shoulder.

Sol nods his head.

"Well, you know, he did build a life for himself here. I don't know if there's comfort in that. For sure not a life you or I could see for ourselves, but it worked for him."

"Worked?"

"He had occupations he enjoyed, friends, Selma. Folks cared about Nat."

"I'm grateful. . . ." Sol started, "to meet someone who knew him."

One wall is brick and unadorned, the other three and the ceiling are covered with his father's postcards in colourful collage. On the worn wooden floor is a braided rug in blues and greens. Art lifts an old cigar box and opens it. Inside is a stack of illustrated postcards of flora and fauna.

"We sold these in our shop," Art says. "Folks loved 'em."

"He made these?"

"Yup. Nat drew and designed them and Selma wrote the captions. Here's one on gooseberries." Art hands the card to Sol who looks it over, as if he is examining a specimen under a slide. The front depicts seven gooseberries glowing in a range of autumnal colours.

"He had an eye," says Art.

Sol reads the caption: *Gooseberries are glowing jewels. Transparent, delicate globes of luminous topaz, golden green, orange, ruby, and deep purple. They were known as "little figs" in England where they were first cultivated. Gooseberries are rich in pectin and make delicious pies and jams.*

"Tell me," asks Sol, "was my father a collector? Did he collect stuff?"

"Oohhh yes," Art answers, his lips curling into a smile, boyish dimples at the corners. "We'll get to those. As he liked to say, collecting helped him hold his neurons together. He left most of his collections to Selma, but one's ear-marked for you. The stamps and album."

"Stamps?" Sol feels he cannot breathe. "I used to collect stamps. As a kid. I was totally into it. You know, not playing hockey, not being a skier, it got me through the winter."

"Yeah, Nat had an idea you liked stamps."

"How? Who told him?" Sol asks, as if a terrible confidence had been betrayed.

Art shrugs. "Want to see more of the place?"

Sol doesn't answer, he's thinking he can't ask his mother any more questions, not that he ever felt comfortable going there. She died two years ago and he had the idea she was not in touch with Nat. She was terrified of him.

"You know," Sol says, "I should make a call." Art points him to the pay-phone at Forest and Sol shuts the door. No answer at home. What kind of message could he leave anyway? He wants a voice, his wife, Ev on the other end of the line.

When he gets back, Art is waiting for him. "Let's go over to the dayroom. We can come back here later and go through things."

Art enters a central brick building, pushing through a dingy corridor to a large fluorescent-lit common room where patients are shuffling about. Art takes a deep breath, bracing himself. He pulls his shining mane out of the ponytail and lets it hang free. "Let's go say hello to Selma. She grew up in Mississippi, but moved up north when she joined the service."

Art approaches the crowd around the television, all men and one tiny, small-boned woman with a long silver braid down her back. On her lap is a needlepoint project which she manages to work on without looking down, the needle darting in and out, tugging plum-coloured thread, her fingers tracing over the pattern, a ball of thread unfurling from a huge tapestry bag at her feet.

Something happens on the game show and she shakes both fists at the screen, with an artillery of swearing. Art squares his shoulders and chews his lip, fidgeting with the silver bracelet he wears on his left wrist.

"Selma?" He crouches down, eye level with her. "I'd like you to meet someone."

"Which someone?" She doesn't look up.

"Nat's . . . son. Dr Sol Stein."

Selma leaps up like a black panther and sidles close to Sol so he can feel the heat of her breath, her tiny black patent-leather shoes bumping against his boots. Her eyes are ice-blue, sparkling in her delicate heart-shaped face.

"You are a very bad man," she says to Sol, spitting on the ground.

"Now, Selma," starts Art, "Sol here –"

"Don't 'Now, Selma' me, young man." She whips back to Sol who has stepped back a pace. Selma closes the distance between them. "I'm telling you you're bad. Why in heck didn't you come and see your daddy? All these years your daddy in here and you never come see him. What kind of thing is that? Your daddy write to you, he ask you to come see him. What, you just land or something?"

The group around the television shushes them and Selma, Art, and Sol move to a corner near the snack table.

"I feel like I just landed." Sol smiles now, his cheeks flush, his ears burn.

"Well, maybe you have." Selma pokes a finger into his belly. "I'm still telling you, you're a bad man."

"Perhaps I am."

"I want reasons," Selma goes on, "I want an explanation." Despite her diminutive size, Selma is daunting in her black dress, a starched white Peter Pan collar, and ladylike string of pearls. She sucks down saliva and Sol thinks, damn, *I could use a cigarette.*

"Well?"

Now it's Sol's turn to sigh. "I guess I've been busy."

"Everybody's busy. Busy, busy. Hmmph."

"I was in school studying to be a doctor and then I got married, had a couple of boys of my own and –"

Selma smiles, impish, her nose crinkling at the bridge. "You got boys of your own. How old?"

"Five and seven."

"Whhoo-hoo! Nat would've loved to have seen those boys. His grandbabes. He didn't know he had grandkids. So why you never come see him? You answer me."

"You're tough."

"I am."

"I've got a million excuses. And none at all."

"Sure you do."

"I guess I was afraid to come. Afraid of him."

Selma broke out in a peal of girlish laughter, like silver hand bells. "*Afraid*? You a big doctor and everything and you afraid of Nat?"

"I heard stories."

"You can't go on believing everything you hear."

"True, but I got here once, years ago, and was warned away."

"Nobody can warn you away if you want to come. No one could keep you away from your own daddy if you had the *courage* to come see him."

"I didn't. I didn't have the guts. I thought I better leave well enough alone, let sleeping dogs. . . ."

"No," says Selma. "He wasn't no sleeping dog. Not Nat."

Every cliché Sol knew rolled in and through his mind like ticker-tape, but he kept his mouth shut. "I've got questions for you too, Selma."

She looks up at him, waiting.

"What exactly was wrong with him?"

"Fear."

"Okay, what of?"

She whistles through her teeth. "Everything and nothing. That's how it goes."

"Why were people afraid of *him*? My mother, for instance. His own social worker years back."

Selma's glittering blue eyes rove the snack table. She takes out two slices of Wonder Bread, screws off the top to the peanut butter, and starts fixing herself a sandwich. When it's done, she cuts it in four pieces, but before she takes a bite, she says, "Fear, it do terrible things to people. Fear, it's the root of all evil. When a person's scared, they wild. Nothing can hold 'em back."

"Are you going to give me any details? I have so little."

"Well, you here now," Selma says. "Somewhere Nat know it, you came for him."

Meeting Selma, this tiny spitfire of a woman, is a shock to Sol, as is meeting Art. He never could imagine the types of people his father mingled with at the VA and had horrible visions of cruel loony-bin wardens and matrons à la *Cuckoo's Nest*. The three walk abreast and head back to Forest and Nat's room to go through his belongings. In the closet, shirts and slacks hang on wire hangers. Everything is in some shade of green, even the pants. Green, green, and only green. And more green.

"So what's up with all this green?" Sol asks.

"Just one of his things," Selma says. "Nat liked green."

"*Liked* it?"

"Well, it is a natural colour. Colour of nature, grass, leaves, the sea some places, even the sky before a thunderstorm. Sky can go green sometimes." Selma takes a rumpled chambray shirt from the closet, a pale mint green and lifts it to her face, inhaling deeply. "Green made Nat feel safe. We all got something makes us feel safe, right?"

"I guess so," Sol says. "Now what would happen if he ran out of green? Or didn't wear green?"

"The bats would come."

"Bats?"

"Rats on wings, special powers, eternal life. . . ."

Sol glances at Selma, chin lowered, out of the tops of his eyes.

"Don't look at me sideways. I don't like it."

"Sorry."

"Bats were his demons."

"Interesting."

Selma shoots him her signature toxic look, burning cold. "Don't you know, Nat's boy, that when you love someone, you live inside their head, you know what goes on there."

Art smiles at Selma and takes her hand. "I love you Selma Winpenny."

"See," Selma says, gazing heavenward. "I already got me a new boyfriend."

Art opens a closet and an avalanche of boxes and papers cascade to the floor, some opening, their contents scattering.

"Nat was careful," Art says. "He taped or rubber-banded most of these. Lucky for us."

Art sits cross-legged on the floor, Sol and Selma join him, and they go through the heap. There are more cigar boxes, shoe boxes, hat boxes, tissue boxes, gift boxes, each filled with a collection of a particular item – the usual things like stamps, coins, shells, rocks – but many others – paper clips, leaves, dried flowers, rainwater, pen caps, dried fruit peels. . . .

This obsessive accumulation of objects disturbs Sol.

"Kept his neurons together," says Selma. "working on his collections. Gathering, sorting, cataloguing. Once he got involved, Nat didn't go off as much."

"Go off?" Sol asks. "Tell me, what happened when he went off?" Selma points to a crescent-shaped scar, a parenthesis that just misses her left eye. "This, for one thing."

"What did he do?" Sol asks.

"Scratched me like a wildcat."

"Why?"

"I told you before. Fear. I couldn't never wear my hair loose because that set him off. Reminded him of the bats, the batwings waiting. So I kept it in a braid or up top my head in a chignon or French-twist style. I can be flexible with my hair," she says, smiling.

Sol puts the paper clip collection in his hand, letting the silver and gold clips, the coloured clips, the small clips and large clips run through his fingers. "Selma, were you scared of him?"

She gathers the clips in her small-veined hands and places them back in their box, a compartment for each type, as Sol imagines Nat might have done. "There were times," she says, nodding, the light leaving her eyes. "Look, I'm no masochist, and when Nat took his medication, we were okay."

She closes the lid of the paper clip collection and stretches a rubber band around it. "There were those times, see, when my own demons plugged into Nat's and we went a little crazy together."

She seems so stable, Sol thinks. "You're strong, Selma," he says aloud.

She whistles. "Everything not like it seem – you a doctor, you should know that."

"Perhaps I should." Sol makes a mental note to ask Art later what's wrong with Selma, is she on meds, which ones?

As they sort through his father's multiple collections, Sol strains for meaning, sinews of connection, bats, coins, batwings, Selma, but these obsessions of his father's, his father's demons, his father's loves, seem hopelessly random, without meaning or poetry. Perhaps if he had met his father, got to know him over time, some of this would make sense. And then again, maybe it wouldn't. Sol has always been impatient with the idealization of mental illness as a higher state of insight and illumination. Instead, he believes that it is pure living hell. At least he had Selma, Sol thinks, maybe that connection redeems some of the rest.

Sol's knees are hurting and he stands up, stretches for a moment. "What war did my father fight in?" Maybe this is the root of his madness, post-traumatic stress, visions of blood, death.

"He never saw any action, never went overseas," says Selma. "But he was in the service during the Korean War. As I was. I was a nurse. And I did go overseas. "

"A nurse!"

"Loved the work, too. Was a nurse back home in the ICU. Didn't love the way folks become their procedure. 'She's a heart, that one's a liver.' It's doctors do that, not nurses. " She looks hard at Sol.

There is a faint knock on the door, seven taps in a rhythm.

"Come in!" Art calls out.

A large disheveled woman with wild red hair appears in the doorway, filling it with her girth. "Selma, I came to fetch you for cocoa."

"Thanks, darlin'," Selma says. "I'll join you in a moment."

Sol and Art stay late sorting through the rest of Nat's belongings, Sol deciding what to keep, what to give away, what Selma should have, and by the time they are finished, he is sweaty and tired, his limbs aching.

"I'm going to call it a night," Art says.

"Me too."

Sol stands, stretches again, a hand at his lower back, rubbing. He puts his hand out to Art. "I want to thank you," he says. "For everything."

Art bypasses Sol's hands and pulls him in for an embrace. The younger man holds on and Sol feels Art's warmth pass into his own body.

Art locks up Nat's room and on his way home, drives Sol back to his car, giving him directions to the Holiday Inn.

"See you tomorrow," Art says.

"Tomorrow," Sol answers.

"Try to get some sleep," adds Art.

It is very late, after midnight, as Sol settles into his room at the Holiday Inn. Tomorrow he'll retrieve his cell. After a burning hot shower, he reaches for the old-fashioned black receiver of the hotel phone, feels an urgent longing to call Ev, to talk to Daniel and Jonah, though they have no doubt been asleep for hours.

Holding the heavy receiver between shoulder and chin, Sol strains to remember his father's face, to bring each waxy feature to life, to imprint his imagining to memory, to hear Nathaniel's voice, what would it sound like in Sol's ears now, as he dials his own home number for the third time that interminable day. The phone rings hundreds of miles away at Sol's restored Victorian in Montreal West, a skylight in Ev's home office, a working fireplace in their bedroom, a windowed sunroom finished in Italian tile, looking out to the cedar deck, the yard and garden. He waits, hoping Ev will still be awake to answer. In his mind, he sees her fair, freckled hand pick up the receiver by her side of the bed. The bed-side light clicks on, the matching ones they picked out in Knowlton, which resemble old-fashioned hurricane lanterns. The phone rings again and he waits for the sound of her voice. At last there is something to tell.

BLOODKNOTS

Shana closed her eyes and everything opened, bloomed. Inner swells rose, breaking heat, and emptying in a rush of blood, the space between her legs like a stretched mouth, her mouth and her baby's gaped black in screams. She felt like she was rising from the delivery table, high and helpless in the wake of pure pain and pleasure.

Already a mother, she'd missed this part the first time.

Her baby girl weighed nine-and-a-half pounds with a tuft of chestnut hair, her eyes squinched shut against this other world. The nurse handed her the baby and Shana held her daughter to her breasts, straining to hear her heartbeat. Dr Zimmer squeezed Shana's hand; her husband, David, kissed the top of her head as if she were a child again. Shana folded her arms around her new daughter, Ariel's warm weight making its imprint onto her emptied belly.

During delivery, David had stood at her shoulder watching the white wall, confirming Shana's sense that childbirth was at its core exquisitely solitary – she was alone, the baby was alone in its passage from darkness to light – one by one, they all left the room, even Ariel was whisked away by a nurse to be sponged clean.

Shana's room was washed with white silences, deep-shadowed snow and glittering pines just outside the window. This winter had held on. Already it was the last day of March, soon the weather would turn. Looking out, Shana thought of her little boy, Azul, picturing her husband's and son's limbs entwined in sleep as they would be that night, just like most nights during her five months of enforced bed rest, her growing belly like a great swelling shield forcing them into a shared space of their own. Shana felt her eyes smart; she couldn't cry.

Shana put Aretha's "Spirit in the Dark" in her CD player, and moved to her voice, lying down. She called family and friends, arranging the dried flowers David had picked in her favourite colours. Plundering through the wicker basket he and Azul had packed with fresh fruit, cheese, and chocolate, she unearthed the plastic button Azul must have buried in there with the food: a photograph of the two of them taken on their last outing before her confinement. Azul sits sideways on her lap, her hand spanning his sinewy brown thighs. Their cheeks touch full-length as Azul slips a treasure into her pocket, a pebble he'd found glinting from the dirt switchbacks leading down to the sea near their summer cabin.

At three-and-a-half, he was still transfixed by his own image. Shana remembered him gravely leafing through the glossy brochure at Penney's, examining all the objects you could acquire to keep a loved one close – frozen in time, fixed in space – buttons and lockets, keychains and keepsake boxes. Azul chose two of the same brightly coloured buttons, each a hair smaller than a half-dollar, a matched set. Throughout her pregnancy, he refused to take the thing off, even to sleep, cherishing this miniature of reality, this bit and piece. She couldn't help thinking that people expelled from their own pasts became the most fervent picture-takers and collectors.

Running her finger over the button's shiny surface, she phoned her older brother Josh, who was watching Azul. Her son was napping and an uneasy relief filled her, not having to face him yet. She knew she should rest but felt high, wired. Blasting Aretha to the hilt, she wrapped a robe around her stained hospital gown and staggered barefoot into the hall.

The shiny hospital linoleum was spongy under Shana's feet, her body suddenly light and buoyant. Needing to feel her body in motion, she twirled down the corridor to "Natural Woman," a take on the number her students would be performing for the spring recital. When she and her sister founded the Auerbach School of

Dance a decade ago, the kids she taught in class were her only children. Back then, David would stop by between patients and watch her teach; no longer a performer, she liked being watched, his dark presence an anchor in the back of the room. Once, on a sweltering August evening, the sky an unearthly violet-gold streaked with black, they'd gone up to the roof where it was cooler to watch the sky change. He'd had an awful day with patients, absorbing the marshy mire of their minds, and she'd promised to cheer him up. "I dare you," she started. "I dare you to dare me."

"Okay." He pondered far too long. "Walk all the way across. On your hands. Naked."

She peeled away her sweaty leotard and tights, tossing them in a ball on the tarpaper, the air cooler on her skin. Flipping to her palms, she made the diagonal, back arched, the tarpaper hot and sticky to touch, David in tow laughing low in his throat. Touching her palm to his cheek, she said in her best British, "How could I ever marry so cautious a man?"

"To make him uncautious."

She patted the flat brick wall encircling the rooftop, which reached her hip. "Right here."

David hesitated again, then lifted her onto the parapet. With her legs wrapped high around his back, she leaned into boundless space as he entered her, moving further and further out as he moved, the pressure of his palms against the small of her back. That's what she wanted, to go to a place she'd never been . . . but when the storm broke, he pulled her in tight against his chest, so her feet touched ground.

Dynamite blasts of water streamed against her neck and shoulders, plastering his hair, heavy and dripping. He'd take her to another place and they would always return again. That was her worst dread, but worse things could happen.

Soon the rain thinned to slanting drops, sun straining through clouds in veins of light. They sat on the parapet, the sandy rasp of mortar against her skin, till the rain stopped, and the sun went down. They talked in desultory drifts about the children they'd have, the trip they'd make to the Isle of Skye, what they'd cook for dinner that night. She knew then that she would marry him. He would take her to a new place and the going would be everything. Now, she wished she could travel in her own past, as if the road went both ways.

Shana whirled around the corner of the hospital corridor, drunk with the newness of motion, as a woman's voice rang out behind her, "You best be doing that dancing lying down." A dark glittering wave shuddered through her falling body, caught by a net of arms and hands. Someone lifted her, propped her to standing. Turning, Shana faced a tall skinny man with black matted hair, a milky substance crusted on his shabby sweater, Ariel's bassinet beside him. A nurse clipped past, craning her neck to watch. "Now me," the man said, feigning a swoon. "Hey, I know that game." Swaddled in white flannel, Ariel was sleeping, her lower lip thrust out.

"I was coming to see you about your daughter, Ariel," the man said. "Hey, I like that . . . from the Bible, some kind of flame, right? Or a horse? No – I know – it's a flaming horse! I thought about it for a girl, a super-different-type name." He spoke in a rush, his thin voice quavering.

Shana reached for Ariel's bassinet, squeezing the clear plastic handle till her knuckles whitened. No nurses in sight. *Where the hell was David?* She breathed out, a sudden nausea clotting the back of her throat. "Who *are* you?"

The man sucked in his stomach as if he'd been punched, then chewed his lower lip, squinting through blue eyes shaded by deep purplish shadows. "Dr Mauro," he said, extending his hand. He had a wide, mobile mouth. His hair was dirty, his teeth bad. Around his neck and wrist dangled brightly coloured paper jewelry, gum chains like the ones she'd woven as a girl in summer camp. His face was round, soft-featured, pale. When she extended her hand, he clasped it firmly and held on. His hand was warm and slightly damp, so large it enfolded hers. "Come," he said, one hand on her shoulder, the other propelling Ariel's bassinet down the hall, its wheels clattering on hospital linoleum. "We'll talk about your daughter."

In her room, he loped over and sat on the bed where Shana had collapsed. Drawing her dressing gown around her throat, she reached for the buzzer on the bedrail, blocked now by his narrow, hunched back. "You don't look like a doctor," she whispered half to herself.

He smiled at her with his whole face, a wide-open loopy grin, unnervingly like a baby's first smile. "You, a mother? You *look* like a mother!" He laughed, then rolled up the sleeves of his mangy sweater. Shana looked at the thin bare arms, a blue-veined strength about them, his hands, one flat on the bedsheet, the other in his lap, graceful and long-fingered, the curved nails short and scrubbed.

"Where's Dr Levine? Dr Levine is our pediatrician." Shana scooted to the edge of the bed and went to the window as if Earnest William Levine, MD, might materialize there.

"Yeah, sure. Well, I'm covering for E.W."

Ariel whimpered from her bassinet, then let out high, warbling screams. Dr Mauro stood; they reached for Ariel at the same time and blood gushed from her, leaving dark red drops the size of quarters in a trail across the floor. The room browned, a cottony rush clouding both ears. Shana started to say something; felt her mouth open, but nothing came out. Within the vortex of sea-sound, she heard the man say, "Come here," and felt the gentle pressure of his hand at her shoulder, his other arm in a shepherding sweep around her waist. Outside the winter winds were howling with an almost human sound. She made a great effort to open her eyes, to see. The man's face was close to hers, his thick lashes fluttering. His eyes were wide and dark blue, like the hearts of small fires.

A grey-haired nurse rested a tray of food across Shana's lap. "Your husband, he was singing to the baby. He has a nice voice." Shana recognized her from the hall. "You've got to eat," she added, lifting the cover from a plate of soup, steam spiraling with a rich salty smell. David made the best soups and Shana missed him; his pensive face and meditative thoughts had a way of enfolding her.

"Where is my husband?" she asked, spotting a note on the night-table scrawled on a prescription pad for Xanax. During her immobility, his calm which normally drew her in, turned grim; David's carefully modulated speech weighed her down, his long pauses were absences, chasms she fell into. (Maybe she'd needed a prankster with a clown nose, blowing horns, banging cymbals.) "Where is my goddamn husband?"

"No need to swear, now. He went home to get your boy, that's what he said," the nurse went on, as an aide wheeled Ariel in from the nursery. Shana wondered if she'd imagined the tall skinny intruder, if he were part of some post-delivery dream. "I've lost track of time," she said to no one in particular, lifting Ariel into her arms. Her daughter felt warm and plush, a pink cast to her skin, still splotched here and there with a cheesy coating. Her pale hair was sparse, her head unbearably soft and warm, the pulse visible through the fontanelle. She had a downy fuzz on her shoulders, back, and bottom. Her plump legs crossed at the ankle, one hand, almost coquettish behind her ear, the other at her chin. Her eyes were teal-coloured and tearing.

"Has Dr Levine been in to see my baby?" Shana asked the older nurse who stood close, admiring Ariel.

"Dr Mauro, he's come in to see you?"

"That man is a doctor?"

The nurse laughed, deep and secretive, covering her mouth. "Gabriel Mauro, he's temporary in the group. Windsor Plains Pediatrics, right?"

Shana nodded slowly.

"Well, they're trying him out."

"Ah, that's comforting."

The nurse laughed again, louder this time. "Some ask for him."

Shana was trying to breast-feed Ariel when Dr Mauro settled his long frame into the floral-covered rocker. "Hey, sorry if I scared you before." His head bobbed like a toy with a coiled spring neck. "I have that effect on people."

As he fixed his eyes on her, Shana draped her exposed breast with a burping cloth she'd slung over the bedrail. She scarcely recognized this body of hers. Her breasts were tender, throbbing, and lumpy, the swelling extending nearly to her armpit; her nipples and areolae were double their size, the shade of blackened plums. Ariel nuzzled Shana's breast with a pathetic sputtering. Frantic, Shana tried the cross-cuddle hold, the side-lying position, the football hold – positions she'd studied from the manuals she'd armed herself with – moving Ariel about like a sack of goods. The baby's head wagged, her mouth zoomed in with a life all its own, a line of spit glimmering. Sputtering off, her screams spiraled; the cloth slipped from Shana's shoulder, crumpling in her lap.

"Nursing's hard," Dr Mauro said, nodding. "Nobody tells you, not those lunatics from *La Leche*. Where are they when you need them? Anyway, she's doing fine. Colour's good, lots of activity, lusty cry." He double-crossed his legs, tucking his foot inside the ankle.

In a moment of inspiration, Shana stuck her pinkie into Ariel's mouth and the baby took it with a sudden grab. Shana's breath came raggedly, sweat beading from her pores. "So . . . she's fine?"

"Her bili levels are a little high, borderline. But not to worry, I don't want you to worry about anything."

"Translation?"

"We'll have to watch her for jaundice. Right now, she's producing more bilirubin than she can handle . . . if it builds up, we'll put her under the lights till we get her levels down. Then you both go home and really get to know each other. Sound good?"

Shana nodded, reassured by his official medical explanation, the sprinkling of clinical jargon, the fact that he sounded somewhat like a real doctor, now. "As long as it's not serious."

He glanced down at her chart. "You had a rough pregnancy."

Shana laughed, more of a gasp. "Yeah. After sixteen weeks, she wanted out."

Ariel sucked furiously, kicking her legs, as if the force of her lips might bring forth food from Shana's finger. Feeling the rhythmic squeeze of her lips, the soft pummeling of her legs, Shana thought of her and David's astonished joy at this surprise baby after so many years of trying, then the precariousness – of the forming fetus, of her body as a safe house – the very real possibility that this longed for child might be born and die, in the same moment.

"Bleeding, some premature labour –"

"I was teaching a jazz class," Shana broke in, "it was the end of my fourth month – I was starting to feel really good – you know how you do." She moved her finger around in Ariel's mouth feeling the firm pink gums, the hard spots where teeth buds were already forming under the skin. "I did a split – and this knife plunged into my gut – Zimmer put me in the hospital on an IV." Shana stroked Ariel's head. "After that, if I tried to go to the bathroom, she assumed it was time."

Although Shana's tone was light, a burst of her old terror returned. She listened to Ariel's heartbeat, high, quick and strong, the curled, cushiony body rising and falling as she sucked.

"Well, we made it. Anyway, it's easier this time."

Dr Mauro shook his head, eyes narrowing. "So you had an even tougher time with –"

"Azul," Shana murmured, remembering the years of waiting, casual lovemaking gone purposeful and joyless, a sperm test for David, dye shot through fallopian tubes for her, fertility drugs, Chinese herbs. Then there was the waiting: as they decided on foreign adoption, selected an agency, prepared their documentation and met criteria for suitability; the waiting after home study and documentation were complete; the waiting for a child to be located for them; the waiting while legal procedures were completed and arrangements made.

At last a baby boy lost and found. From Columbia. Next to nothing known about his parents' or their medical histories, his exact age unknown.

Shana heard the baby before she saw him, before she felt his dense compact weight within the warm swaddling. His cry went right through her, palpable as a tensile hand, reaching. She learned to know him through his cry. When he was hungry, he howled. When he was wet or soiled, he bellowed. When he wanted to be held, he keened. And when he was misunderstood or ignored, he roared. His cry etched a channel in her heart. She knew he would survive.

She tried to nurse Azul, forging the physical connection they'd missed. Yes, you could breastfeed an adopted baby with a will and a way. His suck would stimulate her milk production. For three months, she wore a feeding bottle around her neck, slim tubes leading from the bottle taped down her breasts, extending slightly past the nipples, the bottle filled with soy formula. As Azul nursed at her breast, he took formula from the tube until she produced enough milk to give up the supplementary nutrition system. That was the theory.

But her body said no. Shana tore the apparatus from her neck and the baby took the rubber nipple into his mouth with a greedy snatch.

Now, Ariel pulled off her pinkie, crying out. Stooping slightly, Dr Mauro walked over to the bed, a dip in each gangling step. He brushed past her and put a pillow behind her back, another in her lap. Shana cradled Ariel in her arm, tummy to tummy, the baby's head resting in the bend of her elbow. Shana lifted her swollen and marbled breast to her daughter's mouth and pulled her in close. She heard Ariel's gasp as she seized the nipple in a life-or-death clench, heard her sucking and swallowing, a warmth spreading through her from the baby's mouth, from her soft body. Dr Mauro's eyes were on her and her new daughter. Shana reached out her hand blindly and he took it, her fingers curling into his.

That afternoon, Shana heard Azul's voice, urgent and feverish, from down in the parking lot. Single words floated up: *Mama, magic, luck.* She rushed into the hall as he careened toward her wheeling a red plastic suitcase, cradling his stuffed moose in one arm, a mesh sack filled with books, snacks, and videos dangling from his wrist. "Mama!" he called out, tripping over the suitcase which snapped open, its contents spilling onto the floor: a shiny foil star dangling from a wooden stick, red dice, a lava lamp; coloured rocks and shells; a pad labeled, "My Magic Book," and a drum fashioned from a tin can and piece of rubber stretched over its lid. "Mama," he said, "I have so much luggage."

As she lifted him into her arms, he wrapped his legs around her waist and she saw the button pinned to his red sweatshirt, thankful that she remembered to pin hers to her dressing gown. His sweatshirt was adorned with two snap-on frogs; he'd strung ropes of her beads around his neck, smelled of her perfume, and wore David's tie as a belt. For a moment, they held each other; Azul's head burrowed into her chest, his legs swam seeking bottom. His body was thin, but strong: elastic as rope. His hair fell across her cheek, coarse and sweet-smelling. She held him tight and whirled in a circle, first one way, then the other. One of his sneakers fell to the floor. She stopped and whispered to him, "Put your head down, Az, put your head down on Mama," and he laid his head against her breast as he'd done as a baby. For a moment, everything was right in their world.

David wrapped his arms around their backs, enfolding all three in a family huddle. "At last," he said, kissing her. "Finally."

"I got a idea," said Azul, "a magic star on a stick."

"And what can you do with it, Az?" She swiveled him sideways, holding and rocking him like a baby; Azul squirmed, jumping down. Holding the foil star aloft, he whirled it faster and faster above his head. "I can make anything I want come or go away."

Shana and David looked at each other, then gathered Azul's toys so they could have some privacy in Shana's room. Barely a second later, a sullen nurse deposited Ariel in the room and said, accusingly, "She's hungry," then left abruptly. Ariel mewled from her bassinet, at first intermittently, soon in a steady grumbling.

"Pick me up, pick me up!" Azul ordered, and Shana encircled his waist with one arm and lifted him, scooping Ariel up from her bassinet with her other arm, the baby's head wobbling, unsupported.

"Here," David offered, sliding Ariel from her arms, deftly supporting the baby's head with a broad, splayed hand. Shana watched him as he held the baby close against his chest, rocking her in a vertical motion. Azul glanced up, watching her watch him. He said, "There's a yuk smell."

"Maybe the baby needs a change," Shana answered.

"No!" shouted Azul. "A bear in the woods after bad men shooted him. It's you, Mama." He put a yard of space between them. "I'll stand here."

Shana folded her arms across her chest. There were moments, since delivery, when her own smell wafted toward her, all that was contained now spilling forth, her insides turned out.

Ariel's mewling escalated into cries. David rocked her faster, up and down.

"Hey," Shana said, "watch her head."

Azul stomped up to Shana from behind and shoved her with all his strength.

"Stop it!" She reeled around. "Give me her," Shana said to David, taking the baby. With one hand, she hauled out her breast; she nursed Ariel standing up, circling the periphery of the room.

"I'm hungry," Azul said, beating the toy drum with a coloured rock, then the moose's head.

"Here, bud," David said, laying out a juice box and package of cookies. "You can have a picnic."

"I want pancakes," Azul said. "Chocolate chip pancakes."

"When we get home," David pleaded.

"No, now!"

"Indoor voice," David said. "Remember, Az. Indoor voice?"

"Not my indoor voice!" Azul grabbed one of Shana's arms that held the baby, breaking Ariel's suction on her breast.

"Your mother's got to feed her," David said.

Azul backed away like a bull, then rammed into Shana's stomach. He did it again. And again.

David grabbed Azul from behind, wrapping his arms around his back to confine and contain him. "You stop it. Now."

"When is her mommy coming?" Azul asked. "So she can go back into the egg."

All through the pregnancy he'd asked them, "How does a person make a person?" They'd tried to prepare him, but the notion of pregnancy and birth was a goulash of horticultural imagery of seeds planted in earth, the growing baby in her belly showered with hot soup and pizza, and eggs hatching, like the baby chicks he'd seen on a neighbour's farm.

"I *am* her mommy and I'm your mommy, too," Shana said, her voice so thin and taut, she was almost singing.

"Don't say anything." Azul covered his eyes with both hands. "I don't want to see you."

Shana saw the button with the photo of the two of them hanging on his sweatshirt by a thread. She went to him while still holding Ariel, who in a private world of simple survival was still sucking. While Shana held the baby, Azul burrowed into the space between her legs, falling into the heavy folds of her dressing gown. Shana handed Ariel to David. "Burp her," she said, lifting Azul into her arms, holding him tight. All seemed okay for a moment, then Azul butted his head against Shana's chest, pummeled her back with fists, kicked her shins with his feet while belting out guttural cries. Shana planted Azul on the floor, then grabbed him by his arm so hard he spun around. She raised her trembling hand, heat flashed through her and the room turned harsh, its colours too bright, the outlines of objects black and menacing. She knew if she smacked him, she might never stop. The space between them was charged like a magnetic force field.

Azul looked at her as if he were trying to find her through a many-layered mask. “Mama?”

She couldn’t speak for a while. Finally she said, “You know, I’m a person too.”

“No. You’re *my* mommy.”

Shana looked at Azul, then David. The baby’s mouth was open, her head wagging, rooting at David’s broad chest.

“Maybe I better give her a bottle of formula,” he said.

All the air punched out of her chest.

David handed Shana their daughter and took Azul’s hand. “C’mon, bud,” he said, “let’s explore.” Azul crumpled into David’s side and out they went.

A half-hour later, Shana walked Ariel back to the nursery and found David, Azul, and Dr Mauro in the patient lounge. None of them seemed to belong there. It was a bare room with a green plastic rug made to look like lawn, a large television, a coffee pot, a few tattered Dr Seuss books, a video on making friends, and two wicker bowls on a white Formica table, one filled with saltines, the other with teabags and packets of instant coffee, cocoa, and creamer.

This Dr Mauro seemed to have all the time in the world. The hospital was pretty quiet, but still, Shana was used to Dr Levine rushing around on a schedule timed to split-seconds. She smiled to herself, wondering how long Dr Mauro would last, as he unraveled a length of rope from the neck of Azul’s stuffed moose. With complete absorption, he began tying knots, for Azul’s entertainment. He was deft, his hands quick and graceful. His arms had a tensile beauty, reminding her of plants undersea. He made figure-eights and sheet bends, rolling and clove hitches, butterflies and cats’-paws, weaver and water knots.

“Cavemen tied knots,” he told Azul. “So did the Indians and Eskimos.”

“Did they make magic? *You* make magic,” ordered Azul.

"What kind of magic do you want?" Dr Mauro asked, his hands continuing their fluid motion.

"Make knots go away."

Loosely and with great deliberation, he tied a square knot. While Azul watched, he interwove and tucked the working ends even more "to make it really secure." Pulling slowly on the ends, the knot fell apart, leaving smooth rope.

Azul ran his hand along the rope to make sure the knot was really gone, not hidden.

"Is there somebody you want to keep captive? Your own special prisoner?" Dr Mauro asked.

Azul looked at the ceiling. "Daddy!"

Working quickly with the rope, hand-over-hand, Dr Mauro linked David and Azul together in a set of interlocking rope handcuffs. Azul climbed in and out of the large slack loops linking the handcuffs, which tied him to David. Laughing, he turned somersaults through David's arms in an effort to get free. After watching the captives for a while, Dr Mauro passed the slack length of rope under Azul's wrist loop and then over his hand, releasing them both.

Azul clapped his hands together. "Look!"

"Ever have something – or some*one* – you want to tie to a rope –" started Dr Mauro.

"Something giant big?"

"Yeah, something giant big and heavy where you don't want your line to ever break?

"Like a giant big fish I could eat till I got big and exploded in heaven?"

Working faster and faster with the rope, Dr Mauro tucked the working end through its own loop, two, three, four times, making loop after loop after loop.

Shana watched, as Azul and David stood transfixed. "Bloodknots," Dr Mauro said. "They'll never break. Not ever."

Azul glanced over at the doorway. "Look, Mama!" he called out in his outdoor voice. "Bloodknots. For so they never break."

Soon, Shana kissed her husband and son goodbye, lingering for a while with Dr Mauro in the lounge. "How'd you learn all that?" she asked him.

He twined the length of rope around his fingers, handing it back to her to return to Azul. They picked up a book he'd left behind, one of the snap-on frogs that had popped off his shirt, crumpled cookie wrappers and juice boxes and put them in the garbage.

"So," she pressed, "are you an angler? Or a sailor?"

He smiled a slow secret smile. Though his face was round and soft, like a person not fully formed, there was a stubborn definition to his chin and mouth. His eyes were both dreamy and intense, a quickfire play between his private world and the outer one. "I just like to play around with rope."

"Rope, eh?"

She bent to pick up a few strewn toys, gathering them to her chest, as if they were alive. Every day at about this time, she used to pick up Azul's toys with him, make a game of it – one of the simple daily chores that had been off-limits during her pregnancy – each in its smallness and dailiness unimportant, but the cumulative mass, the foundation of their life together as mother and son.

A sound from deep within her body escaped her throat, involuntary and private.

Dr Mauro reached for the collection of toys she held awkwardly against her chest. "He'll be back."

Shana still hurt all over, exhausted and bewildered from the birth. "You don't know what it's like. I was flat on my back from November to now, Thanksgiving through Christmas, New Year's and Valentine's Day and David's birthday – that's five months – I mean, shit! – one-hundred-and-forty-nine days."

She watched him let her words settle. He stood still, listening, then began to pack Azul's toys into a grocery bag someone had left behind that said *With Love From King's* in green block-print. A nurse paged Dr Mauro over the PA system and he slung the absurd bag over her wrist, holding her shoulders for a moment, as if to steady her before slouching into the hall.

Shana stood in the lounge, remembering the loneliness of immobility, lying in bed, heavy and isolated, hearing David's voice interlaced with Azul's, one room away. For the first time, she was lonely when she was with them, a loneliness immense and unsettling. Her husband and son waiting on her, bringing meals on a tray, letting her rest and rest again. Their solicitude, politesse, as if she were an expensive house filled with breakable furniture.

All motion and growth were within, invisible, except for the rising opaque mass of her belly, a mountain landscape neither she nor David nor Azul could completely access. Shana turned inward.

When the baby kicked, she shaded in the plump toes, the network of lines on the sole of her unborn daughter's foot. Sometimes an arm swam up into her ribcage and Shana imagined the cupped hand, its webbed fingers. When she stood to go to the bathroom, there was the sensation of a hard black ball dropping, and then Shana imagined the developing brain crackle, long wiry cells, staccato bursts of electricity, pulsing waves like currents shifting sand on the sea floor. She'd read about a baby's brain at birth – it has as many nerve cells as stars in the Milky Way. She was still. And waited.

The inner landscape was roiled, alive. Shana existed in an erotic haze, a heavy pent-up tingling inside swollen breasts, the pit of her belly, between her legs, like criss-crossed electrical wires, compressed and bound. Wakeful, she felt David's weight beside her, his lumbering movements jostling the bed. His touches gentle and too tender and solicitous – made her want to bite, scratch, and scream – anything, to pull him back to her, but this, too, could bring on labour. Night after night, she lay awake tumbling into the hollow he made in the sheets, only touching when they bumped, got in each other's way. Until Azul cried out for David. . . .

Wandering slowly back to her hospital room, Shana wasn't sure if she became more dense and compact – self-sufficient – in that pregnancy, or had grown hollow. Some days, she wondered who she was, if she would ever find her way back to herself, to Azul and David.

Dr Mauro fell into step with her as she approached her room.

"It's amazing what you feel," she said, still in her own world. "I mean, to have them inside you –"

She saw him in his clean but cluttered office, dressed in a pale pink shirt and cartoon-character tie, the well-appointed glossy photos of the wife and three or four kids. "So, how many do you have?"

He formed an empty circle with thumb and forefinger.

"I'm surprised," Shana said, as they stood together in the doorway of her room, half in, half out. She wanted to ask why, to find out more about him, but didn't know how. "It's scary to think –" she pictured cavemen eating the still-bloody hearts of rival tribesmen, devouring and ingesting and holding onto their souls. She was losing hold; quickly, she glanced into the room at the wood panelling that concealed emergency equipment – gas, oxygen – "I think I'm going nuts," she confessed.

"That's common," he said, nodding. "After a birth."

Her face must have shown her disappointment.

"I mean," he reassured, "I'm sure you'll do it in your own special way."

They lingered a moment in the doorway. Shana had a sudden urge to touch him, to caress his face. Taken off guard, she turned abruptly and went into her room.

The sky was pearly grey, the trees dusky silhouettes; opening her eyes, Shana wondered if it was late morning or afternoon. Her Early Music CD still played, voices from the hall ribboning into the room. She'd had a stream of visitors, then unplugged the phone so she could nap. It seemed as if she'd been in the hospital for a very long while, but when she glanced at her watch, she saw it was just her second day. Ariel lay asleep beside her and she lifted her daughter, moving to the rocker to sing to her. At birth, Ariel's skin was ruddy, then lightened to a lovely rose; now it was paler, a yellowish cast to her cheeks and chin. She heard Dr Mauro's voice a moment before he stepped into the room.

"I think we'll keep her. Baby girl's got to spend some time under the bili-lights." He walked around and stroked Ariel's sparse hair, his long fingers nearly enfolding her head. "I'll talk to Zimmer, see if we can't get you signed in here a couple more days."

A gift, that's what this was: the promise of several more days in the hospital, alone with Ariel. Shana felt a sudden spasm of guilt, thinking of Azul.

"Right," Dr Mauro said out of nowhere, folding his long arms across his chest. He was dressed more or less like a real doctor now, in a white coat with a pale blue t-shirt underneath. The gum chains were under the t-shirt like a piece of jewelry with sentimental value. His hair was cleaner, his shoes polished. A nurse walked in, depositing a pink wad of telephone messages. Glancing at the phone, she clucked her tongue. "I always did want to be a personal secretary," she said, walking out.

Dr Mauro shut his eyes as if imagining something, as Shana leaned over to plug in the phone. Immediately it rang. As she picked up, Ariel let out staccato shrieks, then an angry cry full of *vibrato*. Shana found herself looking to Dr Mauro, and without saying anything he took the baby from her, threading his slender forearm through her legs, his open hand against her belly as he flew her through the air, whistling.

"He's on strike," David said, and a muscle clenched inside Shana's stomach. "Won't eat. I mean, anything."

"Let me talk to him." Azul was too thin, fussy about food; some days, he lived on air. Shana heard a muffled squeak as the phone changed hands.

"Mama, when you coming home?"

"Azul, you've got to eat."

"Mama, what you said?"

Ariel started crying, her chin quivering, and Dr Mauro handed her back to Shana. Nodding toward the door, he approached it, but didn't leave. The baby took a sharp intake of air and began nursing ferociously, her sucking and swallowing clearly audible, and Shana relaxed within the tingling hot needles, the shivering sensation, as her milk let down and her breast softened, emptying as the baby nursed.

"Honey –"

"Mama, can you see me through the phone?"

"No, sweetie, I –"

"I can see you through the phone, Mama. In my imagination."

"I see you in mine, too, in my mind's eye. So. Why aren't you eating, Azul?"

"I eat," Azul said, "dust from my magic star, so for I can go to heaven."

The baby sucked, pausing and trembling with the effort, which seemed to exhaust her. What Azul said took a moment to register, settling like a black iron hand against her chest.

"What you doing, Mama?" Azul asked.

"Resting . . . Az, if you could eat anything in the whole wide world –"

"A banana strawberry milkshake."

She breathed out sharply as the baby sucked on and on.

"*You* make it, Mama."

"Okay, we'll make it together. You down in the kitchen?"

"You're a hundred percent right," he said. "You Sunday driver!"

"Take out milk, pour a big cup into the blender." The phone crashed to the floor. She heard him opening the fridge, a clattering of objects on the counter. Azul picked up the phone and she went on with her directions. He put the phone down again and Shana heard water running in a hard fast stream. Soon there was the roar of the blender and the welcome sound of Azul drinking the cold rich shake.

She just listened to her son drinking, as her daughter nursed.

Glancing up, she saw Dr Mauro still standing in the doorway; when she looked up at him, he slipped out. On the other end of the line, Shana heard the metallic clink of metal against glass, a crash in her ear as the phone dropped to the floor, then the sudden cut-off.

All evening, she tried to get back through. Frantic, she sent her sister over to the house. No one was home. In thoughtless panic, Shana threw on her coat and started walking down the hall out of the hospital with Ariel in her arms, but a nurse intercepted her and led her back to her room. She lay down on the bed and wept. The nurse tried to comfort her, assuming it was a bad case of post-partem blues. Finally, Shana asked her to leave. That was at midnight.

David called two hours later. "I don't know how to tell you this," he started. "When you were making that milkshake, Az dropped in the button, swallowed it, pin and all."

Shana's mind went white.

"We're at Saint Joe's," David went on. "Got the best pediatric GI guy around. Azul is out of danger, Shana. The metal pin showed up on an X-ray. The button made it into his stomach, but it was too big to pass out. They went in with an endoscope, this miniature TV camera, and they pulled the thing out with a snare."

"I've got to see him – David, I've got to get out of here."

"He wouldn't know if you were here."

She was suddenly so scared, she couldn't think or speak.

"Shana, I told you, they gave him a sedative. Look. Zimmer doesn't want you leaving the hospital yet. It's not safe – for you or Ariel – we'll all be home soon. Together. Everything'll be okay. Okay?"

She felt hollow, mute. David waited on the phone until she said something. Shana made him promise to call back in an hour, sooner. She eased the phone noiselessly back into its cradle and waited for it to ring again.

During her last night in the hospital, Shana walked down to the nursery to check on Ariel. Her baby daughter lay on her back, a black mask over her eyes, a smile on her lips, basking in the heat and light of the bili-lamps. She'd been in close touch with Azul; he was home now, nearly recovered, but she felt responsible for what had happened.

Shana paced the halls, then returned to her room; her belongings were spread out in disarray – she knew she should pack, get ready to go home – but couldn't bring herself to start. Finally, she forced herself to try on her going-home outfit, a loose, plaid flannel dress, all greys, greens, and blues – it pulled across the chest but otherwise was okay. Her ankles and feet were still swollen from the birth, so she slipped on her fuchsia driving moccasins.

Shana saw the wind stirring the pines outside, the bare oak trees dripping, and imagined the feel of cool wet earth under her feet, the soft mulch of brown leaves. She went to open the window, but it was sealed.

On her night table stood the two celebratory bottles, *Nuits-St Georges* and *Pol Roger,* unopened. Shana imagined into the following morning, David and Azul coming for her, as she snapped Ariel into her newborn layers and broke out in a sweat, suddenly frightened. It was as if she stood on a ledge and could not go forward or back; she had no idea what would happen next. Stepping into the hall, she saw Gabriel Mauro dressed in his coat and an olive green hunting cap, its lambswool flaps tied above his ears with a leather thong. He looked faintly ridiculous. She called out to him.

Dr Mauro turned and walked back toward her room. Shana was prepared with some spurious question about the baby, Ariel's jaundice, but dismissed it and asked him if he'd like a glass of burgundy, as she took the corkscrew from her suitcase.

"I need to get out of here," she murmured with whispered force, each word under pressure. "A walk outside."

He opened the closet, reaching for her coat. As he held it open for her, Shana slid the bottle of burgundy and the corkscrew into the deep inside pocket, then the paper-wrapped plastic glass from the bathroom.

They walked down the hall, Shana behind Dr Mauro, turning in the same moment to glance back at the nursery. A nurse said goodnight to Dr Mauro without looking up. They walked out the front entrance of the hospital into the early evening.

Once outside, Gabriel Mauro wrapped his arm loosely around Shana, his palm at the small of her back, guiding her to a wooded path behind the hospital grounds. The path ran alongside a canal, which had risen from rainwater and melted snow. The evening was fresh and mild, a different season from the one she'd left just days before. They walked slowly along the muddy trail, leaves and earth pulpy beneath their feet. They ambled without speaking, the bottle of wine heavy against Shana's hip. She felt the evening breeze lift her hair from her neck and billow the hem of her coat, as it purled the river's surface, a mild breeze with an underside of winter. Clouds scudded across the sky, one star burning white above them. She walked close to the motion around her and was part of it.

"They're trying me out," Dr Mauro said abruptly. "See if I make it."

Shana smiled, a little uneasy.

He shrugged thin shoulders. "I'll just take off maybe, go to China. Adopt one of those throwaway baby girls. . . ."

He suddenly seemed very young to her. "Really."

"I'm contemplating an asexual existence. Nothing adheres, you know? My last three . . . bonds? Liaisons. *Relationships*! Well, they ended badly."

She nodded slowly, uncertain how to respond.

"I mean, I'm not from column A and I'm not from column B."

"What do you mean?"

He didn't answer right away and they kept walking along the towpath. Shana looked at him, his head bowed to the ground. She thought of him deftly tying knots: how quickly he made them; quicker still, his knots dissolved.

"You know when you're born, right?" he said finally. "You just come out. They give you a name . . . but that's not you, it sounds strange in your own ears. You grow up, go here and then there, do this, maybe that. You look around, try to find a space to open up so you can squeeze yourself in but this niche never comes, never quite holds you. . . ."

He glanced at her and Shana felt warm, drawn to his misshapenness.

Along the trail they saw a blue heron wading in the marshy bank, tottering on spindly legs, its bill parted in a hoarse cry. A while later, a flock of geese rose from the water in a V. They walked until the sky turned from blue to black, the lacy silhouettes of the trees blacker still. When she needed to rest, they sat in a mossy clearing on a small rise above the water. Shana eased off her coat and spread it on the ground so they'd have a dry place to sit, then scrambled to the edge of the river, reaching her hand into the current, the water so cold it made her bones ache.

Shana pulled out the bottle of burgundy and opened it, then remembered the plastic glass. Its paper made a loud crinkling in the quiet of the woods. She filled the glass and they passed it back and forth.

"Do you go by Gabriel or Gabe?" she asked, thinking how much she loved that name; it might have been Azul's. Gabriel was feminine, all air and light, Gabe, pure earth. She felt puzzled by him. "So. Gabriel or Gabe?"

"You pick."

The wine warmed her insides, but there was a place it couldn't reach. Shana leaned back against her elbows, her knees up, feet pulled in, listening to the rush of the river.

"What does it feel like," Gabriel asked as he lightly touched her belly, which was surprisingly flat when she lay down, but still loose and boggy, "here?"

His hand sank into the soft flesh, like a print in wet sand.

"Empty." His face above her disappeared. Shana looked into the water, kept looking.

"And here?" He lay his hand across her breasts and she thought of how much she loved nursing, nourishing herself as the baby suckled, reinhabiting her body through Ariel's lips, stroking her soft warm head and dimpled back. Motherhood filled a yearning space inside, but opened another place that was hollow and aching, like hunger or fear. He rested his head between her breasts and she threaded her fingers through his thick matted hair to the scalp. He closed his eyes and she imagined him imagining the birth.

"I can feel the place where she came out," Shana said, "like a ring of fire."

"I'll never have a child," he said.

"Maybe – you can, you *will.*"

"Not a child inside me, growing."

She turned, turning him with her, so they were side by side facing each other. Shana thought of Ariel growing inside of her and coming out and Azul appearing outside of her and coming in, remembering the escort from *Casa del Mundo*, her bright smile pulsing and spinning red as an emergency bulb, as she strode off the plane and passed the swaddled bundle from her arms into Shana's and said, "Here is your son."

Multicoloured balloons rose into the air next to the baggage carousel, the crowd from her synagogue cheered, bumping into cartons filled with mittens, hats, bunting. Shana fumbled as she took the white swaddled bundle, holding it far enough away to see into the child's face. He looked at her with narrow, dark eyes, then squeezed them shut in fury, pain, and screaming.

And now her own terror was back, like vibration before it makes sound. She moved to turn, to get up, and Gabriel held her, in his arms the electricity of tension and want, as if a space had opened within him to take in her raw draining places. His thin chest against hers, she felt the tingling deep inside her breasts and the milk let down, warm, soaking her dress. Her empty womb contracted and she gasped with the pure white blade of pain, as the fluids that had cushioned her daughter, cushioned them both, emptied, rushing down between her legs. He ran his hand slowly across her inner thigh, then his lips. He licked and swallowed.

WISHBONE

Another humid yellow morning. It's winter, not meant to be rank. Dead air meets me as I step into the street, the sky the unnatural sulphur of a tunnel you fear will never open out into light. I wait twenty minutes for a cab, feeling the soft leather of Elia's daybook and the bump of its brass catch through the pocket of my blazer. The black jacket is shot through with threads of blue and green. It's the one Elia borrowed and never gave back. These days, Elia always talks to me with his book open. It grows fatter, more of his life vested in there: notes, names, numbers, line changes for his new play, *The Gloaming*, which opens next week.

At last, my taxi. Climbing in, I see the leaves of a plane tree shimmer in an escape of steamy sun. I lean back, close my eyes, and say without thinking, "The Palace," because Rosalind is behind my lids. She lives in the palace I built, with gold turrets and a moat. I see the pale tint of her ears, like small seashells, the curve of her throat, the living warmth in her eyes, more open than any eyes ever.

Elia's daybook is bulky when I sit, so I slide it from my pocket, checking for the notes he needs, before laying it beside me on the seat. Last night I slept alone, made myself a nest on the floor in the alcove. Rosalind was with me. I'd brought her home from the shop, supposedly to do some final touches; in truth, I couldn't face giving her up. With some of my dolls, I have no trouble, preparing for this with each finger that I mold, with every lock of hair I place on their head. Rosalind began that way . . . but something changed.

This morning, just after I opened my shop, Noel's House, before I even took off my coat, Elia was on the phone. He reeled off places the book might be: bedside, window ledge, medicine cabinet. "Get it to me," he said. Actually, he'd left it in this jacket pocket; I figured I'd get it back to him at lunch. As Elia spoke, I could see him leaning against a wall back stage, hands free so he could motion to his actors, phone resting between shoulder and chin. Elia is not a handsome man, but he commands a room. Wolf's eyes, teal blue. A prominent nose, rough olive skin, short-cropped dark hair. A walnut-sized bump at the front of his scalp, a pause when I caress his head. A dimple below his left eye which gives him a perpetual ironic wince. In our nineteen years together, Elia has come to count on me for every minute thing. I went back to my workroom and placed Rosalind carefully in her case, standing her against the wall, before taking off.

Through the open cab window I smell rain. Clouds pile up, like layers of silt. The Bridge, cars, buildings, even the pedestrians seem to smoke with steam and dark. The tension of the rain sharpens. I smell it, but it doesn't come.

I roll up the window and rest my head against the seat, thinking of Rosalind's hair, auburn curls that reach her heels, hair that shrouds and enfolds her. Later, I will wash it. When we were new, Elia washed my hair with such tenderness my scalp ached. Now I am bald. Growing older does not trouble me, but something else, maybe the future in the present.

It is cool, dim inside the cab, cool and dim as the theatre. Yesterday, I sat in the back row, watching rehearsal. Elia's story had promise. A husband, simply called Him, does not see or hear his wife, Renata. The tangible world she inhabits gives way to a secret life. Into this opus, Elia poured everything he knew, imagined, longed for.

He wrestled with how to enact Renata's fantasy life. At first, it was invisible. She spoke to air; this confused. Then Elia brought out phantoms shrouded in gauze. The effect was comical. Him spiraled puns on *The Gloaming* as Renata said, "Shit, Elia, I can't say this." Lines changed, were still changing.

Last night as I lay in my nest, I drifted, passing into a darkness, not fully asleep, but with sleep's sucking force. Rosalind lay beside me and we talked. Not pleasantries, not assaults. She told me how it felt to be made and I shared with her how it felt to make her, things each of us could never truly know about the other. This talk, just talk, meant something, after what had happened before.

I didn't know if I would ever sit, turn my head. You spent the longest time on my body. Longer than on my face, Rosalind said.

I wanted you to move. To move in many directions, without breaking, I explained.

When you placed the soft moleskin in my neck opening, on my arms, legs, wherever one part of me touched another, that was when I felt the love in your hands.

That was so you wouldn't grate, rasp.

Looking at you now, I see you looking at me on the work table, before I was whole.

This conversation was in the deepest part of the night, when night turns toward dawn. It was after my talk with Elia. We'd had supper in bed on a tray. The low table was set out with cognac and one well-polished glass, dark blue candles that nearly matched the heart of their flame. I know everything Elia likes, the particular details, what comforts him. He brooded. "Tell me really, Noel, what you think." Elia crossed his legs under him, like a boy, while I dangled mine over the side of the bed.

"Maybe it could've been a novel."

"*Could* have been?" His eyes sparked, then went cold.

"An awful lot goes on." I thought of modeling my dolls' faces, adding or peeling back layers of clay to bring forth each feature before making a mold, then pouring the porcelain. "Simplicity's the hardest thing, the last thing."

Elia rubbed his forehead, as if erasing a stain. "Who you quoting?"

I cleared the tray, placing it on the bureau, as Elia stretched out on his back. He is a tall man, on the stocky side. I am nearly the same height, but with fine bones, an ordinary frame. I lay down beside him, but Elia stared at the ceiling. I glanced at him, space for another body between us, then touched his shoulder and rolled over on top of him. "There'll be others," I said, meaning plays. As I bent to kiss him, he held my head between both hands, a few inches above his face, forcing me down the length of his body.

I crouched, face down, between his spread legs. Without seeing, I knew his hands were folded behind his head. Elia's thighs tensed. I know what he likes, a firm tongue, not too wet. I know what makes him crazy, both balls taken into my mouth at once. I love his cock, its smooth weight, the Y-shaped vein that branches from the base, the curve at its tip. I know its solid warmth, its sea-salt taste. All day, I wanted Elia, imagined him fucking me at the bottom of the ocean, my face buried in sand, the bite of grains inside my nostrils, burning closed lids. I was a sunken vessel, blood and flesh washed clean of bone, his cock an anchor, pinning me to the sea floor. (At the shop, I didn't get much done.)

Now I was with him. But. There was an edge between us, a tautening. This tension rose above our bodies and hovered in the air, like silent static. My tongue staggered, stopped; cold seeped into my skin.

I lifted my head and tried to meet Elia's eyes. He shielded them with the back of his hand, as if against a too-bright light. "Do it," he said.

I bent down. My tongue skidded across the ridge of his cock. Running the tip of my tongue down the inside of Elia's thigh – he raked his nails against my scalp – he doesn't like that.

I know what he likes, know it so well neither of us feel it. I know what he likes – a perfect meal on a plate, we can no longer taste.

Tugging the tip of his cock, I slipped, let go. Elia's feet drew up, planted on my shoulders, thrusting me backward so hard, I grabbed the corner post to prevent falling on the floor. "Christ."

Elia sat up and leaned over me. His arm swung around my neck, into a headlock. "Where are you, Noel?"

I put my head down and felt the slam of his heart, the surprising softness of the dark hair that swirls around his nipples and down the center crease of his chest. "So you don't want to make love."

He laughed, a whistling between closed teeth. "So that's what we're doing."

I turned on my side, facing away from him, my hand on the spread, fingers falling over the edge. Then I went into the library, the bookshelves filled with plays and books on antique dolls, a tower room of eight windows, small panels of dark wood, separating glass. A jewel. I always felt soothed there.

The floor creaked as Elia came up behind me. He put both hands on my shoulders as I looked out onto the street where a light was on in the coffee shop across the way. A man and a young boy sat at the window table, maybe father and son. They sat close, on the same side of the booth. The man cut the boy's food for him. The child picked up a taste of something with his fingers, holding it to his father's lips. Without turning around, I said, "Leave me."

All at once, I felt a hand at the back of my neck, forcing my face to glass. Then it was gone.

I turned around and faced Elia. His eyes glittered, not quite human, as his hand tightened around my throat. He thumped my head against wall. Swerved left. With eyes behind my head, I saw the glass, felt its smooth chill, and waited for the shattering. Bump, dead thud of wood.

Elia's fingers pressed into my throat, beneath the jawbone. Man and boy across the street, I'm the little one. Stroked, warm, cosseted. Bump goes my head.

"You bastard!" My arms flew forward, fists jabbing Elia's chest. I held my breath. The glitter melted, flowing over. Nothing stopped him. He moved in a circle around the tower room. *Thump, bump, bump* – my head hitting the panels of wood, just missing glass.

I've left on a journey, gone too far, something's left behind, too late to go back.

I open my eyes inside the cab; what's outside has got to be better than this. The driver pulls over. I imagine I'm holding Rosalind close – she's life-sized, big as a young child – her hair grazing my cheek. I pay, climb out, and find myself at Broadway and Forty-Seventh in front of The Palace Theater with *Beauty and the Beast*, some fifty blocks from The Public, from Elia, from *Gloaming*. My arm forms a protective circle, a loop of shoulder, arm, hand – where are you Rosalind? – a circle back to myself.

I call Elia from the pay phone on the corner. Rain crashes down. No, I didn't notice the driver, his name, number. It's hopeless, finding that book. The downpour lasts no more than a minute. It's still raining when Elia hangs up.

As I head back to Brooklyn, the streets shine. The wind gusts, the air turning colder, and I feel unexpected relief. Winter is back.

It's nearly midday when I open. The green light on my answering machine blinks five times, the phone rings. I don't play back messages, don't answer. I've missed Rosalind's pick-up, orders for repairs, Christmas commissions. I set a pot of tea to brew, Lacas darjeeling, letting it steam on the low table beside the counter, before going back to my workroom.

I find Rosalind on the floor, face-down, her auburn hair flung above her head, her gown hitched up. One exposed leg stretches out, the other is bent to her chest.

Under the work bench is a small mud-caked boot; I spot its mate by the kiln. Rosalind's fur muff and tippet, the wax flower tiara she wore to her sister's wedding, and her mother-of-pearl mandolin are strewn about the workroom floor. It hurts to see her things like that. I go to Rosalind's Plexiglass case, which leans against the wall by the window. A pair of black eyes stare out at me, pale chapped lips roll in, and my chest closes up.

I turn the latch of the case, swing open the door, and lift out a small child, folding her into my chest. Her breath is warm and smells sweet, a bit acrid. I support her neck with one arm and hold my other hand beneath her knees, carrying her to the couch. Her chin is sharp against my chest, the soft curve of her cheek, cool and wet from the rain. She is light, but hard as flint. "You okay?"

She nods slowly, studying my face. Her corduroy pants are stiff with mud. A wool jacket of red and black checks is tied around her waist and her torn white shirt is soaked through, clinging to her skin. Dry brown leaves are caught in her hair.

I draw the space heater to the couch and wait until the coils glow. Casting about my workroom, I go to Rosalind's wardrobe, flipping hangers, impatient with the stiff frocks, jet-trimmed tasseled jackets, and bustled overskirts I've sewn for her. At last, I find a sweater. I pull it out and hand it to the child. She sweeps her hands over the red wool, plucking at the pearl buttons. With furtive motion, she unties the damp, muddy jacket from her waist and lays it over the arm of the couch. Turning away from me, she peels off her shirt. The skin of her back is blue-white, the bones of her spine like links of a chain.

"Go on," I say. She crumples her wet shirt into a wad, then pulls the sweater roughly over her head; it catches, and for a moment her features are hooded, inside wool. I stretch the neck, easing it over her head. She smooths it down.

"How'd you get in?"

The child sniffs and stretches her arms out stiffly from either side. "I closed your window for you." Her voice is tremulous and indecisive; words float in the air.

I look out to the alley at backs of brick buildings, fire-escapes, rusting dumpsters. A grey cat cringes under the eave of the back steps. Through the dull and dirty glass across the way, I see a faint glimmer of green, potted plants and painted crockery arranged on the sill. I don't remember leaving my window open. "I'll call your parents," I say, "to come for you."

"No phone." The child wanders around my workroom, then heads up into the shop. She looks around five or six, but I'm not a good judge. I'm startled by the ragged ends of her coarse, black hair, which look sawed off. She has this way of walking, her right arm held out from her side, fingers barely grazing her hip. Her elbow is a point, the space between her arm and body filling with a triangle of light, a space meant to hold something. My eyes run across my shelves, searching.

The child walks to the glass case containing accessories and examines the portrait buttons, sterling mirrors, perfume bottles and lace hankies. She takes Esmeralda off the shelf and strokes her hair, fingertips tracing Esmeralda's arched back as she bends in the hunchback's embrace. Picking up Jumeau, my snake charmer, the girl touches her jeweled eyes and bare feet, putting her back in the wrong place. "Where's my troll?" Her eyes set on me. "The one with black hair stuck out, horns, his own fox to pet."

My elfin ogre. "Sold."

The child chews her thin lips. "Why?"

"A lady in the Heights fell in love with him."

"We came to visit, Wishbone and me. Every day." The girl looks at me without blinking; she has hard, wide-spaced eyes, black and shiny as their pupils. Onyx eyes. I don't recall ever seeing her in my shop, even looking through the window.

The child opens my Lady Fleur's beaded bag, tracing a finger in the crevice between her lips; she touches Pierrot's teardrop, then licks her fingertip. Turning to me, she screws her eyes shut and thrusts out her lip. I usually warn children to look, not touch, but something stops me. I watch her and words freeze in my throat. It is her face, this knot. The girl lifts Caleb from the shelf, my delicate Parian, and examines his features close up. He is a pale boy with a moon face, dressed in seafoam green with a black velvet jacket and matching hat. Caleb is slender, always hungry. The child sets him clumsily back on the shelf and Caleb topples over. I prop him back into his usual stance – his left foot a little behind the right – then I see his wrist is cracked. "Careful!"

The little girl shrugs.

I examine the crack, not too bad, and slide Caleb into my pocket. It won't take but a minute to fix. "Can I *help* you?" The tired phrase sounds wrong, like I'm asking her to leave. "Is there something you want?"

"The doll for Jesse."

"So . . . your name is Jesse?"

She nods.

"Which doll?"

The child smiles, her lips closed. "I don't see her." She walks back to my workroom and sits on the couch near the heater, as I place Caleb on my repair shelf. Outside, the wind keens through nearly bare trees. My shop holds the chill; some days, it's colder indoors than out. There's nothing worse than being cold indoors. I'm wondering how to get in touch with her family when she says, "I saw the baby." She draws her feet up and wraps her arms around her knees.

"What baby?"

"The head was hard. When he kicked, I counted every toe."

"Your mother is expecting?"

Jesse glances at the ceiling. "Christmas Eve. That's when I want Wishbone born. My Mommy is having her baby, Wishbone's for me."

"You have her name picked out. After the friend you mentioned before?"

Jesse shakes her head, and her mink black hair swings back and forth, shielding her face. "*I* didn't pick it." Her mouth draws into a thin line. "Last night we had roast chicken with crispy potatoes. I got the wishbone. Mommy and I closed our eyes and snapped it. My piece was longest. We made the same wish, so it'll come true. You like chicken?"

"When I'm in the mood." I wonder what Jesse's wish was, but know I can't ask; this would break the spell.

"Every night, we sit in front of the fire. Me and Wishbone, Mommy, the baby inside –"

"And your father?"

"Him too." Jesse walks to the window and looks out onto the alley. With her back to me, she says, "Mommy likes to listen to the radio. Mostly a person's voice singing. The Roches, she likes."

"They're lovely."

Jesse turns, stooping in front of the heater. "We listen to *everything*. Jazz, rock, opera too." She stretches her hands out toward the glowing coils. "Mommy holds the radio to her belly, so

Rory can hear. He kicks when he likes something. You know what's his favourite? Pavarotti. Rory's from Roderick."

"It's an elegant name." Once I'd chosen names, not only for my dolls. Leafing through books, I liked to discover their origins, meanings you would never otherwise know. Roderick sounds like a king, someone famous who lives forever. Once, I knew something about babies: a newborn who hears a dog barking while in the womb won't be startled by the sound; playing with a knee, patting a head, can forge a bond between mother and child. I have no way of using what I know: they're just useless facts, swimming about my head.

Before I met Elia, I was with a woman, Katherine Spencer, a collector who brought me her dolls for repair. Katherine loved delicate dolls, but had the habit of toting them around with her. Broken or bruised, I could make them nearly whole.

We've kept in touch. Katherine is married to a manufacturer of doll eyes. She has five sons and raises Angora goats. Katherine shears them twice a year and cleans and sorts the hair. From her, I get most of my dolls' eyes and their hair.

Jesse goes to my work table where I've arranged a series of eyes. I've put them close together on a strip of velvet, so I can compare. Oval and round, almond-shaped; green, sky blue and topaz, all of antique and figure-blown glass. Jesse rolls the eyes under her palm; flicking her thumb and forefinger against an emerald one, she scatters the others, some rolling onto the floor.

Before I can gather them, the bell chimes and I go up front, where two women are browsing. "I'll be with you in a moment," I say.

Back in the workroom, Jesse has settled on the couch, her legs drawn under her. The floor is clear, the scattered eyes clustered in my unused teacup. In Jesse's hands, she holds a small book of shiny vinyl, pink with gold threaded quilting, which seems to belong to another girl. Seeing it in her small, rough hands, the nails edged with black, gnaws at me. I sit down beside her and she bends her head, running her finger under the print. On her third finger is a ring I hadn't noticed, a trinket one might find at the bottom of a cereal box or in a gumball machine. The plastic squeezes the inside of her finger, making a small bulge, and as she moves her hand the stone slowly turns colour, from brown to green.

"I'll read you," she says, "from Wishbone's diary." *The light hurts my eyes, gives me a headache. When it's bright, I stay very still. . . .*

As Jesse reads from the diary or speaks of Wishbone, her voice changes; it is no longer thin and tentative, the words have weight. Her voice is modulated and strong, almost grown-up. I hear the customers leave the shop and don't really care. "What do her eyes look like?" I ask.

Jesse holds up her hand. *I have magic eyes, can see in the dark. Nightmares, dreams. Ghosts, too.* Jesse pauses, looking up at me.

"Whose?"

"Mine. Maybe yours."

"If you have a bad dream, what can Wishbone do?"

"Make it over."

Some nights, I don't let myself sleep. I had nightmares as a boy; now they've come back. In one dream, I can do only hands: newborn, old, young, using every possible material. These hands take on a life of their own and shatter my dolls, which are whole. Then they turn on me – my hands – until my hands can only mar, not mend, and on no account, make. The bad dreams are like this, bald: no hidden magic, no secret messages.

"There's more stuff here," Jesse says. *Jesse helped her mother yesterday with the letters and notes. She made some up herself. I helped. She was good at sympathies and please-forgives. Monique, her Mommy, can't do these. Love letters are her specialty. Most people don't want those.*

Listening to Jesse, I feel the vague longing of looking for a missing object I've lost, though what it is, I can't say. Jesse nudges my shoulder, calling me back to her. "She's going on about yesterday," she says, reading from the diary once more. *Jesse was helping Monique with a forgive-me. Not husband to wife, mother-son. Jesse wrote in red pen because it helps her think. Monique walked one way, then back. The lights went out. Total black-out! Jesse didn't need a candle, my eyes lit up the room. We finished the letter, the three of us.*

"Why did the mother want her son to forgive her? For what?"

"She left him soaking in the tub."

"How come?"

Jesse closes her eyes. "Forgot."

The heater rattles, giving off a burnt smell; I turn it off. "So what became of him?"

Jesse sighs, laying the diary on her lap, face-down. "Whenever Mommy and I have a fight, we write, using the most beautiful sealing wax to close up our notes. I like pink pearl. Can you make Wishbone today?" From the back of the diary, Jesse pulls out a soiled and crumpled bill.

"You hold onto that."

Insulted, Jesse pockets the bill, gathers her things into the paper bag I offer, and goes up front. I follow, standing in the doorway, and before she leaves I ask for her full name and address, so I can get in touch with her family. She lives a short distance from my shop, in the heart of the Slope. "Will you be all right?"

"Wishbone's always with me."

I call out to her, wave. Jesse turns and waves back, such a childish gesture, her wrist loose, fingers curled inward. As she walks down the street, she holds her right arm out from her side, leaving that triangle of light. I watch her until she fades into a patch of red, a patch of black.

In the workroom, I pick up Rosalind from the floor and stand her up. Jesse's presence made me forget her. Rosalind's hair is tangled and dirty and the weight of these masses have given her a headache. At the sink, I wash her dark red curls with brandy and egg yolks. Then I tie her hair up with ribbons to lighten the weight and let air circulate through her scalp.

I feel Caleb's eyes, without turning around. I lift him into the crook of my elbow, supporting the split wrist, and take him to my work table. After I fill in the crack, I lay him on his side, so his wrist can set, all the while thinking of Jesse, when or if she'll be back.

As I'm playing back my messages, the bell chimes. Penny Mitchell, a student from my Apprentice seminar comes into the shop, straight back to my workroom. "Noel!" she calls out, kissing me on both cheeks. "You're the elusive one."

I nod, without explanation or apology. Penny made the Phoenix Bébé in my class. She had a terrible time dying the mohair locks, meant to be a mix of black, brown, and auburn; her Phoenix emerged with purple hair and eyes too centered, giving the doll a drugged, bug-eyed look. Today, Penny wears a poppy print dress with eggplant and pink flowers pinned to her breast. From her oversized tapestry satchel, she pulls out a bundle swathed in blue tissue, unwrapping a pair of Christmas snow babies, and hands them to me with a flourish. The children appear to be mates. The boy carries a lamb in his arms and pulls an empty wagon. He looks to be about five inches and is not incised. The girl is giving her own doll a drink from a teacup; she is a little over five inches and incised 4613. I think these are Galluba and Hoffman pieces, but want to have a closer look.

The afternoon passes quickly. I catch up with Penny, attend to repairs, and take a storm of Christmas orders. A blessing, being busy.

After closing, I take a long walk around the outer boundary of Prospect Park, then stop in at the notions shop downtown. I often go there, lingering over the antique buttons, bits of fabric, and accessories. The place inspires me, but today the buttons slide through spread fingers; I flip through swatches of fabric without noticing their colours or texture.

Jesse lives nearby and I find myself stopping in front of her brown brick building on Polhemus, a block-long side street. Coloured lights, wreathes, and white candles adorn the windows; on the fifth floor, hers, I see the blue light of a television flickering, just as a pregnant woman comes out of the building. She is huge, making her way down the cracked cement steps of the stoop, bumping two bags of laundry along. I can hear her hard, ragged breathing. She stops for a moment, putting her forehead down on the broken bannister.

"Need a hand?"

The woman nods, barely lifting her head. She is wearing a black sweatsuit, torn sneakers, and a long, cherry-red robe. Shaggy black hair, threaded with grey, hangs about her broad face.

I carry the woman's bags down to the street. She follows me, making her way down backward, painfully slow. Standing at the curb, she thanks me, bends to pick up the bags, only to put them down again. "Have a cigarette?"

"I don't smoke." My hand goes to the breast pocket of my blazer, where I feel a bulge: Elia's pack. Dark eyes peer out from the woman's jagged bangs. Jesse's eyes. "This isn't my jacket," I say absurdly. "I mean, someone else usually wears it."

The woman bites her lower lip. I take the pack, shake out a cigarette, and hand it to her. She folds it tightly between her lips. I give her a light, then hold out the pack, the book of matches. "Take them."

She slides cigarettes and matches into the deep pocket of her robe, then folds her arms across her chest.

"Your daughter's all excited about the baby," I say.

The woman just looks at me, a flat stare. She shakes her head, as if coming to, her thick black brows knitted across the bridge of her nose.

"Jesse came into my shop." I point back toward Seventh Avenue. "She told me about you. You were almost all she talked about. The baby due for Christmas."

The woman lets out a low whistle. She shakes her hair back with a flip of her head. "I don't have children. Neither are they expected." Putting her hands on her belly, she breathes in sharply, not safeguarding what's inside, warding it off. "Jesse doesn't have a mama. Neither is she expected. No time now, not anytime."

I wonder where Jesse is, who's looking after her.

The woman holds her hands beneath her breastbone, fists pressing inward. I see now her shape's all wrong, she's just thick around the middle.

"Jesse's mama slipped her coat on over the paper gown, just took off."

I glance up. Now there's no blue light on the fifth floor; the window's black. I am tempted to go up, to knock, and check on her. Instead, I offer to carry the woman's bags to the laundromat down the block. She walks beside me with a wide-spaced, halting gait.

We enter the brightly lit laundromat, which is too warm, thick with steam and the smell of bleach. In back, an old man listens to the radio, staring intently at the black box, seeing its voices. "Does Jesse go to school?"

The woman shrugs. "Sometimes."

"And the father?"

She looks puzzled, then says, "He's all right. But Jesse's too much on her own."

We say goodbye without exchanging names. I head to the diner on the corner, have spinach pie and greek salad without tasting it, and return to my shop. Anywhere but home.

In the workroom, the sudden quiet unnerves me, and I brew a pot of tea, just to keep busy. I miss the warm clamor in the coffee shop, the noise on the avenue, people coming and going. It's been so long since I've spent time alone. I look about for my old transistor radio, then remember I took it back to Elia's. I gave away my cat, Lewis, because Elia was allergic to her hair. My golden retriever is now a part of Elizabeth Spencer's family.

I sweep up the flour-fine plaster dust coating the work table, scrape a bit of hardened clay from the floor. I feel the urge to work, the anticipation and fluttering nerves of getting started. It's always scary, that never changes. Cleaning the workshop calms me a little. Everything must be in order, before I begin.

Once, I thought Elia was my beginning. Before we met, I worked as a clerk in a doll shop, doing repairs when business was slow: fixing cracked skulls, split limbs, badly torn cloth, and kid bodies. These were the best-loved dolls, the ones owned by children, dolls who were slept with and taken everywhere. Evenings, I took a sculpting seminar with the dollmaking team, Lothar Grossle and Gudrun Schmidt. Working the clay, I knew this was what I was meant to do. There were so many hidden faces only I could find – as long as I knew when to stop – or a face would be forever lost.

I also cleaned other people's houses, saving toward my own shop: on the Slope, in the Heights, townhouses and brownstones on quiet, lush-leaved blocks. Houses I'd never be invited into. I liked the moment of stillness and darkness, standing in a stranger's house, just after entering with my duplicate keys. This was the time I was most free. I felt a power, access to secrets. I liked to see what books these people read, what music they played, the kind of food they kept inside the refrigerator. Sometimes, I'd taste their liquor, feel the soft stack of pajamas inside a drawer, pocket a button or shell. I didn't mind getting down on hands and knees, wiping grime off floor moldings, grease beneath the stove, shaking sand and crumbs from sheets.

Elia Abraham walked into the room just as I was whisking a starfish out from under his bed, along with an odd sock, and a pen without its cap. I was about to pocket the starfish, the perfect pendant for Natalie, my mermaid. Instead, I blew off the flanneled dust. When I gave it back to Elia, he cupped my hand in both of his and said, "It's brought me good luck."

I was caught.

We became lovers that night. Elia Abraham was the one I loved best, the love of my life, the love I hoped would prove me to myself.

In three months, I'd given up my job at the shop; I had no place to make dolls or do repairs. I told myself I could always go back to it. Instead, I spent my days searching for hard-to-find props, typing drafts of Elia's plays, mailing letters, making our house a home. Reaching to understand Elia, to please him, was like trying to catch fish with my bare hands. I was groping my way in the dark. Two years ago, my Grandma Sayer died, and left me a small legacy. With that, I opened Noel's House.

Tonight, I feel ready to get started on Jesse's doll. Wishbone. I set up my sculpting tools and start working the clay, making the head. Later, I'll do a mold, pour it, and reproduce the sculpture in porcelain. I've used many media: paperclay, cast resin, polymer, even tin – but keep returning to porcelain. I have faith in its durability. Porcelain has been found – intact – in one-hundred-year-old shipwrecks at the bottom of the sea.

I sculpt Wishbone's head – square-shaped – then carve her finely molded chin, her strong jaw. It's strange, searching for a being who already exists, finding and feeling out her shape. I indent deep hollows for her eyes, lay in the bone structure for a nose and cheeks, then shape her ears. Using my palette knife, I mold her sinewy neck, tilting her head to the left, a posture of watching and listening. I see Wishbone with a long, thin nose, flared nostrils, unusual for such a shape, a deep furrow in the centre of her upper lip. Her lips are full and wide, slightly parted, with a beautiful downward curve. I build her forehead – high and broad – working from the top down, then deeply furrow her brow. She has deep grooves on either side of her mouth. When I look at the face that's emerging, it startles me: Wishbone has a wizened face, old or newborn.

As I pour out my tea, there's a rapping at the window. My whole body tenses. Elia, after me. I'm afraid to look into the darkened alley.

A pale white face presses against the glass, Jesse scrunching her nose flat, and I relax. She draws back, laughing.

I throw up the window, lift her under her arms, into my workshop. As I raise her to me, she draws her legs up, and I feel the sharpness of her knees against my stomach, her elbows at my ribs, each bone like a point of light. I'm struck again how light she feels, yet how strong.

Jesse is breathless and says, "I forgot to tell you things about Wishbone." She studies the head forming on my work table, then thrusts out her chin. "Wishbone is old, *very* old."

Jesse comes closer to the work table, throwing her coat on the couch. Glancing at me, she fills in Wishbone's parted lips, builds up her browbone, gouges crow's feet at each corner of the hollows I've left for eyes. Her work is rough, clumsy.

"What else?"

"Her ears. They're bigger."

I form pieces of clay like the letter C, enlarging the ears, shaping the outside channels and lengthening the lobes. Jesse smooths the head of any hint of hair.

I look at my watch, see it's gone seven. "I'll walk you home. Tomorrow, after school. You'll help me then."

Jesse frowns, but puts her coat back on. As we leave the shop, I take her hand; she clutches her fingers tightly around mine. I leave her off at her weathered brick building, watching as she enters the foyer, looking through the glass doorway as she runs up the narrow stairs. I wait until I see a light up on the fifth floor. I think I see Jesse wave, but I'm not sure. A moment later, she runs out of the building, her eyes streaming.

"Where's your father?"

"Can I sit with you? *Please.*"

I don't know what to do. We stand for maybe ten minutes in the street.

"My Daddy isn't home," Jesse says.

"Where is he?" I ask.

"At work."

"Do you have his phone number?"

Jesse shrugs.

I scribble a note on one of my business cards, telling her father where she is, and leave it in his mailbox. As we make our way back to the shop, wind gusts against our faces, then our backs, with sudden, violent changes of motion. All at once, there's a flat, hollow crack, which rips through me, then horrible silence. I grab Jesse's arm and run.

At the shop, I heat milk and make Jesse a cup of cocoa. In a tin, I find some oatcakes and spread these with jam. While she eats, Jesse examines Wishbone's head from every angle. She runs her hand over the smooth head. "The baby," she says, "it's not coming."

"You'll have Wishbone soon."

Jesse smiles, wan and tired, then curls up on the corduroy couch, her chin resting on her elbow. She watches me work a while, then closes her eyes. Her white lids flicker. Having her there with me, I feel a joy I can't explain.

I search my apothecary chest, rooting through odd eyes, unused hands and feet, tiny feathers and fans, copper tubing for piercing ears, bits of moleskin and squares of soft leather, strewing them on my work bench. In the bottom right-hand drawer, I take out the pair of amber gems I planned to give Elia for Christmas. I thought they'd make lovely cufflinks.

I set the gems aside on a swatch of black velvet: smooth ovals, a deep honey colour, each threaded with gold and black filaments. Watching Jesse sleep, I remember the day we met – *today* – as if it were some time ago. Jesse said, *She's always with me,* yet she wants Wishbone given form, made whole, visible to the world. It seems a risk, shows faith I don't know if I have myself.

I have no idea what will happen to her, what I can or should do. Get in touch with Social Services? Go see that neighbour, find out what's what. For now, she's here, safe, where I'm safe. I can't think of last night, or the night to come, each day folds up into itself.

I look over at Jesse, her eyes half-open. Rubbing one of the amber stones against my sleeve, I hold it a few inches above my work bench. Bits of paper, lace, and velvet, fly up to it and adhere.

"Look," I say, "Wishbone's eyes."

Jesse smiles.

I start on Wishbone's body, molding arms, thighs, hands, feet. As with Rosalind, I spend the longest time on her body, much longer than on her face. As I work on each separate part, I feel Elia, the sharp rasp of his hip against mine, the pressure of his presence. I don't know how much time or distance will change that. I have no mold for Wishbone; the clay is damp. Still, I place one eye, then the other, into each hollowed space.

Ami Sands Brodoff is the author of the novel *Can You See Me?* Her short stories appear in leading literary journals and anthologies, and she has contributed to *Vogue*, *Self*, *Elle*, and other national magazines. She's received a Pushcart Prize nomination and has won fellowships to Yaddo, the Virginia Center for the Creative Arts, the Ragdale Foundation, the Julia and David White Artists' Foundation, and the St. James Cavalier Center for the Arts in Malta. Ami is from New York, but lives in Montreal with her husband and children, where she writes and teaches creative writing. She is currently working on a new novel, a love song to Montreal, entitled *The White Space Between*.

Praise for *Can You See Me?*:

"Heartfelt, ambitious; one family's way of coping with the trauma, shame, and secrecy of mental illness. A genuinely moving novel."

– *Publishers Weekly*